calendar
of regrets

Also by Lance Olsen

NOVELS
Live from Earth
Tonguing the Zeitgeist
Burnt
Time Famine
Freaknest
Girl Imagined by Chance
10:01
Nietzsche's Kisses
Anxious Pleasures
Head in Flames

SHORT STORIES
My Dates with Franz
Scherzi, I Believe
Sewing Shut My Eyes
Hideous Beauties

NONFICTION
Ellipse of Uncertainty
Circus of the Mind in Motion
William Gibson
Lolita: A Janus Text
Rebel Yell: A Short Guide to Writing Fiction

calendar
of regrets

lance olsen

FC2

Tuscaloosa

Copyright 2010 by Lance Olsen
The University of Alabama Press
Tuscaloosa, Alabama 35487-0380
All rights reserved
First edition

Published by FC2, an imprint of the University of Alabama Press, with support
provided by the Publishing Program at the University of Houston–Victoria.

Address all editorial inquiries to: Fiction Collective Two, University of
Houston–Victoria, School of Arts and Sciences, Victoria, TX 77901-5731

Design: Lance Olsen, Andi Olsen, Kyle Schlesinger, Lou Robinson, and
UHV Graduate Students
Typeface: Sabon
Cover Design: Lou Robinson
Produced in the United States of America

∞

The paper on which this book is printed meets the minimum requirements of
American National Standard for Information Sciences–Permanence of Paper
for Printed Library Materials, ANSI Z39.48–1984

Library of Congress Cataloging-in-Publication Data
Olsen, Lance, 1956–
     Calendar of Regrets / Lance Olsen.
          p. cm.
     ISBN 978-1-57366-157-7 (pbk. : alk. paper)—ISBN 978-1-57366-819-4
(electronic) 1.Psychological fiction.   2. Experimental fiction.   I. Title.
PS3565.L777C36 2010
813'.54—dc22

                                                2009041860

Acknowledgments

The author would like to thank the publishers of the following journals and anthologies, in which some of these chapters first appeared in slightly different form: *Best New Writing 2007, Black Warrior Review, Brooklyn Rail, Closets of Time, Gargoyle, Detroit: Stories, Iowa Review, Perigee, Serving House, Weber Studies, Writers' Dojo.*

Collage/text chapters and photographs created and manipulated by Andi and Lance Olsen.

for Andi,
co-author of it all

Once upon a time I was someone then that stopped.
　　—Laird Hunt, *The Exquisite*

This too is erotic—the anticipation of the pleasure of making sense.
　　—Lyn Hejinian, *My Life*

To hope is to contradict the future.
　　—E. M. Cioran, *All Gaul is Divided*

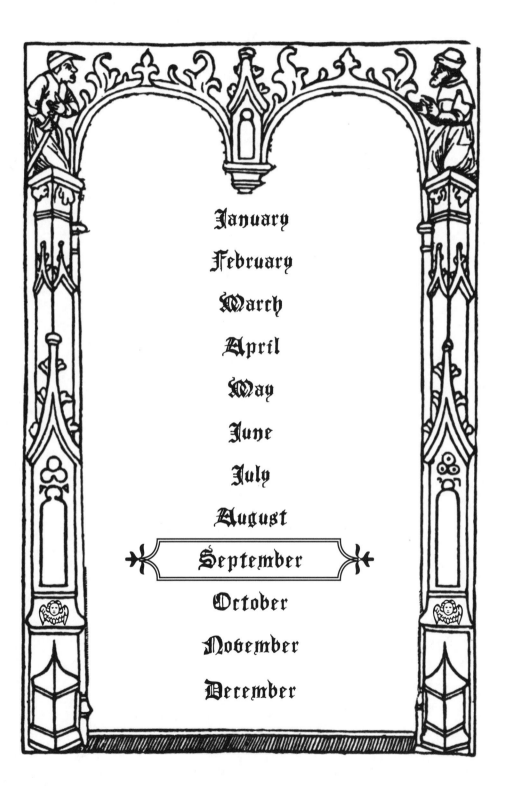

January

February

March

April

May

June

July

August

September

October

November

December

Hieronymus Bosch dabs paintbrush to palette and confers with the small round convex mirror floating alone in an ocean of bonewhite wall on the far side of his studio. Sharpness of eye, thinness of lip, satirical rage, he thinks: his whole family of attributes, God willing, will be out of this mess soon enough. Rotating back to his work at hand, he touches color flecks to the insectile legs rooted in the dwarf's shoulder. Appraises.

Travel is sport for those who lack imagination. Bosch is sure of it. Take, by way of illustration, that huge hideous Groot. That huge hideous Groot does not possess a nose. He possesses a greasy vein-webbed tumor partitioning two puckered purple assholes. A homuncular likeness of him hunches in the dark sky above the rendered Bosch's raised left hand. Groot appears piggish as a gluttonous priest, ears donkey-large with gossip. The heavens churn with hell smoke. Below, the hilly countryside blazes with the firewind of belief.

Yet, despite his mass, the noisome emissary from the Brotherhood of Our Lady cannot stop moving. 'S-Hertogenbosch to Tilburg, Tilburg to Eindhoven, Eindhoven to Brussels, and back again, busying himself with business. What Groot's sort does not know, cannot fathom, is that movement is nothing more than a forgetting, foreign landscapes forms of amnesia, journeying a process of unstudying.

One must learn to stay put in order to see. Become a place. A precise address. Lot's wife, that salty pillar.

Huge hideous Groot dropped by this morning, unannounced. Bosch is still trying to figure out why. Prattle over coffee before heading to Helmond. A shared prayer for the Virgin through a cheek squirreled with sugar cubes and ginger snaps. Scuttlebutt about Brinkerhoff, the Brotherhood's banker, between slurps. Groot's sticky mouth sounded like a sea-creature oozing in a fishmonger's bucket.

Bosch knew the boob would not recognize himself in the painting. No one ever does. Every man believes it the next who is worthy of scorn. So Bosch left his easel unveiled as the two sat opposite each other like chess players on the two chairs, stiff-backed as Groot's personality, that comprised the better part of Bosch's cramped workroom.

Because behind the heavy green curtains (he has had them manufactured especially for this severity of space) hovers a window out of which Bosch is proud to say he has not peered for almost sixty-six years. His days are nights lit by eleven lamps. Beyond the window hovers a reeking market square through which he cannot at this instant remember ever having ambled, although he has done so to bring his humors into balance every day since he was thirty at precisely two o'clock with his wife, skeletal Aleyt, and every day at precisely five o'clock, alone, in preparation for the evening meal. He cannot remember the neat rows of slender two-story whitewashed and redbrick houses adorned with stepped gables, tiled roofs, glossy black highlights. He cannot remember the cobblestone lanes shiny with horseshit, wet hay, rotting vegetables, foamy piss, shabby beggars, and ballooned rats rigored under the autumnal mizzle, or, as must be the case on this warm summer afternoon, were he to allow himself the luxury of a glance, the fly-hazed heifers dumbly raising their heads not to reflect a little longer throughout the pastures beyond that slide toward infinity beneath a sky sewn from Siberian irises.

Bosch consults the mirror again. He specks ochre along the dwarf's beak sparkly with slobber.

His grandfather was a painter. His father, too. His big brother Goosen. Three of his four uncles. Yet for the life of him Bosch cannot comprehend whence his own style swelled. It resembles that of the other members of his clan not in the least. Unlike them, unlike his peers, from the instant Hieronymus Bosch kissed brush to canvas he took the greatest pleasure in leaving a faintly rough surface behind him that announces *this is a picture of my mind's picture,* which is, he believes, as it should be: the world alla prima, a single sketchless application.

Underpainting, he is convinced, is the technique of genius gimping.

The skin of any one of his paintings is more Bosch, more fully himself, than the graying disgrace presently stretched across his bones. This is why he has signed only seven in his career, and then only under duress, only because that is what it took to cache coins to pay bills to paint further paintings. Aleyt sometimes asks why he does not want additional wealth, a larger house, a more elegant wardrobe, although she already knows she already knows the answer. She is the one, after all, who taught it to him. It is the same reason he writes no letters, keeps no journals. Such things are paper children, and why produce paper children when one refuses to produce the screechy, selfish, reeking variety?

Sail nowhere save among the continents of your own soul, and, when your body at long last gives up its war upon you, sloughs away, returning you to infancy, the final hinged panel of the polyptych called yourself having been reached and rushed beyond, leave the useless remainder behind on the wicked midden heap it is.

Let your stunned spirit lift. Drift. Bolt. Soar. Because—

Because—

Because, in a phrase: *Doeskin brown. Watermelon red. Sandy summer soil the tone of sandkage.* These are the only exotic municipalities a man needs visit during his delay on earth, so long as he pays attention, keeps his inner eyes open, learns to listen to himself, which is to say to the noise light makes within the head.

Life's foe is distraction. This is why Bosch has never stepped beyond the lush pastures embracing 's-Hertogenbosch. He does not see the advantage. Journey is attempted breakout, and yet, down behind the liver, the spleen, every human knows no one leaves this town, any of them, alive.

Bosch mentioned as much to Groot in passing. He could not help taking note as he did so of the pink speckles constellating the emissary's bald pate, the bad hide beneath his patchy fog of beard. Their peculiar meeting lasted less than half an hour. A rap arrived upon the front door as the town clock tolled ten. From his studio, where Bosch had been orbiting his easel, endeavoring to see his self-portrait from the vantage point of another solar system, he could hear clatter and commotion in the foyer, his wife's artificial trill, Groot's bass outshout caving into that chronic gluey cough of his. Hope cringed. Bosch could hear Aleyt usher in the intruder, offer him a cup of coffee, could hear Groot accept. Hope bit its own cheek. Aleyt called brightly to her husband that his colleague was here. Bosch watched hope hobble away.

Aleyt showed Groot into the studio where Bosch set down his brush, dabbed his fingers with a nearby rag, revolved stiffly on stiff knees, reached out, and wobbled Groot's chubby hand. Aleyt disappeared, reappeared with a hectic silver serving tray, then vanished for good, leaving the painter to fend for himself. He felt like the last soldier on a battlefield, the enemy of thousands descending.

The huge hideous Groot half-cleared his gluey throat and began boring Bosch with details concerning his imminent departure to Helmond. From what Bosch could tell, it had something to do with finance and dry goods. Bosch loathed finance and dry goods. He slipped into his mask of feigned interest while privately calculating this afternoon's labor on his piece-in-progress. Groot worried aloud about having to travel so soon after a resurgence of the plague in the region. Quarantine had been declared in Breda and Oss. The burghers had taken it upon themselves to aid the Lord's wrath upon the peasants by islanding their neighborhoods. The idea was to let the buggers cull themselves, thereby hastening their atonement. It was the least decent people could do.

Bosch stared stonily over Groot's right shoulder at his canvas in the fidgety lamplight. He would, he decided, fork a cinnabar serpent's tongue between the homunculus's lips. Alter the ears from donkey to rabbit to signify the unholy Catholic exuberance for bottomless proliferation.

A miniature nun, unclothed but for her headdress, breasts girlishly pert, rode a large mouse with horse's skull bareback and upside down across the shadowy ceiling. Bosch raised his chin slightly and studied her with interest. A portwine stain in the shape of a crucifix ornamented her bare left flank. Her tongue, a good meter long, flapped behind her like a purple scarf.

Such waking visions did not especially surprise him. They had visited ever since that night more than five decades ago when he was awakened by his mother's screams down in the street. Never till that moment had he heard raw terror tear through a voice.

Lord save us! he came to consciousness hearing his mother cry. *The End Times are here! The End Times are here!*

He lurched up in the bed, his muscles thinking for him, and—

And it occurred to Bosch that Groot had just asked him a question.

Bosch's thoughts had been wandering down their own paths and now they were lost. His attention flicked back to the halfwit's face. Ginger snaps crumbed the whiskers at the corners of Groot's groupermouth. His dewlap toaded him.

Silence unfolded through the studio.

Bosch attempted to follow the thread from Groot's slack expression back to what his question might have been, but came up short. Apologizing, he asked the lummox to repeat himself.

I don't suppose, Groot began again. That is, I wonder if I might, you know, entreat. If you would be so kind, that is, as to consider.

Well, not to put too fine a point on it, Mr. Bosch, if you would contemplate giving up, you know . . . all *that*.

Bosch shut his eyes and watched a small wooden ship packed with fools flirting, eating, drinking, gaming, cheating, begging, singing, carousing, and puking over the side, waft through blue-green time, aimless, never nearing harbor.

Opening his eyes again, he reached up, scratched a wild white brow, responded, deadpan:

I'm afraid I don't know what you're talking about, Mr. Groot.

Please, Mr. Bosch. You receive my meaning perfectly clearly. You know as well as I do what your neighbors and friends are, you know. What they have. Begun, that is. Behind your back.

Bosch raised his china cup, sipped, set it down in its tinkly saucer.

The ship sailed on through the years.

If they are whispering anything about me behind my back, they are whispering rumors. Rumors, as I am sure you are aware, are bad air in words' clothing. Bad air is malice in gaseous form. It disappoints me greatly that you pay heed to such bodily functions gone public.

A member of the *Cathars*, for Christ's sake, Mr. Bosch. Affiliate of a *cult*.

Clothesline comments. I should be interested to hear what tangible evidence your blatherskites and quidnuncs might have provided you in support of such accusations.

You call charges of heresy *rumor*?

Bosch, I'm afraid, Bosch replied, is Bosch. People trust and repect him, or they do not. Regrettably, there is nothing poor Hieronymus can do about it.

I am sorry to hear that.

I am sorry to hear you are sorry to hear. But there it is. Now, if you'd be so kind, Mr. Groot, you must excuse me. He nodded in the direction of his self-portrait. I ought to be returning to my toddler.

Bosch made to hoist himself out of his chair.

Groot's stubby arms became upturned porcine legs erect beside his ears.

But *why*? Tell me that, at least. *Why in the world* . . .

Bosch paused. Bosch sighed.

He took in the brownblotched back of his hands starfished on his trouser legs, then lifted his head to meet Groot's anal eyes and answered, as if answering an imbecilic child:

Because, Mr. Groot. Because—

Because when he was thirteen his mother's panic voice shredded his sleep like a swirl of scythes. Bosch had been a cat curled on the hay mattress beside his big brother Goosen, so far submerged in unconsciousness he had left even his dreams behind. Next he was a finch flitting around his small hazy window, straining on tiptoes to peer over the sill at a nightworld swallowed by flames.

Buildings burned all the way to the horizon. Houses. The guildhall. Barns. Schools. Stables. Depots. The globe itself was ablaze. A dense umber cloud roiled above the bedlam like an inverted sea, its behemoth belly glowing orange. Ash snowed down through air thick and acrid with brimstone, cooked horsehide, clamor, clangor, whinny, bleat, bay, bellow.

Chickens flapped along the street below, hugging shop fronts, trying to gain altitude, cackling torches.

Bosch's mother, still in her nightgown and bare feet, white hair witch mad, tiptoeing among a gathering crowd of burghers, was right. This was what she had always warned Bosch about, what he could never bring himself to believe. But now, watching existence explode around him, watching his father, a goosenecked man with fierce eyes and flared nostrils, throw on his trousers, shirt, and shoes, and plunge, determined, into the throngs trying to hold back the conflagration with picks and axes and sloshy buckets of water, Bosch saw how Doomsday came calling on those who refused to take heed of its inevitability. His mother stood in the doorway, back to the boy and his brother. She refused to retire, refused to shed her nightgown for a dress, refused even to slip into her clogs. She forgot the presence of her own sons looping around her. Her thin lips just thinned a little more every minute with the recognition that what she had assumed was life, wished was life, was not, it turned out, life at all. This was life, the world whirling.

The boys clambered back up the ladder into their attic room and spent what felt like weeks at that window, staring out at reality shredding in bright strips, talking about how they had always supposed hell's upsurge on the final hour would somehow be fast as a cannonball, a lightning strike, an epiphanic burst, and over. On the contrary, its advent had come to pass as a protracted smoke-swamped scramble.

The beautiful angel with the blue eyes, it turned out, came at you, came at you, came at you.

She was everywhere at once, forever.

That evening they beheld the steeple of their church collapse into itself in a billowing rush of sparks.

The next afternoon they craned to catch sight of three large hogs gnawing at the buttocks of a charred corpse lying facedown half a block up the lane.

The following night Goosen shook Bosch awake from an exhausted doze to show him a group of men hurrying along with a naked girl carried between them in a quilt employed as a stretcher. She was eight or nine. Agony rocked her head. Her blond hair was firefrazzled and most of the tissue down the right side of her body had blackened and slipped away. To Bosch, she was nothing save glisten and blister and skinned hare. At that moment, she happened to look up briefly, or perhaps only appeared to do so. Their eyes locked, then broke, or maybe not. She was, in any case, it occurred to Bosch as he balanced there beside his big brother, the first unclothed girl he had ever seen.

When his father finally bobbed to the surface again four days later, Bosch's mother pitched forward to shawl herself around his spindly neck, and two thirds of 's-Hertogenbosch had subsided into smoldering charcoal knolls of wreckage, more than four thousand homes had been destroyed, three hundred townspeople perished, and Bosch had become himself. In an effort to comprehend what it was he had seen, he soon applied brush to canvas and realized with a jolt that he had learned how to paint. That the purpose of the act was to capture and convey the details of the soul's geography, not the world's. That the world's was worthless, was wind, because the soul was where the only bona fide cosmos breathed.

Bosch began an apprenticeship with his father, but soon moved into the house of a stern wall-eyed master from Mechelen who had established his studio several blocks away. Although Bosch worked diligently, earnestly, people refused to take him more than lightly. He was too young, too boyish, too pleasant for such bleak apparitions. Too prolific to be considered sincere. And his paintings? They were too eccentric, unnerving, cluttered, out of step with custom to be considered worthy of anything approaching serious attention.

It did not ultimately matter to another human being, it dawned on him one day, that Bosch was Bosch, and it never would.

Every Sunday he towed his spirit to church to hunker apart from the others in a pew at the rear, better to despise those around him, wondering why he had made the effort to show up in the first place. When it became inevitable, he grudgingly joined the Brotherhood of Our Lady, not because he felt a lint fluff's weight of devotion to its lessons, but because he knew that joining was what was expected of him, tacitly demanded, the sole means for a business-man like himself to get a leg up in this incestuous city. And that, at the end of the day, he also knew, was all he really was, all he would ever really be: an entrepreneur of bad dreams and devils that no one wanted hanging on their walls. Bosch had the misfor-tune of reminding the world of itself, and that was something the world simply would neither tolerate nor forgive. There are some things, the world asserted, at which people should not become too accomplished.

Slowly, Bosch came to admit that he would never be famous. He would never be the talk of this town, or any other. The recognition ached like a body full of bruises. He could hardly wait to take his place before his easel every morning to find out what his imagination had waiting for him, yet he had to make peace with the bristly fact that recognition was a boat built for others. He had to content himself with the rush of daily finding—the way milled minerals mixed precisely with egg whites create astounding carmines, creams, cobalts; how the scabby pot-bellied rats scurrying through his feverscapes were not really scabby pot-bellied rats at all, but the lies flung against the true church day after day.

There were, that is, lives behind this life, messages murmuring within nature's minutiae.

Look closely: everything is webbed with everything, existence an illuminated manuscript you walk through.

All you have to do is study.

All you have to do is learn how to read.

And so he prepared to live his life as a bachelor, faithful to his art because he had nothing and no one else to be faithful to. Shortly after informing his shaken parents of his decision, he attended a small dinner party at a well-heeled patron's home. There he met the angular patron's angular daughter, Aleyt Goyaerts van den Meervenne. She was three years his senior, serious as a sermon, beautifully pale, blond as a pearl, frugal as a friar with her words. Her clothes hung off her loosely as they might off two broomsticks fashioned into a cross. Over the course of the meal, Bosch noticed Aleyt evinced the habit of closing her wisterial eyes whenever he addressed her directly, as if she were trying to will him away from her. It took him most of the evening to puzzle out that just the opposite was the case. Aleyt was concentrating on each syllable he spoke because she wanted to understand precisely what he had to say.

In that meeting's wake, they began to court, first in the family sitting room, then strolling through the pinched streets of the city, conversing about music, painting, the quality of cloudy light on snowy mornings when 's-Hertogenbosch softens into bluegray reverie.

Bosch opened his eyes fourteen months later to find himself kneeling before an indifferent priest with a chancre on his grim lower lip. A wafer was thawing on Bosch's tongue. The painter was thirty years old and he was deep in the midst of articulating his wedding vows.

Because, he ruminated, attempting to nail down the language of it—

Because—

Because late one motionless autumn afternoon, sitting side by side on a stone wall overlooking the pastures at the town's edge, powdery gilt sun backlighting the dying trees, Aleyt asked Bosch, apropos of nothing, if by chance he had ever considered that he might be holding his painting of the universe upside down.

Bosch had not.

Pressing his hands between hers, staring straight ahead as she spoke, Aleyt suggested in a tender, even voice that he unfasten his mind and heart to the prospect.

Imagine for a moment, just a moment, that the reason the earth-ball is swarmy with transgression lies not in the fact that Man has foundered, failed, fallen, but that he has never risen, flourished, revised his basic constitution in the slightest, has always been, in a word, exactly what he is now: sin lodged in skin.

Imagine, further, she suggested, that the reason is as obvious as the stunning honeyed suffusion across this afternoon's sky. That Satan, not God, is responsible for what we see. The explanation for why you set your eyes upon Lucifer's labor everywhere you look is that there is nothing else to set your eyes upon. What you observe is no illusion, no lamb in lion's clothing, but the genuine shape and heft of things. The globe really is about what it appears to be about: war, crime, bigotry, covetousness, spite, deceit, disorder, sloth, sham, meanness, mischief, misery. Living tallies up in the end to nothing more than ceaseless vinegary letdown. You are promised this. You get that. Without end.

The gold-dust sky, Bosch noticed, consumed three-fourths of his view. If he held up his right thumb sideways just so, he could effectively blot out any one of the sparse trees or slavering cows in the foreground.

Beyond them hazed a large still pond the same hue as the sky, only glassy.

Imagine, in a word, Aleyt pushed on, that this planet is product, not of God's intellect, but The Fiend's fancy. We are living in the devil's dream.

Bosch parted his lips to speak.

Pressed them closed.

The grass was too green by half.

It may not be easy to do so at first, Aleyt said. Such notions go against the grain of our education and predilections. But try, just for the wink of an eye, and you will sense sense start returning to the senselessness surrounding you. Satan, not God, sired what we see. He stole our souls from heaven's radiance and boxed them in these inky containers.

Astonished, Bosch turned to examine her. Aleyt did not return his glance. She was busy examining something on the gauzy horizon that remained imperceptible to him. For Bosch, distance simply gave way to more distance.

Would it not therefore perhaps follow, she continued, should we grant such a surprising premise, that, in order to escape our night dungeon and reunite with light, we must leave our fleshy selves behind as swiftly as possible? Let us think of the model lives lived by those called *Les Parfaits*—men and women who welcome the pure ascetic refusal of corruption, whose modest and unfussy acts reveal the antithesis of the church's opulent duplicity and obese comfort. Eat less, they say. Drink less. Avoid all things stemming from sexual reproduction, since sexual reproduction's mission is to burgeon sin and thereby suffering: meat, milk, cheese, eggs, progeny.

Be fretful to multiply. Live frugally. Leave life with dignified haste. Stand back and let humankind do what it does best—battle, blunder, and besoil itself into oblivion. Then we can all go home.

Bosch looked back at the pasture, the polished pond, the sky bullying his awareness. The inside of his mouth tasted like chicken shit. What he studied before him seemed, all at once, diaphanous, as if it were a sketch some artist had begun to erase.

You will not hear me speak of these things again, Aleyt said beside him, tender, even. With this my beliefs, my family's, become invisi—ah, *look*!

She let go of his hands with a squeeze and lifted her left to point at the blenching sky.

A crested lark! she sang.

Bosch squinted, squinted, strained, but could make out no bird, no blot, no movement up there whatsoever, no matter how hard he tried, because—

Because—

Because in that temporal throb he made out something else altogether: something that struck him with the force of an idea he had always known to be true, yet one he could never quite have brought himself to articulate until now. Until now, it had remained a poppy-seed notion wedged between two molars, a nagging semi-thought, an almost-philosophy, like a semi-solid, an almost-animal, a unicorn awareness. He understood the evidence had always been everywhere: in those speckles constellating Groot's bald pate, in that plague chewing across northern Europe, in that ship of fools drifting through his consciousness.

Not long after, Aleyt's father invited Bosch to dine with the family, solo, and, once everyone was comfortable, everyone sipping his or her pea soup, the patriarch began explaining to the painter how, sub rosa, they had fashioned their house into a Cathar girls school;

taught reason behind closed doors; studied numbers, the lute, grammar, logic, rhetoric; struggled through scriptures, rehearsing the intricate art of the fourfold interpretation: the literal or historical, whereby what happened happened; the allegorical, whereby every detail in a tale releases a symbol that whispers Christian doctrine into your ear; the tropological, whereby you glean the moral of what transpires as it relates to your own life; and the anagogical, whereby the import of what took place is applied to the largest Christian concerns: death, judgment, heaven, hell.

Privately, Bosch took up Cathar habits one by one. Publicly, he continued to embrace The Brotherhood of Our Lady, continued to tow his spirit to church every Sunday and sometimes more. He introduced Aleyt to its members. They took her under wing, lent the young couple a hand in securing an agreeable dwelling on the market square into which Bosch and she moved the day after their nuptials. When no children were immediately forthcoming, their friends began murmuring among themselves, treating Bosch and Aleyt with the same patronizing solicitousness good Catholics set aside for the penniless, pitiful, and palsied, in an attempt to make themselves feel better about themselves, more deserving of what they didn't deserve.

On occasion, Bosch still saw his older brother Goosen. The man had married an amiable possum-faced woman with a high forehead named, hideously, Griseldis. Griseldis was so fat, so short, so indelicate that she trundled through existence without bending her knees. Sometimes Bosch found himself wondering, his brother nattering on about this or that in the sitting room after dinner, if the two had in truth enjoyed different mothers and fathers. What else could account for such egregious dissimilarities? After all, Bosch found Goosen's paintings humdrum, merely competent, nostalgic as a Christmas tree in June. At their most successful, they were talented in the way a wicker basket can on occasion be said to be talented. His canvases depicted flat fields, feathery clouds, half-baked haywains. Evidently, the man was incapable of facial particulars, so each of his subjects stood either some distance from the painter's vantage point, or nearby, but with his or her back turned squarely to the viewer. All you had to do to see better examples of nature was look out your own front door—and what sort of art was that?

Not, needless to say, that Bosch would admit as much to the fellow. Rather, he was painstakingly polite, scrupulously diplomatic, altogether reserved in his remarks. He strained to seek out a reasonably well-executed white willow or beige heifer cramped in some corner of Goosen's canvas and compliment its execution, all the while searingly envious of—of what, exactly? Not his brother's talent or achievements, no, but rather of what others had mistakenly imagined that talent and those achievements to be.

Worse, when Bosch showed Goosen one of his own works, Goosen stood before it in speechless perplexity. His wide shoulders slumped. His dim eyes partially closed in partial contemplation. It appeared as if he were teetering on the very brink of thought, that the approaching intellectual breeze had cost him no little bodily discomfort.

What is the point, Hieronymus, I wonder, he would say after a time, of such hellish visions? They bring . . . they bring *mischief* to the mind.

Of *course* they bring mischief to the mind, you dolt, Bosch did not say. Instead, he watched Goosen become increasingly well known and respected while he watched himself become increasingly tolerated. His hair faded from the color of butter to the color of ashes to the color of babies' teeth. He could not grasp the upended reality of the odd aging man glaring back at him from that small round convex mirror floating alone in an ocean of bonewhite wall in his studio. Yet, as if to convince him of the apparition's authenticity, his knees began to ache, pissing syrupped into extended acts of dedication.

His backside deflated so thoroughly that one day it struck him with a twinge that he had come to resemble nothing so much as a frog reared up on its hind legs.

Nor was growing older any kinder to his wife. Aleyt's skin drooped, crimpled, crinkled, browned, stained. Her breasts emptied and flattened. Her periods perished. Headaches and flushes flocked her. She found herself unable to sleep.

Be strong, the world told the aging. Be brave and obdurate.

But the world was wrong.

Growing old turned each day into a small catastrophe shaded with just enough wisdom to allow one to understand wisdom changed nothing.

Bosch and Aleyt tucked into themselves, embraced, huddled against time's uncaring weather. They watched acquaintances thrash against the bloody flux, St. Anthony's fire, typhoid's poisonous patches. They watched friends lose life's footing, topple out of contentment, go bankrupt, become the object of their offspring's derision, fall prey to highway bandits, drunken soldiers, mountebank monks, and—

And what—

And what in God's name do you call all *this*, Bosch wonders, back with himself in front of his easel, if not travel? A journey that is no journey at all, yet one that undoes you as you race along on your way to nowhere, and—

And—

And, in the midst of this thought, Bosch becomes aware of himself again because something in his chest slips.

The surprising sensation arrives between inhalation and inhalation, a bluewhite spasm sluicing through his left arm, billowing down his back.

He is perfectly well.

He is anything but.

His hands become anvils. His legs become lather.

This is not, he is certain, as it should be.

Somewhere below him he hears his paintbrush clitter across the wooden planks.

Stunned, he tries to locate equilibrium, rotate fussily, take a step toward the heavy oak door that will lead him directly to Aleyt. He can hear her footfalls in the hall. She will know what to do. She always does, only—

Only—

Only something is sitting on his shoulders. Something is sinking him. At the edges of his flustered vision, he glimpses talons.

A hairless tail rubs his neck.

No dreams, Hieronymus Bosch thinks. These are not dreams, not at all, not for one—

With his next breath, a strut of his easel leaps up beside him, huge as an elm. The mirror on the far wall shrinks to the size of a silver fly. His paintbrush becomes a broom chafing the tip of his nose.

It strikes the painter he is no longer on his feet. No. He must be on his elbows and knees, ridiculous froggy rump raised in the air, dizzy as a blizzard, crawling, endeavoring to crawl, but making very little headway.

If only he could revolve slightly in a counterclockwise direction, he would place himself in a propitious position to push off toward that door which seems to reside, all at once, in another country.

He shores up his resources, takes a crack at it. The effect is not at all what he had anticipated. Bosch's right cheek is caressing cool floorboard. Wet strands dangle off his chin. Watery mites slip down his neck. The situation shames his prim northern European sensibilities, but not as much as what his body dares do to him next.

What his body dares do to him next is soil itself in a hot murky rush.

A dike fails without warning, and his soggy trousers are suddenly steaming.

Good God, he tells himself, eyes closed, head down, ass up, in an effort to buoy his spirits, circumstances could always be less satisfactory than they are in fact at present.

One should never disregard such significant information.

There are, all said and done, Bosch is sure, no more than two and a half meters between him and hall. It is a fairly straight shot. On a middling day, he could traverse the expanse in three strides, four seconds. He merely needs signal Aleyt, and help will reveal itself. Frozen there, Bosch pictures his wife going about her everyday industry on the other side, wiping off a lamina of dust along the mantel, perhaps, or, perhaps, settling back in her sitting-room rocker to read a line or two of scriptures before lunch, oblivious of what is happening just a few steps away.

Bosch channels the sum of his psychic fuel toward burrowing himself into her awareness.

If ever there were a time in his life for the telepathy of love to prove itself, pull hope out of its hat, this most certainly would be it, and—

And—

And nothing happens.

Nothing happens some more.

Nothing, that is, save the coalescence of a crisp understanding within him. Bosch, Bosch now fathoms, has been mistaken.

Absolutely.

For the last thirty-odd years, he has existed in error. The truth, he comprehends in a blast of searing lucidity, is just this: he does not want to die. Concluding is the very last thing he wants to do. He is not indifferent. No. He is passionate. He wants a bath. He wants a bed. He wants to see his wife again.

His present plan is to stay married to her for another ten thousand years.

What could possibly be any simpler?

And so—
And so—

And so, once again, he assembles his strength and sets off.

Instead of gaining ground, however, he finds himself examining the ceiling.

He has ended up turtled on his back.

Far above him, wood slats do not resemble wood slats any longer so much as an eddying mist. Stranger still, he can pick out, if he narrows his eyes sufficiently, concentrates, a collection of shady shapes up there. Human silhouettes. Rough. Amorphous. Like charcoal sketches.

Six or seven of them hanging in chairs around a hanging table.

They are laughing. They are having a party. They are sharing conversation and drink over dinner. Corks thwop. Glasses clink. Knives clatter. Bosch narrows his eyes further, listening, becoming no more than his attention.

One voice lifts in exasperation above the rest.

A man's.

No! it exclaims. *Good God, no!* That may be many things, Jerome, it is saying, but

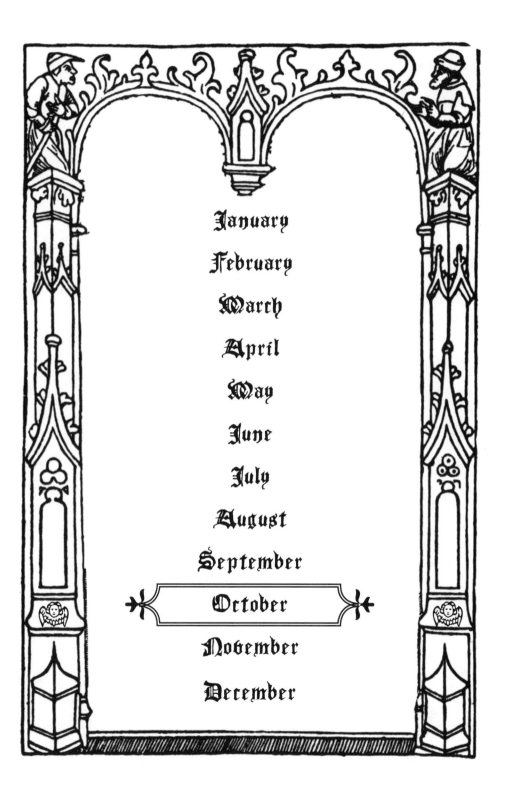

January

February

March

April

May

June

July

August

September

October

November

December

art? Surely art isn't one of them.

Of *course* art is one of them, dear boy, fleshy Jerome said reaching for his wine glass. He sipped, turned to Estelle: Your husband's certainly being contrary this evening, isn't he? Then back to Robert: The delicious red, green, yellow? The heavy black outlines? The pleasure that pair of monkey men in the painting exude in the face of just, well, *being*? It's like making your way through a spring street fair down in the Village. What could possibly be more wonderful?

Don't mind him, said Estelle. She raised her last forkful of salmon risotto and her busy turquoise bracelet jangled. Robert's contrary *every* evening. Why should this be an exception? She slipped the fork between her lips.

Mirth broke out around the table. Everyone faced Robert, eager to hear his rebuttal. He leaned back in his chair, chewing, taking in his dinner guest with a deliberately exaggerated look of befuddlement.

Jerome, he said. Jerome. They're sucking each other's *dicks*, Jerome. Two guys are sucking each other's *dicks*. They're *sixty-nining* each other. That's not wonderful. Longo is all right. Tansey is tolerable. But Keith Haring? Please. And the execution? Why don't you ask me about the execution. Go ahead, Jerome. Ask me.

Jerome sighed and answered as if answering an imbecilic child: You know what somebody once said the difficulty with the idea of utopia is? There's no red-light district in it. Fine, Robert. Fine. Why don't you enlighten us all about the execution?

The execution's execrable. It has about as much sophistication as an episode of *Pee-Wee's Playhouse*.

I love you exceedingly, dear boy, but you're really quite mad. And, if the truth be known, I rather enjoy Mr. Herman and his nutty theater. Larry Fishburne as Cowboy Curtis is almost enough to make one want to wake up early on Saturday mornings.

Robert didn't like joking at his expense. Patting his mouth with his napkin, he said, toneless: Keith Haring isn't about art, Jerome. Keith Haring is about doodles. Doodles and those posters hanging on sophomoric dorm-room walls alongside *Starry Night* and that Duran Duran gang. Anyway, how in the world can you take that schlemiel seriously? He wears his baseball cap *backward*, for godsakes.

I believe we refer to that as *being camp*. And everyone knows bands like Duran Duran exist for the sole purpose of being made fun of, bless their silk suits and three-note melodies. What's wrong with that?

Robert rolled his eyes, opened his mouth to speak, and the maid, a shy Puerto Rican elf with overlapping front teeth, appeared and commenced clearing away dishes. Estelle asked if anyone might like an espresso or cordial. She wore a baggy grayblue dress with a large crimson rose just below the collar and possessed a left-leaning jaw. Robert extracted a cigarette from his case lying on the tablecloth next to his plate and lit up. In the midst of exhaling two spikes of smoke, he caught himself.

Look at me, he said. I'm a heathen. Anyone?

Naomi palmed her high oily forehead. Recently she had started wearing wigs because she said she was tired of taking care of her own hair. Tonight's was a ginger Jennifer Beals that shifted unnervingly side to side as she rubbed.

I shouldn't, she said, but, oh, well, fuck it.

Please, Dan said, leaning forward. Thanks, Bob.

Did you hear, by the way, Naomi asked as she passed a match

beneath her Dunhill tip, that Keith just opened his own boutique?

God save us, said Robert.

The Pop Shop, I think it's called. I pass it on my way to the Foundation every morning. It sells Keith buttons, Keith watches, Keith t-shirts, Keith ties, Keith bandanas, Keith bubblegum—and, should there be any question about it, Robert, Keith baseball caps. The idea, evidently, is for Keith to make Keith accessible to the masses.

Naomi crossed her eyes goofily and took a drag.

You can't help adoring a populist with a good sales sense, Robert said. Please tell me you're kidding about the bubblegum.

They may have been Tootsie-Pop-like objects, but comestibles were definitely involved. Same color, I'm afraid, as those shlongs you speak of so fondly, Jerome.

I speak of all shlongs fondly. Each is a parade waiting to happen. Present company excepted, he added, winking at Robert.

My dick's a veritable cavalcade of pomp, Jerome, thank you very much. But you have to give it to that guy. He certainly does know how to turn himself into the aesthetic counterpart of a Big Mac. Good for him. Bravo. What an admirable accomplishment.

Where is it? Estelle asked.

What? asked Robert. Haring's conscience?

The *shop*, Robert. The *shop*.

Lafayette Street, Naomi said. Two-hundred block.

We should pay a visit, Estelle suggested to Naomi. What are you doing for lunch next Tuesday? Ethan's bar mitzvah is at the end of the month. I could taxi down after the editorial meeting and pick you up. It'd be fun.

For his bar mitzvah we're getting our poor nephew a piece of Keith Haring crap? Robert asked. I would have expected so much more from us.

Not to worry, darling. We're getting him many other kinds of crap as well.

Ethan should be prosecuted for turning thirteen, you know,

Jerome said. Does he have any idea how old that makes the rest of us?

Enjoy your firm asses and baby fat while you can, my pretties, Naomi said.

The maid returned with liqueurs and coffee. Silence distended through the dining room as she served. She smiled at her hands while she worked. Everyone took stock of the tulip glasses and mocha-colored cups being set down before them.

Oh, come now, Jerome said at last. What in the world's so terrible about *that*?

About what? Naomi asked, watching the maid round the corner back into the kitchen.

Keith Haring opening his own boutique. I mean, *really*. He's simply a business-savvy artist. The opposite would be . . . what? Hank Fürstenhoff?

Robert eyed him, gauging.

Okay, I give up, he said. What the hell is a Hank Fürstenhoff?

My point exactly, dear boy. What the hell *is* a Hank Fürstenhoff? No one knows. That's because he was an *artiste* who refused to compromise his work for commerce. The result being he died a drug-addled pauper in Hoboken. *Quelle horreur.* Mind you, he was utterly inspired. Dazzling, even. He redefined the very concept of painting in our age. Critics often used the word "postmodern" when speaking of him. Predictably. Yet he left the planet unknown. Or would have, if I hadn't just made him up.

Haring's work is . . . Look. It's simply too goddamn easy to like. *That's* the problem. In the same way, say, Vonnegut's last fifty or sixty novels have been simply too goddamn easy to like. They're about as complex, emotionally and intellectually resonant, and revealing of the human condition as a tube of Prell.

What's so horrid about being a playful and pretty shampoo? Shouldn't everything be tried? I can imagine worse. Our current commander and chief, for instance, and his troupe of dancing Muppets referred to as the Supreme Court. Bring on *Galapagos* and *Deadeye Dick*, I say.

Do you know what Haring does best, Jerome? Ask me. Ask me what his real contribution to the world of art is.

Jerome closed his eyes and grinned as if trying to make Robert dematerialize.

Okay, Robert said. I'll tell you. Haring is excellent precisely at imitating himself. Once upon a time he stumbled upon the single thing he could do relatively well: create colorful pieces of eye-candy that allow people to feel mildly, fleetingly edgy and urbane. What a fucking genius. Right up there with the inventors of the pet rock.

Granted, Jerome replied, it's moving to see a man pretending to believe in something these days. Still, you continue to miss the point entirely. One never *likes* such things. He raised his chubby arms and stroked the air with his index and middle fingers. One *"likes"* them. Every American adores *The Jetsons* and Jeff Koons. *Sort of.* That's the key—that *sort of,* in a there-may-or-may-not-be-a-Wizard-behind-the-curtains way.

Robert snorted.

You're saying this hideousness is a uniquely American affliction?

What other culture could possibly be arrogant, vulgar, and facile enough to produce such art and then "enjoy" it?

You can't possibly be suggesting someone like Haring is in the same league as a real artist.

Perish the thought. I just can't conceive of living in a world where there's only one or the other. What a place *that* would be. A never-ending ballgame at Yankee Stadium with cheap beer and William Rehnquist singing the national anthem.

Jerome performed a hyperbolic stage shudder. Everyone laughed and to his relief Dan could feel the conversation preparing to move on. Softly dizzy on the wine, he settled back with his cigarette to wait out the others. It was already past ten. He would give them a few more minutes and then excuse himself. He was looking forward to the chilly night air on the stroll home.

Dan's attention coasted leisurely from the shelves lining the living room—paperbacks, hardcovers, records, paperweights, jade statues, and bulky manuscripts were piled haphazardly in formations more geologic than bibliographic—toward *Paradise of the Blind*, the odd book he planned dipping into before falling asleep tonight. A correspondent friend stationed in Calcutta had sent it to him as an early birthday present. Ten years ago, a strapped American novelist landed an assignment writing a travel piece about Rangoon. Soon after his arrival, his scheme began hazing into something else altogether. He jotted notes on a pad he carried with him, tore them out, and wrapped them around Polaroid snapshots he took along the way, tucked the packets into envelopes, and sent them to a woman who wasn't quite his girlfriend back in the States. A few weeks later he vanished. The woman eventually edited the result and found a publisher.

Dan had never been to Burma. The idea of the writer's disappearance and relationship with his semi-girlfriend intrigued him. If he continued to like what he read, he planned to float the idea of doing a story on it at Thursday's editorial meeting.

It occurred to him in the middle of that thought that Estelle had just asked him a question. Everybody had turned his or her attention toward him with obvious anticipation. He met their expressions with a hangdog smile and tried to reenter the evening. Sorry, he said. Jetlag.

You're in luck, said Estelle. That's exactly what we want to hear about. How in the world did it go over there?

We begin editing tomorrow. We plan to run a segment Wednesday. Wednesday or Thursday. We've got a lot of footage to sort through.

But we demand nothing less than a preview from our intrepid newsman this very moment, dear boy, said Jerome.

Dan examined his empty coffee cup. He decided to sketch in a couple of details and then bow out. No one liked hearing about someone else's trip anyway. It was like listening to an acquaintance recount the intricacies of his recent house repairs.

Okay, he said, looking up, so: picture no one around for miles except cleanup and construction crews. The military's cordoned off a thirty-kilometer area called The Exclusion Zone. Towns inside are one-hundred-percent vacant. It's like driving through a series of desolate Eastern European sets in the back lot at Universal Studios.

Estelle leaked smoke between her lips.

Everyone just *left*?

You can still see laundry hanging on balcony clotheslines. Baby strollers lying in the streets. These scrawny cats wandering around the apartment blocks, living off irradiated mice. Otherwise, there's just this eerie, steady wind.

How ghoulish, Naomi said.

They wrap up work on what they're calling The Sarcophagus next month, Dan continued. The structure looks a little like the Battersea Power Station, only bigger—this huge windowless *thing* with what appears to be a chimney towering out. It's supposed to seal in the damaged reactor, a hundred and eighty tons of uranium, and a thousand pounds of plutonium. Only here's the problem: it can't be built on a sturdy foundation, not with all the radiation the crews would be exposed to. They can only work shifts a few seconds long. Even so, they're losing their hair. Their lungs don't work right. You know what they call themselves?

. . . ?

Biorobots.

All right, said Jerome. That's it. You've had your fun. Now be a nice boy and tell us what's *really* happening.

The cameras used to document their work? They're so radioactive they have to be buried. You can't stand anywhere near the fire trucks that initially responded to the accident because they're oozing curies. Dozens of workers have already died, but the government forbids listing radiation as the cause on death certificates. And there are already cracks over more than five thousand feet of the surface area of the building. A guy I interviewed in Helsinki told me the crews see rats running in and out all the time, birds flying through holes in the roof. Inside it's swarming with radioactive mosquitoes.

You want I should sleep like shit tonight? asked Estelle. She blew out a long cone of smoke. Because let me tell you something, mister: mission accomplished.

You're right, Dan said. Maybe I should stop.

No way, said Robert. You're in the middle of telling us a ghost story. We have a right to know how you can possibly reach a happy ending from here.

I'm not sure it's one of those kinds of ghost stories, Dan said.

Everyone stared at him.

I've got to give it to you, said Naomi. How do you come up with this stuff?

It gets worse, Dan said. He took a drag off his cigarette, let the hot smoke hang in his lungs. Because of all those cracks? The old reactor hall's going to be covered in snowdrifts this winter. Put that together with the tremors that occur regularly in the area, and there's a good chance of an accidental blending of fuels.

Which means? Jerome asked.

Pretty much another chain reaction.

And Jerome here bitches about the stupidity of *Americans*, said Robert. At least we keep our radioactive catastrophes within the bounds of decency.

Or maybe the powder from the breaches simply keeps filtering down and mixing with the fuel little by little over the years. There's a ton piled up inside already and the thing isn't even finished yet. If it collapses, this geyser of irradiated particles lifts into the atmosphere. On windy days, there are localized radioactive dust storms. Stay in one for three minutes, and your organs start falling apart.

Robert stubbed out his butt in a large glass ashtray swirled with orange.

You call *that* a happy ending? he said. He turned to Jerome: This is why people delight in Haring, you know.

Jerome looked like a student called on unexpectedly.

I've lost you, he said.

Who wouldn't rather gawk at a stupid painting of two guys draining each other's little Elvises than listen to this sort of thing? Robert asked. And it's people like *you*, Dan, who are ultimately responsible for people like Haring's success.

Me?

You should be ashamed of yourself, bringing all this goddamn reality into the American public's living room night after night. No wonder art is going to hell in a handbasket designed by Basquiat.

Oh, my gosh, Naomi said, checking her watch. Look at what time it is. I've got to get going.

Nonsense, said Robert. The conversation's just getting interesting. Another cup of coffee?

I wish. I promised my parents I'd drive them to Van Saun Park for a picnic tomorrow morning. It's becoming a Sunday tradition. Boiled hotdogs, squishy duck turds, and a dead lake in Paramus, New Jersey. What could scream family togetherness more forcefully? Estelle, Robert: you're angels.

It's been great, said Dan, rising. Jean's going to be envious. Hey, I hope I didn't depress everybody too much.

Baloney, dear boy, said Jerome, hoisting himself out of his chair as well. He tugged down his olive-green knit vest over his bright yellow shirt and bright blue knit tie. What are a few Doomsday scenarios among friends? Share a cab uptown?

Thanks, but I think I'll walk. I could use the exercise.

Chattering and laughing, they all moved up the hallway to the foyer. The elfin maid distributed coats and scarves. The guests arranged themselves amid a flutter of thank-yous and flamboyant hugs, then Dan, Naomi, and Jerome were descending in the elevator together, talking about what a nice evening they had had.

Out on the street Dan waited while first Naomi, and then Jerome, hailed cabs, and soon he was walking north by himself. It was one of those instants in the city where despite the intermittent flow of traffic everything seemed to become strangely motionless, hushed, as if all the people usually around at this hour walking their dogs or coming back from the theater had gone inside for the night. The air smelled lightly of swamp water. Central Park looked shadowy, overgrown, the leaves still left on the shrubbery black and shiny.

Strolling past the Met, he relived parts of the evening's conversations and worried he had probably shaken people up with his story. But in a real sense this was why he existed: to shake people up. This was his job. Every night at six o'clock he took his seat before the cameras, straightened his tie, and made people feel uncomfortable. He was the guy who told the country that their thirty-fifth President had just been assassinated, that they couldn't win the war they were waging in Southeast Asia, that the space shuttle had shredded seventy-three seconds after liftoff and yet the crew survived for an additional minute, maybe more.

That's what Dan did. Then he got paid for it. He thereby got to travel, meet movie stars, murderers, athletes, heads of state, models, refugees, ordinary policemen on the beat. From time to time he got to employ those signature metaphors of his that had become inside jokes with his fans. *This race is shakier than cafeteria Jell-O. In the southern states they beat him like a rented mule.*

Dan understood he wasn't supposed to enjoy his slow shading into a pop-culture figure, but he did anyway. Every day the news became a little less about itself and a little more about the people reporting it. That was okay with him. You worked the ratings or the ratings worked you.

On East 86th Street he turned right and came across a pizzeria. He ducked inside and ordered a slice of pepperoni and a can of Coke and sat on an uncomfortable orange stool looking out the window. "Walk Like An Egyptian" was playing on the boom box behind the counter. Peeling back his straw, luxuriating in this cramped steamy space, Dan watched the reflection of the slim man with a

Fu Manchu mustache glide in after him and order a plain slice. The guy seemed agitated, preoccupied with life inside his skull. He wore nice khakis, a crisp tan jacket, polished brown loafers, and one of those hairstyles.

What did they call them? Short on the top and sides, long in back. There should be a name for that.

Lately people had begun making a big deal out of fancy kinds of pizza. Goat cheese, chicken, asparagus, pineapples, white sauce. But that wasn't real pizza. Real pizza was about simplicity, and you found simplicity in places like this. Hard orange plastic seats. Harsh lights. White and red delivery boxes stacked on top of the ovens. It was like Houston Heights where Dan had grown up. It was like a good piece of television journalism: unsurprising, easy to follow, satisfying. When you wanted real pizza you wanted doughy crust, tangy red sauce, plenty of mozzarella. You wanted grease pooling on your slice, seeping into your paper plate. And most important—this was the secret nobody on the other side of the Hudson seemed to get—you wanted absolutely no skimping on the oregano. There had to be lots of oregano. Otherwise the point was what, exactly?

Dan stepped onto the street again, heading for Park Avenue. This was often the time of night when loneliness started sifting through him. Jean and he were carried on different currents all day long. She worked on her own art, saw her friends, visited her favorite galleries. Dan worked on his stories, saw his colleagues, got ready for the next broadcast. Often it was past midnight before they convened over scotches on the living-room sofa to reintroduce themselves to each other.

This evening Jean was home with a bad cold. She had caught it while Dan was overseas working on the Chernobyl story. They hadn't wanted to let down Estelle and Robert, so Dan had attended the dinner party alone. Now he wanted to see his wife. He believed he could jet anywhere in the world so long as he could imagine her waiting for him when he returned.

When they had first met, Dan hadn't become Dan yet. He was still this skinny eager guy with a B.A. in journalism from Sam Houston State Teachers College. His father laid oil pipeline. His mother bagged groceries at Weingartens'. Dan never kept a job very long because he was always looking for something that made him feel awake and most of them did just the opposite. He started each believing it would be his last, only something better always seemed to come along.

For some reason, he could never bring himself to think much about his coworkers as coworkers. He conceived of them in simple terms, as impediments to his prospects. He wasn't mean to them. He didn't wish them anything but good. He treated them cordially, as if each were an acquaintance he had just bumped into on the street while late for a more important appointment. Every time he came across them standing around someone's desk or at the water cooler, he smiled, maybe asked a question or two about their families, and remembered his father telling him about locusts. Locusts were usually solitary insects, but they had a secret trigger built into them. When they saw more than two of their species facing a certain direction, they would also start facing that direction. That was how swarms appeared to swell out of nowhere.

Dan did some work for United Press International, some stringing at a couple of local radio stations, a two-year stint at *The Houston Chronicle*. Jean was game every time the scene changed. They had a little girl named Dawn and a little boy named Danjack. Then in 1961 Dan got his big break. He ended up covering Hurricane Carla live from Galveston. TV stations didn't own radar systems back then, so Dan took his camera crew to a nearby Navy base and got a technician there to draw an outline of the Gulf on a sheet of plastic and hold it over the radar display to give viewers a sense of the storm's size and position. CBS executives in New York saw the piece, enjoyed Dan's audacity, and offered him a job.

But Jean never stopped treating him like that skinny eager guy from Sam Houston State Teachers College. Dan appreciated that. It helped keep things spare. With other people he always felt different from himself. With Jean he could be whoever he had to be outside his apartment and then inside be himself. Sometimes at gatherings he noticed her looking at him from across the room, wine glass in hand, trying to figure out who he was supposed to be this evening, who she was supposed to be in turn.

Recently she began cutting her graying hair short like middle-aged Midwestern women did so they didn't have to deal with it. She wore large tortoise-shell glasses. Dan could see where sun damage stained her face with small brown clouds. She had gone slightly swaybacked, developed the beginnings of a potbelly, something until it happened Dan didn't know women could do. That was okay with him, too. Jean and Dan had earned their bodies. Although he had become more handsome in that rough way men do as they aged, he had also become thicker around the middle, puffier around the eyes. His lower teeth had started migrating around inside his lower jaw.

Whenever he thought about Jean and him, he imagined two overweight cats sharing the same couch. They enjoyed not so much interacting with each other as simply being aware of each other's presence.

Dan turned north on Park Avenue, deciding when he got home he would slip into their bedroom and see whether Jean was still awake. If so, he would ask her if she needed anything and sit with her for a while. He wanted to tell her about how Jerome and Robert went after each other. Jean and Dan would have a good laugh over that. Next he would change into his pale blue pinstriped pajamas, crawl in beside her, and read *Paradise of the Blind* until he got too tired to concentrate.

The first punch came from behind him, landing at the base of his skull. Dan stumbled forward and a bluewhite surge overflowed his vision. He semi-straightened, began to rotate, and the second punch caught him square on the cheekbone and ear. He went to his knees.

Instinctively he raised his hands to protect his face.

Hey, he said. Hey. Stop.

Someone was beating him up. That's what was happening to him. Someone was beating the shit out of him. Dan heard fast heavy breathing and fast shoes scraping pavement behind him like someone was doing boxing moves. Maybe there were two sets of scraping. He couldn't tell for sure. Things were going by too quickly.

A fist knuckled him hard in the right temple and Dan went down on his side. He curled into himself, knees to chest, head tucked.

The footwork ceased.

Kenneth, the voice above him said, panting, what's the frequency?

Dan didn't understand. He opened his eyes and saw polished loafers and white socks.

I said what's the fucking frequency, the voice said.

You've got the wrong guy, Dan said. I'm not the guy you're looking for.

The mugger kicked him in the back, tentatively at first, then with increasing zest. A few seconds later he stopped again, winded. Maybe he was examining his work. Maybe he was thinking about his options. Dan couldn't believe no one was coming to help him. There had to be someone around who had noticed what was going on. He heard cars passing by on Park Avenue, but none of them was even slowing down.

Tell me, the voice said.

You want money? Dan asked from beneath his arms. Let me up and I'll give you all the money I've got on me.

Tell me the fucking frequency. I wanna go home now.

I've got like a hundred bucks in my pocket and a nice watch. A ring, too. Let me up and they're yours.

Fuck you.

A Rolex. Self-winding. Just let me up here, and—

Tell me the fucking frequency, man, or I'll fucking *kill* you.

Dan didn't say anything else. He just lay very still, collecting his energy, tasting the blood where he had nipped the inside of his cheek and tongue. Next, he exploded up and was hobblerunning along the block.

His shoulder hurt and his coat and pants were torn and somehow he had twisted his ankle, but he knew he couldn't stop moving.

He heard the guy's footsteps closing the gap between them. A hand brushed his shoulder, scrabbling for a place to grab on. Dan sidestepped it, bobbed and weaved, and a set of glass doors welled up in front of him.

The footsteps fell away as Dan found himself in a marble lobby, palms on knees, inhaling and exhaling frantically.

Behind the main desk a security guard looked up, taking in this new information in his environment. He was massive like Marines are massive. His head was shaved. Dan opened his mouth as if he were about to say something.

Then he was on his back, staring up into bright fuzzy fluorescent light.

He heard someone talking very quickly on a phone across the lobby, and, next, talking very quickly right beside him, telling him to take it easy, pal, take it easy, an ambulance is on the way.

Listening, Dan wafted in the over-lit white space. He watched as black words solidified before him like they were solidifying on a movie screen.

Gradually, they formed a sentence.

Dan had to study it for some time before it made any sense.

Well, it said, *I'm here.*

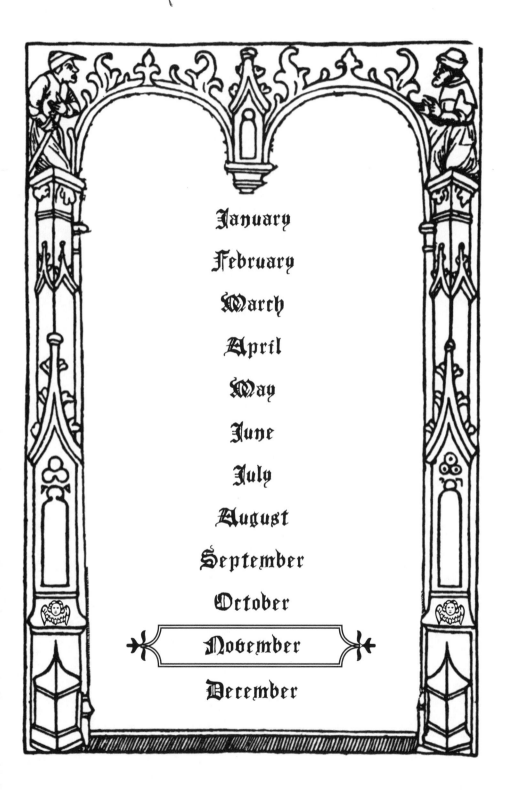

January

February

March

April

May

June

July

August

September

October

November

December

11.02.76. Well, I'm here. Third floor. Right set of shutters. I thought it couldn't get any muggier than in Thailand, Taru, and then I stepped off the plane in Rangoon and lost the little appetite and desire for sleep I had. A two-inch-thick mattress on a narrow bed, damp sheets, a pillow smelling of someone else's hair, a rickety side table with one leg shorter than the others, a lamp without a shade, flaking white walls blossoming with mildew. At night I lie here sweating, crashingly jetlagged, listening to people jabbering nearby in a language that doesn't sound as if it could possibly be a language. Now and then insects built like ~~tanks~~ miniature heavy-duty assault vehicles drop off the ceiling onto my legs and belly. Handcarts, shouts, the giant mosquito engines of tuk-tuks starting up outside the moment the light ashes toward dawn. Yesterday I crossed this border and suddenly became a blurrier version of myself. That's how it works.

11.03.76. Wandering through Shwedagon Pagoda complex this morning, note-taking. No sandals allowed, even though the marble floors are blistering. They call this "the cool dry season." Lower stupa plated with 8,688 solid gold bars. Upper with 13,153. The tip is set with 5,448 diamonds and 2,317 rubies, sapphires, other gems. At the top, a single 76-carat diamond. All that for housing eight hairs from the Buddha. People check you out with sidelong glances when they think you're not looking at them as if you were missing your hands. These monks refused to see my Polaroid and me. They treated me like I was invisible. It hit me this morning: yesterday was my birthday. I'd forgotten. Must have slid into travel's elastic time. Wish me a happy 33 when you get this, okay? Man, do I miss our late-night conversations at the bakery. Man, do I miss you.

11.03.76. More Shwedagon this afternoon. The sweeping women go round and round the complex clockwise, cleaning. Out front, vendors sell wooden dolls, good-luck charms, books, incense sticks, gold leaf, prayer flags, Buddha images, candles, warm cut-open orange melons crawling with flies. I bought a bottle of water from this cute kid, sat down to drink it on a low wall outside, and noticed the seal was broken. When I returned to show him, I discovered him refilling plastic bottles at a spigot around the corner with his friends. Women and children wear pale yellow bark powder on their cheeks, foreheads, and noses as makeup. It occurs to me, sitting under the shade of this banyan tree, drinking a warm Coke, beige dust fogging the air, perhaps the greatest thrill of traveling is to be the one to tell.

11.04.76. The reclining Buddha at ~~Chu~~ Chaukhtatgyi Paya is nearly 200-feet long. Its gargantuan feet are covered with 108 sacred symbols. I have no idea what they mean. No one who speaks an approximation of English in the vicinity seems to know, either. The plaque at the base is in Burmese with its string of half-circles and round doodles broken by abrupt right angles. Studying it, another case of reading blindness comes on. As with the rest of the signs in this country, there's no chance I can tease the script into meaning. I find that sort of sight loss appealing. Most tourists prefer the guidebook to the confusion before them. They want those Michelin reductions that impersonate knowledge, even though the day after tomorrow they'll have forgotten everything they wanted to believe they took in. But isn't travel, Taru, all about the opposite of that? Call it the Aesthetics of Misreading, a continuous reminder of the disorder of things.

11.05.76. What I guess I'm trying to say is that movement is a mode of writing, writing a mode of movement. So it suddenly feels like I'm cheating when I try to picture the travel article I'm supposed to be putting together. You know what I mean? Its heart seems diminishment, its prose the kind unaware that *travel* was originally the same word as *travail*, that *travail* originally referred to an instrument of torture made with three stakes forming a conical frame to which the sorry victim in the Middle Ages was tied and burned alive.

11.06.76. A few beers with these three German trekkers last night amid the surreal polished teak, rattan furniture, chandeliers, and black-lacquered ceiling fans at the fancy bar in the old colonial Strand Hotel down by the river. The woman of the trio so blond she seemed made out of light. They told me the real Burma is north up the Irrawaddy. That's where they're heading. ~~You don't worry about visas, apparently. No one checks outside Rangoon.~~ Today the markets: aged women, teeth stained dark red from betel-nut juice, sitting cross-legged along the streets, frying mutton, asparagus, onions, beans, green peppers, and ginger in heavy iron two-handled woks. They wrap the betel-nut leaf into a triangle with a smear of slaked lime, insert it between their gums and cheeks, let it soak there for hours, spit the excess onto the sidewalk. The air around them carries this pungent fecal reek. Came across a vendor selling fried tarantulas stacked high in a bowl like black potato chips. He spoke wrecked English. I asked him what tarantula tasted like. He thought some, then asked me, expectant: *You ever have scorpion?*

11.07.76. Hans, Werner, Leyna. The Germans' names. A couple more rounds of beer, a teetery stroll through the unlamped streets swarming with rats after dark, Leyna laughing every time one darted out of the shadows. Asked if I wanted to join them on their voyage. My flight back to Bangkok tomorrow. My visa runs out. Have plenty of notes for my piece, but zero motivation to write it. I've been dreading that disengagement one experiences upon arriving home. Remember when I returned from Cairo? *Who was the person who went over there and did all those things? What in the world was he thinking?* You end up maintaining a fever-distance between where you are and where you've been. As if you've been sick. Yeah. That's it. As if you're recovering from some sort of illness.

11.08.76. What the hell, right? Landed a cheap ticket on the ferry to Mandalay. Bought a secondhand sleeping bag stinking of mothballs from a trekker named Jules on his way back to London. Will mail the next batch of these from Bagan. We're living on the noisy, crowded upper deck with the natives. Below, the Irrawaddy is the color of melted chocolate ice cream. A bloated pig's carcass has gotten sucked into our wake. It's been clinging to the side of the ship for miles. Werner is taking bets on how long before the thing parts company with us. He's winning.

11.10.76. Pretty cool, huh? The horizon low flat jungle at sunset today. The reflections Giacomettis shaped out of glistery light. Germans passing around a bottle of rotgut ~~vodka~~ they bought before leaving. Lenya laughing. Hans staring down at the water, sullen. He shaved his head this afternoon to look like a monk. For the hell of it. Werner busy arguing with no one about how Buddhism is the perfect religion for impoverished countries and authoritarian regimes. It teaches you how to put up with endless shit, he says, then ask for more.

11.11.76. You open your eyes this morning, Taru, and see the same scene a man a thousand years ago saw upon opening his.

11.12.76. Among other provisions on his trek across Africa, do you know Dr. Livingstone carried 73 books in three packs? Together, they weighed 180 pounds. Because of his porters' growing fatigue and complaints, Livingstone finally agreed to jettison a small part of his traveling library—after putting more than 300 miles behind him.

11.13.76. Pulled into a village this morning for supplies and passenger exchange. Disembarked to have a look around. Hans in grim
mood. Something's going on among the three of them. My tinea
versicolor's flowered again. Fuck. Light reddish patches across my
shoulders and chest. I'm genetically wired to produce such epidermal junk in these climates. A reminder of where I am, worn on the
skin. And me without my antifungal. The village kids ~~follow~~ dog
us along the dirt paths as if we were the best movie they've ever
seen.

11.13.76. The women fire hundreds of pots at a time under smoldering knolls of hay like this one. Werner strolled up behind me as I was watching and patted me on the back. Hand loitering, he said under his breath: *Every culture contributes what it can to world history, nicht?* Then he wandered away.

11.13.76. I understand Sigmund Freud almost always had to be accompanied by someone on his trips because he had difficulty reading a railroad timetable.

11.13.76. Sorry about the blurriness. She wouldn't stay still. Did we ever talk about how Columbus lied to his crew on their maiden voyage west? It's true. They didn't know where they were, where they were going, how long they'd be at sea. ~~Try to imagine what they were feeling.~~ From their point of view, reality could end any minute. In order to reassure them, Columbus created two logbooks. The private one gave the actual distances covered as he reckoned them, the public shorter ones designed to lead his crew to believe they were closer to home than they actually were. In retrospect, though, it turned out the falsified figures had been more accurate than the authentic ones. When he returned to Spain, Columbus brought with him several captured natives, some gold, some tobacco, and a few specimens of pineapple. But you know what his favorite discovery was? The hammock, Taru. The *hammock*.

11.15.76. Arrived in Bagan at dawn. The view's astonishing. As every tourist says. Unavoidably. But in this case there's really no other way to put it. Five thousand pagodas from Burma's golden age clustered in sixteen square miles of dry central plains. The place thrived from the eleventh through thirteenth centuries—until, that is, the population refused to pay tribute to Kublai Khan and Bagan was sacked and abandoned. Because the current government doesn't think the architecture will attract enough visitors, it's planning on putting in a world-class golf course.

11.16.76. Ducked away from the Germans long enough to picnic by myself atop one of the tallest stupas, spend a little time imagining what we might talk about, Taru, if you were sitting beside me. You can go pretty much anywhere you like here. There aren't any guards, almost no locks. The stone-block steps are so steep you have to use your hands and feet to scrabble up. It's like rock climbing. Every so often you come across the milky translucent skin of a cobra shed on the sandy ground among the ruins. Found a quasi-room for all of us in town this afternoon. Looks like a garage missing its front door: three unpainted cinderblock walls and a cement roof, one side entirely open onto the street, bare floor, one gas lamp, no beds or tables, the outhouse a short walk around back. Dinner at a nearby café. Werner annoyed that it took 45 minutes to get a bowl of lentil soup while seven waiters keystone-copped for nearly 15 in an attempt to change our tablecloth. Hans told him to stop whining. Werner told Hans to go fuck himself. Lenya's artificial laughter becoming increasingly prevalent and unpleasant.

11.17.76. Market day. Warm wet blackred slabs of meat lying out on wooden planks. Piles of unidentifiable spiky fruits, vegetables, dried fish. Open gutters used for everything from pissing to chucking out food scraps, empty potato chip bags, shreds of cloth. A vomity medieval rot general in the air. Leyna struck up the semblance of a conversation with one of the locals, asking him what the Burmese thought of Westerners beginning to descend on his country. The guy smiled madly and hemmed and hawed. She pressed. Eventually he admitted he thought we were foolish for throwing away so much good money to travel halfway around the world to be worked so hard. *But your sneakers very good*, he added. *VERY good*.

11.17.76. What I saw sans Polaroid this afternoon: a skeletal dog missing large patches of hair and covered with crimson pustules who'd had both its hind legs broken at some point. They'd mended so misshapen he had to sort of drag-hop them behind him. Yet there he was busily trying to hump an equally skeletal bitch in heat. Every time he mounted her, his bad legs caused him to slide off, only he wouldn't give up. He just kept draghopping himself after her, rising briefly, clutching her around the waist, losing his balance, toppling to the side.

11.17.76. I feel like I am always moving, Taru. Like I am never exactly where I am.

11.18.76. At sunset they begin burning off garbage across the plains. Smoke rises like mist in front of the bare mountains. Since the government doesn't see a future in these buildings, it restores them haphazardly, ignoring the architectural styles, using materials bearing no relation to the origi

Atop a temple teeming with European tourists, a sweet little Burmese girl holding a single postcard in her hand just sat down next to me. Her postcard shows the same view I am witnessing. She blows her nose into the fingers of her free hand, distractedly wipes the mess across her belly, turns to me and says: *Where you from? You want buy postcard?* All I want is to live these next three minutes by myself because I won't ever get to live them again. I give her a quick mechanical grin and return to the sunset, try very hard to pretend she's not there. *Where you from?* she says, undaunted by my indifference. *Hello. Hello. Where you from? How long you be here? Mister, mister, where you from? Hello?*

11.18.76. Finally gave up on me and left. I'm guilty. I'm relieved. Each of the Germans has gone, too, dispersed to watch the sun sink from a vantage point away from the others. They've gotten on each other's nerves. Tourists approach this scene with their cameras raised, framing, trying to control what and how they'll remember when they return home. In the process, they block other tourists trying to do the same, elbow the local Burmese out of the way. What in the world do they do with all the photos they take? Look at them once and stash them away in a shoebox, an album, a drawer? Show them after a nice dinner to a group of captive friends who feel the event nothing if not an imposition? Or maybe they just forget to develop them altogether? Maybe at the end of the day the simple act of arranging the shots in the viewfinder, cropping the world over and over again, is the only thing that really matters.

11.19.76. Remember Jean and Geoff, Taru? How they planned on going to Penzance, of all places, for years and years, then at the last minute decided not to because they'd read so much about it, seen so many pictures of it in travel catalogs, they said it felt like they'd already been?

11.20.76. Last night the trio came in ~~stumbling~~ drunk. Hans and Werner arguing about something in German. Out of the blue Hans threw a punch, catching Werner below the eye. Werner launched from the floor and tackled him. They went after each other briefly, until Lenya and I could break them up. This morning I woke to discover everyone gone. I'm pretty sure for good. Maybe they got tired of each other. Maybe they got tired of me. Maybe they got tired of this uncanny country. Maybe they got tired of the very idea of traveling. When you're on a trip, every day begins as a possibility. It will either be one of most memorable you've ever lived or it will be one of the most easily forgettable. You never know. Nobody knows what's going to happen next.

11.21.76. I'm thinking I'll hang around here a little longer, then continue on to Mandalay. I've always wanted to see that place. I suppose I should be unnerved by them ditching me like that, maybe even hurt, but, shit, all I feel is let loose.

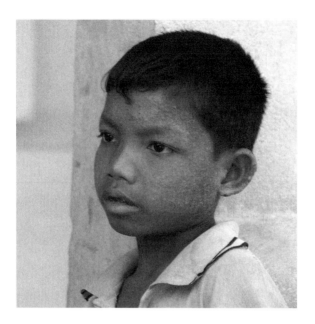

11.22.76. Decided what I really want today, Taru. I really want to sit down across from you in our bakery on Bleeker and Cornelia like we used to do right after college, order almond croissants and lattés, and talk about how the saddest thing is how every McDonald's smells the same no matter where on the planet it is. ~~How some people travel to shop, some to do business, bond as a family, be alone, meet strangers, run away from something, find something they can't articulate, experience the feeling of new data rushing in, help locate the limits of their own minds. How travel is an exercise in imagining the unimaginable. How every journey has a secret destination of which the traveler is always unaware.~~ How I had that roommate at NYU. Dennis. Remember? Dark curly hair, glasses, an upper lip that protruded over the lower, a goofy smile that dropped his IQ a handful of points? He toured Europe for six weeks, had a great time, visited tons of countries, returned to the States, and never traveled again. Can we do that, Taru? Meet at our bakery? This afternoon? Let's say at two? Love, me.

11.23.76. What do you imagine the schoolkids in this photograph made of the ~~raggedy blond~~ bearded American who stopped them in the dusty street to ask if he could take ~~there~~ their picture? What's going through the head of the one on the far right? It's beyond a visitor's capability to hazard a guess, I guess. I find myself remembering how you can sometimes feel like you're taking one logical step after another on a journey, only when you look up you discover yourself lost—not as in gone astray, but as in over your head. And the thing is: it feels completely right. You would never have done this thing had you known in advance where you would end up. Yet under the circumstances it would never occur to you to do otherwise.

11.24.76. At lunch I ate several tables away from these two American women with sun-mottled skin who could have been in their mid-forties or their mid-sixties. Having ordered, I went over and asked if they'd mind taking my photo. It was only after they'd agreed, after I'd thanked them and returned to my table, after the couple had reentered their conversation, that I realized I'd interrupted the story the short brunette was telling the tall redhead about how one day her older sister had just up and disappeared. It was unclear when this was, but the short brunette was still clearly shaken. I picked away at my food, pretending I couldn't hear them. The short brunette explained that, because of the age difference, they had never been that close. *It was an ordinary day, then it was a horror.* Those were the words she used. She said everything became something else in her life with a single phone call. It felt like moving while standing still. *How can such a thing happen?* the tall redhead asked her, leaning forward on her elbows. *Like this,* responded the short one, snapping her fingers. *Just like*

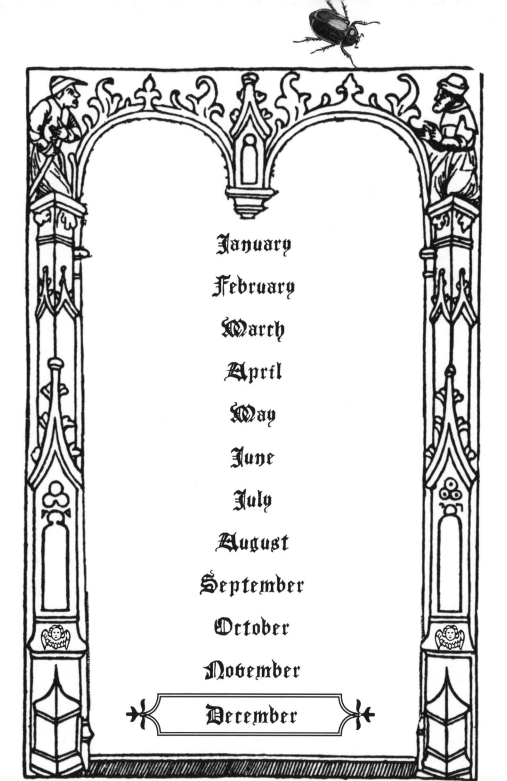

January

February

March

April

May

June

July

August

September

October

November

December

this: it makes me feel like I'm doing something for others, being useful, you could say, the same point I was able to make about my monkeys and me once upon a time—when I was fresh out of college, fresh in the classroom, when everyone needed saving and could be saved. After a while, naturally, such thrills rinse into something much paler. I like to imagine I can recall the specific moment of the modification, the stillness between one breath and another when everything became other than it had been. It was, I want to say, a rainy afternoon in November, the maples outside the window bare and bony, the palette having weakened into shades of wet black and gray, the classroom yellow and steamy with teenage hair, soggy sneakers, and Right Guard, and there I was jotting an equation on the chalkboard that answered the question: *What do butterflies do in a downpour?*

As it happens, the answer is *they get the hell out of it* because, if you do the algebra, you learn that for a 500-milligram monarch with wings only a few cells thick getting pelted by a 70-milligram raindrop is the equivalent to you or me being battered by water balloons with twice the mass of bowling balls.

I thought this sort of knowledge, if any, would net their attention. I was wrong. You're always looking for ways to fake their lingo while pretending not to fake it, ways to carry information from your solar system to theirs . . . and then some chimp was chittering behind me, another joining him, and I slipped on my stern expression, began rotating, but, in the adrenaline boil that that rotation took me, something metallic pinged off the chalkboard several inches from the back of my head, paper and books shuffled like crazy, a whootle rose and was answered by a fleeting hodge-podge of honks and howls, and presto:

By the time I faced them, there my class sat, silent as spite, staring back at me decorous and blank and pitiless as a murmuration of Methodists.

The real news took some time to burrow in, as real news does, yet from here, on this mattress in this windowless room half a life later, it feels fast and unexpected as the first flinch in an overweight businessman's left arm.

My hope was in it.

My hope was out of it.

Ping.

Don't get me wrong, I'm not saying I suddenly hated them, it wasn't that, there was nothing sudden about it, and I didn't hate them. I didn't like them, either. It was more—

It was that they saw me, I came to understand in that capsize, as a piece of furniture, a television set with legs, say, even if not quite as surreally amusing. They saw me as something to be endured until they could locate the remote and click me out of their heads, drag their ennui into another channel several hundred yards down the hall in order to think the same thing about the harried woman or man who greeted them there—who, naturally, was thinking much the same thing about them, retaliation being what it is, exhaustion being what it is, although it was inconceivable for such a notion to penetrate their airtight faculties.

And so I may have been turned into a piece of furniture in that first flinch, sure, but it was also the case that they had been change-linged too, becoming a sea of hobbits, homo ergasters, little green lunarians, in my eyes. I felt toward them what any rational being would toward a species she could no longer quite recognize as her own, one that paid homage to voluminous costumes, preposterous customs, shrill plumage, thumpity-bump music, supersonic films in which things went bang in the night, and shiny silver nuggets stuck through eyebrows, noses, nipples, lips, clits, tongues, cocks.

It's a cliché, I know, they're a cliché, I am too, but there you have it, there you will always have it, what a strange tug in the chest.

Unsurprisingly, each of my monkeys saw him or herself as an *enfant terrible*, a sensitive antihero, a profligate lone wolf, while none fathomed she or he had been and always would be in lockstep with all the other putative *enfants terribles*, sensitive antiheros, and profligate lone wolves in his or her pack, difference for them amounting at the end of the day to just another way of being the same.

I'm unique! their anxious eyes exclaimed across the classroom every time I glanced up at them from my work. —*Aren't I?*

Well, of course you are, dears.

Of course you are.

Our entire popular culture is in essence about high school: about reliving it, about its social relations, about the fears it hammers into your plans.

What I knew that they couldn't, know that they can't, what covered such scenes with a gauzy membrane of regret, was that in three years, or five, or ten, tops, when their own hopeful hype had eventually lost heart, they would become precisely the run-of-the-mill lawyers, bankers, pastors, podiatrists, receptionists, accountants, nurses, cooks, clerks, engineers, office managers, rental car agents, taxi cab drivers, electricians, machinists, bartenders, realtors, chefs, stay-at-home moms, deadbeat dads, and—god forbid—high-school teachers whom they sneered at now and believed, ho-hum, they would sneer at forever. Over a relatively short period of time, they would forget completely who they had been in my class, forget my class, forget me, forget that metallic ping, forget that rainy afternoon, just as I would forget them, forget the subtle traits they believed differentiated them from others of their breed—despite the 182 days a year, give or take, we spent staring each other down—and they would grow into the very people they openly ridiculed with that desperate and desperately hackneyed cool.

At least, I remind myself, there is always some minor satisfaction in that.

The metallic ping, rainy afternoon, flip-flop inside my faith took place more than thirty years ago. These days it arrives as no shocker, no pronunciamento, that from one September to another my abecedarians remain basically alike as a boxful of white-headed thumbtacks, you scarcely teach one batch how to parse an unadorned differential and off they toddle, leaving you to start afresh with the next batch slouching through the door, taking in my classroom like a charm of convicts their new digs. Oh, sure, perhaps each autumn the latest troop knows a few grams less about the world of numbers and nominatives than the one that eyed me charily the September before, perhaps they wear nearly imperceptibly different angry identities corporate executives bamboozled them into plucking off shelves at that bright nightmare called the Mall of America, and yet, still, all said and done, they remain, fundamentally, living constants in my own ongoing equations. They remain firm believers in concepts like autonomy because they're the sort that swallow whatever they're told like a handful of colorful gummy bears while pretending to question every dust mite of fact and authority, the sort that play the role of rebels and renegades because they want nothing more than for someone like aging, plumping, drooping me to plop down a few do's and don'ts before them, draw a couple of lines in the regulatory sand, and then tell them they are forbidden to cross at the risk of detention, suspension, expulsion, tamp them down, spell out exactly what they've got to ape in order to fatten into that farrow of adults called *us*.

Each day I look a little more like the kind of person they're wired to distrust and shit-talk behind her back: the math matron, the Latin Club lady, the increasingly block-shaped old bag in beige slacks, outrageously beflowered blouse, and large tortoise-shell stereotypes with distorting lenses who appears to them a short prim flautist in her fifties. She's the nervous type who measures time by the weeks between one hair-coloring and the next: Moira Lovelace, the ogre most of them, their green theories notwithstanding, will wake up one morning to meet in their own bathroom mirrors. Blink, and you're smacking your panty-pink bubblegum, fidgeting with the combination on your locker, obsessing about those designer jeans with the cute red-thread highlights you just *have* to have. But blink again, my pretties, and a ball bearing is snapping off the blackboard fewer than a twelve inches from the back of your head and you're standing there thinking: *What the fuck did I do to land in a place like this?*

It's that quick, that astonishing.

The extinction of experience, I want to say.

An existential smear.

Sometimes they remind me so much of myself at that age I can barely stand to glare at them, destined as they are to inhabit screenplays they trust they're scripting, only to discover one day they've really been written by somebody else, some*thing* else that you can't actually point a finger at because its pen is scribbling everything and everyone from everywhere all at once.

Here's a bowling ball for you, my monarchs.

Happy flapping.

They can't help themselves, I can't help myself, any more than those young, short-skirted, blue-eyed, blond-haired schoolteachers can who sneak a couple of quickies back at the ranch with their wonder-eyed fourteen-year-old faunlets and later call the hanky-panky an affliction, a sickness, a disease, a sin, true love—on national TV, no less, the sluts.

What's so hard to figure? They're not bonking little boys. They're bonking themselves, their webby age lines, their saggy fannies, the adolescence they're losing a sliver of every day, skin flakes from a psoriatic. Bonk hard enough, they're frantic to believe, and maybe it won't fade so fast. Bonk hard enough, and maybe they can make it linger a few bumps and grinds longer. The least they can do is own up. They're as bad as those Christian fundies who claim to be opening their wombs for God, reproducing like rabies, swarming the globe with Jesus Camp fodder, bunging up the place with a glut of progeny in a masterful act of selfish, thoughtless, righteous insular idiocy. Like my big sis, Sarasa, who found herself with four kids, two dogs, no husband, a foreclosure, and an unbounded devotion to the Almighty who'd done all that to her. Her answer? Sprinkle said kids and dogs among church chums and hightail it to Southeast Asia on missionary work to convert more cretins to her messed-up lifestyle. Way to go, sis.

My own weaknesses subsist on another continent altogether. They have nothing to do with narcissism or nympholepsy.

They have to do, as I say, with making myself useful.

The camcorder didn't come cheap, you could call it my one genuine extravagance in life, but the rest—my makeup, toys, wigs, outfits, blank cartridges, software, faux silk leopard sheets—I collected over time the same way nerds do stamps and southern grannies those hair-raising darky cookie jars.

My modus operandi: Friday afternoon shuffle through my apartment door drained, drawn, stunned by the week behind me, wanting nothing save to sink into a protracted slack-jawed hibernation. Order out for pepperoni pizza, watch self-important Dan Rather deliver the news, spend the evening surfing the web for nothing in particular, vaguely curious about where the next click will escort me, always a little taken aback, a little disappointed, even, by where it ultimately does, at the end of the line some dumb ad for spam filters, cheap financing, affordable friends, unable to retrace my breadcrumbs back to any awareness of how I got there, and then, bushed, beat, to bed. Saturday things start looking up: curled on my living room couch, pot of green tea and tin of Walkers shortbread beside me, grade pop quizzes until three, plick down my pencil, stand, stretch, clear my head, and stride into two shots of bourbon on the rocks at the liquor cabinet, a Jenny Craig dinner, a lounge before whatever happens to be happening on TV. I prefer the reality shows, where life is scrupulously edited to look like life, only with midgets, has-been female wrestlers, geeky dates, appalling singers, and skinny rednecks setting themselves on fire in their underwear in shopping carts while they ride down ski slopes into unforgiving geologic outcroppings—all for a handful of shekels and six seconds of mild public interest mixed with open derision.

What childhoods those guys must not have had.

Dishwasher sealed, steam a-hiss inside, fill my tub with lavender-harvest bubble bath, light three coconut-scented candles, and settle into the lush cadences of Celine Dion's *Falling into You.*

Let people say what they want, my monkeys would rattle their cages in malicious delight if they only knew, yet the truth is this: you simply can't bring yourself to feel anything like cynical about the world when "Because You Loved Me" is playing on your boom box while you slosh in sweet foamy warmth and bird-wing flickerings.

I've learned lots these past two years. How a whole evening can be dedicated to a worthy sixteen-second clip, how the right lighting is hugely harder to attain than it may at first appear, how a plastic bag taped over your liquored-up head—just you and your caught breath and the distant whir of your camcorder—can begin turning damp and scary much more quickly than you might have initially presumed. I've learned that making is always a mixture of danger and discovery, meaning always a story, and how worthwhile it all feels sitting there Sunday morning before your computer screen, snipping, shaping, copying.

Post proelia praemia, as I always used to coach my miniature Romans. Relentlessly. *After battles, the rewards.*

A thought that makes, that made, Monday the most vivid day of the week. I woke early and spry, mind spiky as three cups of caffeine, downed a bagel runneled with cream cheese and orange marmalade, primped, and drove to the local library, where I waited in my Corolla the color of desert sand till the front doors unlocked. Everyone knew me there. Hands raised and smiles magnified as Ms. Lovelace bustled through the metal detectors. She waved and beamed back, beelining for the shelves stacked with phonebooks at the rear of the third floor: every major city in America, many large towns, most minor ones, a landslide of Lilliputian names rilling down page after butterfly-wing-thin page. It's heady stuff, all that data speeding by.

I lifted a finger and jabbed it down at random: *there* and . . . *there* and . . . *that one, too.*

A lust lottery.

Passion packages.

Moira's love letters to the world.

Outside the post office several minutes later, I'd pause an extra heart whoosh in the incessantly unpleasant Minnesotan wind before letting an armful of them drop down the chute, picturing the sizzle they would put into the spines of people I would never meet: the middle-aged housewife with chapped lips who innocently unearths my offering among the otherwise featureless mail mountain on her husband's desk; the doe-eyed sophomore in a fuzzy rose sweater unwrapping one surrounded by her sorority sisters in her Alpha Kappa Alpha den, assuming she's unwrapping a thoughtful weekly present from her parents in Peoria; the beetle-backed preacher in pressed jeans and plaid shirt humming to himself, swaying to his own celestial music on some suburban street corner, lifting a bubble-padded envelope out of the black aluminum tube and believing he's just received a lovely little daybook or Whitman sampler from one of his flock in Fredericksburg; the friendless widower; the blue bus driver; the waitress who feels she's waited long enough; or, luck being what it is, what it isn't, another teacher, an educator not unlike myself, only, say, male instead of female, younger instead of older, taller instead of sadder.

Puritanism is at its most diabolical when, as in this perilously unimaginative nation, it somehow trusts that it's being its opposite.

Swedes would swoon at my enterprise, Danes dance, but all my fallow Americans can do is pray on, preying on. Moira intended to show them what change feels like, that there remained alternatives to this alternative, and so, standing at that postal chute, she couldn't help wondering who might be thinking about her this very minute in Pleasantville, Iowa, and how . . . and then it was bombs away, fire in the hole, the prim squat schoolmarm barging back to her car, sliding in behind the wheel, thumping shut the door, flipping on NPR to see what progress isn't being made in the Middle East, and rolling happily out of the parking lot onto the boulevard lined with fast-food joints and bus stops and used-car lots that led toward her quadratic equations and third conjugation i-stem verbs.

Last month I received out of the blue an email from the wife of a high school semi-boyfriend named Flynn. We had semi-dated for six weeks, which in eleventh-grade is just this side of an ice age. We had exchanged bead bracelets. We had held hands, although never in public. We had gone to exactly one movie together, whose title I've forgotten, as I'm wont to do these days, and perched in the dark, untouching, learning what a date wasn't likely to be about.

Because we lived in the same town where we'd grown up, Flynn and I had stayed in indistinct contact with each other ever since, said hello through intermediaries, occasionally face to face in the ice-cream aisle at the supermarket or in front of the cash register at the gas station. Flynn played football and piano well at Jefferson Senior High, but not as well as we all wanted to believe, not well enough, for instance, to do more, when the time came, than to slip himself through the nearly shut doors of an underwhelming state school up the 494 on a scholarship that entitled him to very little when he graduated, six years later, with a BA in musicology. Next I heard, he was serving as amanuensis to a distinguished pianist in Paris. Next I heard, he was back in Bloomington, coaching at the community college. And that's where he remained for the following thirty years, married to a disappointed French lecturer named Franny, father to an easily addled son with bad self-esteem, committed to making what he ended up doing for a living sound to others like something other than a poignant misstep.

Flynn, Franny explained in her staccato e-note, entered the hospital for routine hip-replacement surgery to fix his fullback years. The operation went off without a hitch—until, that is, an infection flowered within him, one of those virulent bacterial strains that chew through a patient's every prospect. One week Flynn was perfectly fine, minus the limp and a certain throbby stiffness. The next he was on a ventilator. And the next Franny was emailing acquaintances like me in an attempt to drum up something that looked like an acceptable audience for the memorial service I had absolutely no intention of attending.

I had never been especially close to Flynn, had already lost my own mom to a brusquely failed heart eleven years ago, looked on helplessly as an unfamiliar physician signed away my increasingly dreamy dad into an assisted living center, lamented my aunt's execution by aneurysm and another unvigilant colleague's by Jeep Cherokee.

Somehow with all those passings I had still been young enough, middle-aged enough, to sidestep their full-metal impact and busy myself into distraction, but Flynn's going flapped at me enormous and inky, arrived with a blow of recognition about how one day, no matter what you do, no matter what you don't, you begin to experience a lack of light from the inside out. There's no elaborate way to say this. I got scared. I got scareder. Over the next few days, I retreated down the hall of my apartment into my office, a dark eight-by-eight cubicle spartanized with two aluminum filing cabinets, desk, swivel-chair, drawn blinds, and bare walls, and bathed in the bluewhite glow of my computer screen, eating choco-choco chip Häagen-Dazs and clicking aimlessly, then less aimlessly, then finding myself navigating one of those sites dedicated to explaining whatever happened to your high-school classmates. Did they shrug on the flab, make a fortune, hunt down a mate, become a cosmetician, move to Malibu?

I was there, it struck me, to make sure they were all all right.

And they all were, more or less. The majority had never left town, or had left, toed the void at the edge of their flat earth, and scurried back, drawn inexorably homewards by Bloomington's safe, corn-fed, suburban gravity. Some had bought their parents' houses or moved in down the lightly leafy lanes from them. They swam with their hatch in the same backyard pools they had swum as tots and teens. They traced the same routes to the same soccer fields, bakeries, pizzerias, dry cleaners, dance studios, music lessons, jujitsu classes, orthodontists, churches. The science superstar, a good guy named Gyong-si, whose parents were unimaginatively from Korea, secured a PhD in physics from Cornell and then, at the very brink of snatching a research post at a company somewhere in the new south, decided instead to open his own simulated Nepalese new-age wellness center in Chicago, while the wrestling luminary went on to impregnate and marry—in that order—a second-string football cheerleader, chub into the Michelin man's brother, and open his own 7-Eleven on American Boulevard. The queen of the flower children mellowed her way cross country and landed in Oahu, where by chance I caught her late one night in the first episode of *Real Sex*. She was into group groping on sunny verandas as a means of personal discovery.

Nearly every one of the other women had had kids, nearly every one of the other men had taken positions they never would have imagined taking, not in a million years, back in high school, and many used their crannies of the website to effuse about the dwindling number of days till next year's thirty-fifth reunion at the local Holiday Inn, a gala that would include a cash bar, catered finger food, a sixties cover band, a driving-range diversion for the guys, an expedition to the nail spa for the gals, and a smorgasbord of melancholy, longing, schadenfreude, and remorse for everyone concerned.

From that grayish sea of names, some of which I recalled, some
of which I could convince myself I recalled if I tried really hard, but
really didn't, some of which I would swear I had never seen in my
life, one in particular bobbed to the surface: *Aleyt*. I had forgotten
until I came across it, floating there, that she and I had been something like best friends through the better part of tenth grade. She
showed up framed in our homeroom door one morning, fresh from
Faribault, looking antsy and skinny and misplaced, pearl-blond
hair in pigtails, complexion a Scandinavian dough, eyes a wisterial
blue, bellbottoms too short, primrose tube-top too flat and rhine-
stoney by half. She was going to be, if she wasn't careful, a sitting
duck. By the end of calculus, I had made a point of striking up a
six-syllable conversation with her, five of them mine. By the end of
lunch, we were buddies. By the end of the month, we were hanging
out at the sweetshop together, biking through the park, phoning
each other while ticking through homework, sleeping over at my
house every other Friday night. We blew up an aluminum balloon
of Jiffy Pop and peeked out at monster movies on the black-and-
white set with the bent rabbit ears from beneath a shared blanket
on my unfolded castro convertible. The creature from the black
lagoon mooned for Julie Adams, gigantic radiation-mutated ants
skittered across cityscapes toward Joan Weldon huddling in James
Whitmore's arms, and my father owned an old Eastman Kodak
8mm Brownie.

If I pleaded with him annoyingly enough, harped at him cutely
enough, he would sometimes relent and let us borrow it, so long as
we used our allowances to buy the film, develop it, and swore cross-
our-hearts that we would be super-duper watchful with it. Friday
afternoons we became screenwriters, directors, actors, stuntmen,
choreographers, costumers, editors, property masters, producers,
and sisters that should have been but weren't, turning a short roll
down a small hill into a three-minute experimental investigation
into the notion of motion; a Barbie, a can of lighter fluid, and a pile
of twigs into a blazing vision of daring Joan stuck on the stake,

praying without moving her lips as she liquefied blackly. And once, lacking a male lead for the love scene we had composed, Aleyt put on a black construction-paper mustache and we smooched. It felt very good and very strange and we had never kissed anyone on the lips before and, by the following April, Aleyt had unpigtailed herself, lengthened her gauche jeans, and started plumping out less humdrum tube-tops. Boys caught her scent.

There was never a specific day we deliberately became less than friends. We never had what you might call a falling out. We still saw each other through the summer, through eleventh and twelfth grades, too, but always less and less, always as increasing strangers, passing each other in the halls with artificially cheery smiles, chatting each other up among colorful sweaters piled on display tables at the Gap, bumping into one another (Aleyt nearly always hand-in-hand with some polite boyfriend with a Lutheran aura and vaguely glassy eyes) at the hamburger joint, the mandatory pep rally, the town library, the lavatory tampon dispenser, yet I kept a soft spot for her, never wished anything but good for her, failed to remember her for months at a time only for her presence to materialize before me in the midst of a tricky math problem or handful of Raisinettes at the movie theater.

And then she left me. Aleyt dropped out of my frame of reference. My viewfinder went vacant.

Her profile on the website proclaimed she had traveled east for college, studied film and psych at Sarah Lawrence, alighted briefly in the Village to see if she could make a go of it there and, when she realized she couldn't, flew back here, where a few years later she wound up marrying a cop with a buzz cut. They churned out three children, now all grown and gone.

I got up to refill my bowl of ice cream, ate it leaning against the kitchen counter, paid a visit to the bathroom, paced up and down the hall two or three times to rouse my legs, took my place before the computer screen, got up to refill my bowl of ice cream, ate it leaning against the kitchen counter, stood in my living room with the lights off and my eyes shut, listening, mostly to the creamy pulse behind my lids, took my place before the computer screen, and, without a single further thought, clicked on Aleyt's email address, typed her a fast message, and hit send.

I told her I was glad to discover she was doing well, I was doing okay myself, I would really like to hear from her sometime and imagine together the size of the numbers that had collected between us. I didn't tell her it was unlikely we still had anything in common, anything whatsoever, unlikely we ever had had anything in common, even back in tenth grade, if we had taken the time to think about it—apart, perhaps, from a certain fascination with my dad's camera and a certain frenzied need to claim friendship at any cost, and that, I've learned since, is precisely as sad as it sounds.

Next morning Aleyt's reply was waiting for me. She couldn't believe it, she wrote, she simply couldn't believe it, she was so glad to come across my name in her inbox, how weird it seemed, how familiar, how many memories it brought back, how many years had rushed us since high school, more than thirty of them, and what was I doing these days, where was I living, what was I thinking about, because wouldn't it be great to get together for a cup of coffee someday? It would be. I don't know why, but it really would be. I don't believe I believed we could rekindle an extinguished familiarity. I wasn't *that* naïve. I believe I believed, instead, that I just wanted to know what Aleyt would look like and be like, how at least one story in my life had drawn toward a finale, what it would feel like to complete some kind of circle, knowing, naturally, how homiletic all that sounded, how in real life the only circles are the snaky species that can never quite seem to locate their own tails.

Two more exchanges and we had set a date for Saturday at four at a local coffeehouse. That's when Aleyt's husband Jerry usually slipped out for a couple of brewskies with the boys. I showed up at three forty-five, a blindingly bitter day outside, the first of my school's winter vacation, early sunset already buttering the blue atmosphere with night cold. I ordered a latté and a slice of banana-nut bread, and I curled up with the *Star Tribune* in a cubbyhole toward the front packed with two oversized plush, homey, purple chairs that had been painstakingly manufactured to look like they had seen much better days.

Next thing, someone was palming me on the shoulder, saying *Moira, is that YOU?*, and my heart knocked and I looked up and saw a woman I had never seen before, or maybe a woman I *had* seen before, it was difficult to tell which, it had been a very long time—a woman, in any case, whose identity blurred in and out of focus like jumpy video footage. She had quadrupled in heft, thickened into middle age, her hair wasn't blond but black, wasn't long but bobbed, her complexion had mottled, roughed up, reddened, olived, her eyes had darkened, and her nose was someone else's. She wore large wire-rimmed glasses, a wide squinty smile, and a heavy red holiday sweater with a herd of happy green reindeer cantering across from front to back and around from back to front again.

It IS you! she exclaimed. *It IS! OH! MY! GOD!*

There were only a handful of other patrons, an elderly parkaed man with cadaverous cheeks and an aluminum cane no doubt out for his daily excursion, a clique of cute college co-eds caffeinating over a shared computer, a trio of galpals in their early thirties passing time passing around photos of some exotic cruise they had taken to San Juan or Saint Maarten and chirping at the glossy results with glee. They all stopped what they were doing to see what we were doing without making it appear that that's what they were doing, and I was on my feet, my newspaper flapping down behind me, and Aleyt and I were bear-hugging like people in sitcoms and L.A. bistros do, exaggeratedly familiar with each other while not really familiar at all, a display of practiced friendship-fervor you want to be ten times truer than it is, though you think maybe you're at least fooling those around you, if nothing else, though you know you're not, no, not at all, not for a second.

Aleyt went up to the counter to order. I took my seat and

commenced rearranging myself, head weightless as helium. The others around us coasted back to their own continents. Above the parking lot and brick buildings outside, the sun wasn't so much setting as dissolving into a nordic yellowgray haze. Aleyt returned holding a Toffee Nut Crème and a napkin-skirted Brownie Immorality before her. She had bought me a second tall latté, too. She set her loot on the pale wood palette-shaped table and collapsed across from me. Lounging back, studying me, she took a big bite of sugar, chocolate, butter, eggs, and walnuts, smacked away, and, mouth full, teeth gunked, half-cleared her throat and said: You look *soooooo* good, girl. You know what I'm going to do here? I'm going to just sit back while you tell me *every*thing. I'm all ears, honey. All ears.

Somehow that was what I needed to hear, evidently, because I did, I told her everything, or at least almost everything, you know how it is, you can never be too careful, about how after high school I majored in education at the U., minored in math and Latin, student-taught up near Medicine Lake, entered my very own menagerie, have been feeding my little ones, whom I don't hate, whom I don't hate and don't especially like, either, baboon-knowledge ever since, how I dated a few guys, slept with fewer, raised my head and realized I was in my late twenties and still had plenty of time left, how I dated a few more, slept with a few fewer, raised my head and realized I was in my late forties and that all the time had run out, quick as a shiver, you're one thing and then you're another, even though you feel like you're not, even though you feel like you're really the same thing from one month to another, only a different size, a different weight, a different outlook with different skin conditions, and yet *whose life turns out the way you thought it would?* I asked, *name me one person, just one*—but, despite all that, I said, it feels okay, doesn't it, it feels right, even, sometimes, other times not so much so, only do you remember those crazy films we used to make, those video letters to ourselves, how goddamn creative we were back then, how our Friday afternoons used to blaze by behind the lens? What happened to those kids? I know you can't tell me, but tell me anyway. How strange, isn't it, that I can remember the year we were best buddies more vividly than what I did the day before yesterday, regardless of the fact that I'd be the first to admit I'm romancing the whole deal here, sure, nothing remarkable about that, is there, nostalgia being what it is, being what it isn't, only you have to confess there was a certain *density* to our high-school years, wasn't there, a certain extension in time and space, you could say, with which last Thursday can't begin to compare, it feels as if we've been half asleep for most of our lives, everything gray and gritty, while back then, before this librarian or that internist, we really *were* awake, and it was morning, and we had just woken up, and we were lying in our beds, dug into our quilts, and even before we opened our eyes we could tell, we really could, I don't know how, that it was a stunning day outside, the sky unconditionally blue . . .

January

February

March

April

May

June

July

August

September

October

November

December

It was a stunning day outside. Even before I opened my eyes, I could tell an unconditionally blue sky would greet us. I took it as a sign. A prophecy. Events would go as they needed to go.

I rolled over to wake Iphi and found her already lying on her back under the comforter, right arm cocked behind her head. She wasn't looking up at the ceiling. She was looking up at the unspoiled Sunday morning beyond it.

It's here, she announced to herself. We're here.

We arrived the day before yesterday. Minneapolis to Kennedy, Kennedy to Heathrow. This was what we were told to do. This was what we had been told to do twice before, our flight routes different each time.

My ideas still gauzy with jetlag.

My lower abdomen tingling.

We lay in the B&B across the street from Marylebone Station. Our bed took up so much space we had to shuffle around it sideways to reach the bath. In the next room, a man and a woman jabbered in a language that didn't sound as if it could possibly be a language. We listened because we didn't have a choice.

I snuggled my nose into the skin between Iphi's neck and collarbone and took long deep breaths. I mounted her. She was dry. I got off, rummaged through our suitcase, returned with a tube of KY.

I tried again, but the moment was behind us.

At the bathroom mirror, trimming my beard with scissors. Touching up the black in my hair with the kit I purchased yesterday. Stepping into the shower.

Soaping up, rinsing off.

Soaping up, rinsing off.

Farsi, I think.

Loose black slacks, white knit sweater, a pair of highly polished black shoes. I flipped on the television to the morning shows. A famous young underfed woman who was famous only for being famous and underfed stood before a congested counter watching a fat man in an apron and chef's hat make flamboyant waffles with whip cream, strawberries, banana slices, blueberries, maple syrup, large lozenges of butter.

She wore a silver mini-skirt and frilly white blouse and looked tired and lost.

The shower tunked off. The hairdryer roared. I couldn't hear what the famous underfed woman was saying or wasn't saying. The hairdryer stopped. Iphi appeared and began dressing in her burqa and black slip-on shoes. She was careful to braid and tuck back her long black hair first.

I clicked off the television set, and then we kneeled and prayed silently at the foot of the unmade bed.

Eyes shut.

Listening to the worlds inside us and out.

It was difficult to say whether the people in the next room were fighting or just talking loudly. This is what their language had done to them.

Beyond their commotion: doors opening and closing up and down the hall, footfalls thumping. Engines thrumming on the street three floors below. Horns. Air brakes.

A police siren ululating.

Above us, a plane either gaining or losing altitude.

All this noise.

All this doing.

For what?

Sitting across from each other at the tiny table in the cramped dining room in the basement. The air damp and pungent with bacon fat. It seemed to us our words described things other than the things that seemed important to us, and so we didn't use them.

Iphi studied her eggs. Beans on fried toast. The surreally red wedge of tomato and three fried mushrooms.

I reached over and picked up a newspaper a businessman had left behind on the chair at the next table and tried reading. Nothing from its pages reached me. I folded it again, returned it to the chair, sipped my espresso.

Staring over Iphi's head, I waited for her to finish.

9:37. Flossing and brushing. Spearmint mouthwash. A longer urination followed by a shorter one.

9:51. Iphi standing framed in the bathroom door, eying the ugly gray rug.

Language was never important for us. It isn't what comes out of your mouth that matters. We understood such things from the day we met three years ago at the church retreat in Voyageurs National Park. I was seventeen, Iphi sixteen. We happened to sit together at the campfire one evening during the sing along. Next morning we either deliberately or not sat side-by-side at first prayer.

Her dark brown eyes, long shiny black hair.

The unadorned goodness of her spirit.

You don't need many words.

Who can explain how over lunch we discovered we both lived in Bloomington, both attended Jefferson Senior High, yet had never met each other before?

Who can explain how love happens?

Who can explain why your father, a butcher covered in blood no matter how many showers he took, no matter how hard he scrubbed under his fingernails, didn't show up for dinner one evening, how his bright metallic blue pickup vanished from your life, although you continue to remember every detail of it, how your mother and you found yourselves living in a motel room smelling of pizza and onions on the outskirts of town, how she used to scour toilets and disinfect countertops and mop floors to make ends meet while you used to bump into your father and his scrawny new girlfriend at the supermarket, the gas station, the McDonald's?

How he refused to look at you, refused to meet you eyes, your father, walked past you as if he was walking past a fire hydrant without seeing?

How, when you were six, perched in an uncomfortable aluminum-backed chair next to your mother's in another tent at another church retreat, you suddenly felt the waterfall of voltage ripple down over you, the voice not so much whisper as merely begin to exist along your spinal cord, felt yourself without warning learning things language could never teach you as chance became a superstition?

After evening prayers, I caught up with Iphi, escorted her back to her tent across camp. Somewhere along the path, in a blast of darkness that turned me invisible, in a cloud of sweet piney fragrance, I asked: *Would you maybe like to go to a movie sometime?*

My din hanging in the shadow air.

I'd like that, she responded after I waited so long I thought she hadn't heard, or had already said no, and seven months and seven days ago we married.

Seven months and seven days ago we learned what it meant to become the Lord's lightning.

How is it possible to cherish anyone more than this?

Knowing too much leaves you knowing nothing. I learned this in eighth grade. All those straight lines. All those sandpaper definitions. The teacher who walked as if both of her knees had been soldered in place laughing at me in front of the classroom when I raised my hand and pointed out that evolution is just one theory, that there are plenty of others.

You stop those thoughts of hers right now, you hear me? my mother said when I told her that evening over dinner. *You stop them cold. Let them things into your head, and I don't know what.*

I tried, but I couldn't.

I tried and tried.

Because words are designed to confuse. They don't ever tell you this, but you figure it out. Because all you have to do is listen.

Go ahead.

You can hear the devil's lisp in every sentence a human speaks.

By tenth grade I couldn't take any more. The voice that isn't a voice visited me in my sleep, arriving as a huge black bird with broken wings flapping in the grass below my window, and, when I awoke, the idea of high school had become something you only remember, like the Old Spice, like the blood scent of your father, the grit of his unshaven cheek against your forehead as he carried you to bed after you fell asleep on the living room couch, the way the cab of his pickup was stained with cigarette smoke and the television in our motel room picked up just three channels—and even those in a hail of static.

My mother knocked on my bedroom door.

You all right, hon? she asked. Breakfast's ready. You got to get a move on or you're gonna be late.

I'm not going, I said.

What?

I'm not going anymore.

A slow silence hanging in the hallway.

My mother saying:

Well, praise the Lord. It's about time, babe. It's about time.

You ready? I asked Iphi.

I was sitting on the unmade bed.

She nodded.

I rose, moved to the window. When I pulled back the drapes, the crisp blueness was so concentrated I winced.

The red brick Victorian station with its slate roof.

The modern glass overhang that reminded me of the greenhouse in Kew Gardens we visited yesterday for a chilly picnic. One of the flowers there was tall as a small tree, green on the outside and a dark burgundy bread loaf on the inside. It rarely bloomed, but when it did it stank of rotting meat for twelve hours straight to attract the flesh flies that pollinated it.

Then it folded back into itself to wait years before unfolding again.

I remember a dream, Iphi said, standing there.

A dream? I said.

I didn't think I had any, but I did. You were gliding next to me. We were both gliding. We were going very fast, very high, but it was warm and sunny and magnificent. We held our arms outstretched like wings. Everything looked small and featureless below. Like this rug. The landscape looked like this rug. That's what reminded me. The perspective was totally off. I was thinking: *I've never been so fortunate.*

Zipping our suitcases shut, fastening their locks, carrying them to the closet and stacking them inside.

Taking down our long baggy black coats, shrugging mine on, helping Iphi with hers, stepping over to the door, opening it, standing back.

Iphi hesitating.

Iphi hesitating.

Iphi stepping through into the rest of her life.

We rented a small white farmhouse with black trim on two acres of barren land on the outskirts of town. We didn't like our neighbors. We didn't like their trash-strewn lawns and rusty cars propped on cinderblocks and pot smoke drifting through our windows, the way their dirty children ran in dirty packs, whooping and cursing, knocking over our woodpile repeatedly, making faces at us from a distance as we walked down to check the mailbox. We didn't speak to them. We didn't look in their direction. Our brothers and sisters from church were the only company we needed to keep.

Their kindness, their thoughtfulness, their comfort, their tidiness.

When the weather started turning colder, a skunk burrowed into a broken bale of hay in the shed. Iphi told me she was scared to fetch the lawn chairs and grill we stored there. She asked me to take care of things. I asked her how. She told me she didn't want to know how. She just wanted her lawn chairs and grill back.

Who can explain how it feels buying a shotgun, fingering the crenellated yellow plastic shells for the first time, sitting on your bed reading the directions over and over until you're sure you have them right?

How awake you feel crossing the yard the next morning, frost dusting clots of dead grass?

How careful you are opening the wood-slat door, slipping inside?

How seeing the shiny black flank nestled in the straw, unmoving, arrives as a palm pressed against your chest?

It didn't have time to shift to see what was happening around it.

The thunder struck out that fast.

The thunder kept striking.

Then fur and blood and bone were spattered across the walls, through the hay, on my boots, and I was standing in the middle of the aftershock.

This, I remember thinking, shaken, proud, high-pitched whine in my ears, *is how vengeance works.*

This is exactly how it works.

It was cold outside, but not nearly as cold as Minnesota at this time of year. The pollution smelled tinny like bad water and made the back of my throat burn. We walked north half a block. The black cab was waiting just like they said it would be.

The driver didn't acknowledge us as we climbed in back. He had the broad hunkered shoulders of a wrestler and was bald except for a thin band of long whiteblond hair skirting his head. His radio was tuned to a classic Christian rock station. Sanctus Real was singing about how much everyone will eat and drink when they finally reach the Promised Land.

We turned left at the first corner, then right into a series of narrow winding streets. I lost my sense of direction, settled, watched buildings slide by. I reached for Iphi's hand. It was moist.

None of that, the driver said matter-of-factly over his shoulder.

I caught a glimpse of his eyes in the rearview mirror. They were the color of staples, only glassy.

I let go.

The fraying neighborhood rolling past.

The streets deserted under the rare blue sky.

Each window a black square, a black rectangle.

I thought about how in Mark it says: *And when Jesus was alone, those present along with the Twelve questioned him about the parables. He answered them: "The mystery of the kingdom of God has been granted to you. But to those outside everything comes in parables, so that they may look and see, but not perceive, and hear and listen, but not understand, in order that they may not be converted and be forgiven."*

I thought about how in Job it says: *God covers his hands with lightning, and commands it to strike the mark. Its crashing tells about Him.*

We rented a small white farmhouse with black trim on two acres of barren land on the outskirts of town, and I got a job working at a 7-Eleven on American Boulevard. There was nothing to do there except wait for time to pass, then wait for time to pass again.

During lulls my boss, a fat man who always looked like he hadn't shaved for two days, told me about how good he used to be at football in high school. *I was a fucking diety*, he said. *You should've seen me throw, man. I know it sounds like I'm bullshitting you, but seriously. You should've fucking seen me.*

He would toss me a football that didn't exist and be winded.

I mopped floors and thought about nothing and two hours would disappear. I cleaned the Slurpee machine and the toilets and the sinks and there would go another one.

The teenage women left used tampons on the floor in the lavatory and giggled because they knew I had to clean them up.

Transparent, I sorted and stacked candies, beverages, sandwiches sealed in plastic, potato chips, nuts, crackers, jars of salsa, pet food, soups, cat litter, ice, cleaners, newspapers, magazines, cigarettes, packages of beef jerky, cheap CDs, maps, key chains, postcards.

Sometimes people would reach in front of me while I was working to get what they wanted without saying excuse me.

Sometimes I could see reflections of classmates I left behind in high school making faces at me when they thought I wasn't looking.

Did you know 7-Eleven licenses more than 7,200 stores in North America alone? my boss asked me across the store as I was disinfecting the handles on the refrigerator units one evening. *32,000 worldwide?*

I did not.

It's like it's its own fucking country, man, he said, *only not.*

Petra singing about how Christ will love you after the rain stops falling, after the sun forgets itself, after the world scalds clean for the last time.

Eyes closed against the brightness.

Disciple singing about how today is already yesterday, tomorrow already come.

Listening.

I thought about how in Psalms it says: *But God will smash the heads of his enemies, crushing the skulls of those who love their guilty ways. The Lord says: "I will bring my enemies down from Bashan; I will bring them up from the depths of the sea. You, my people, will wash your feet in their blood, and even your dogs will get their share."*

The cab easing to the curb past a zebra crossing on a road lined with dingy brick housing projects.

Mews, the driver saying. First block of flats on the right.

The door slamming shut behind us. The front window rolling down.

I stooped and peered in. The driver continued staring straight ahead. There were two dark purple stains on his neck. Birth marks, maybe. It looked like something with pincers had gone after him.

Bless you both, he said.

The window rolling up.

The cab beetling forward.

10:59. We waited in the foyer like we were told.

The front door had been bashed in. It hung off its hinges at an angle that suggested exhaustion. There were holes the size of soccer balls in the plaster like someone had taken a sledgehammer to them for fun. An upended desk missing its legs. A headless cobalt blue mannequin lying among garbage bags, newspapers, crushed beer cans, empty liquor bottles, ceramic shards, rebar, shreds of clothing, an overturned lamp, a torn-open teddy bear.

A wiry guy with a gray ponytail stepped out of the doorway at the far end. He was wearing jeans and a heavy beige Irish wool sweater and sneakers. His hands were in his pockets as though he were out for a stroll in the park. He gestured with his chin.

Back here, he said.

Five of them in what once had been the kitchen. Three men and two women, all in their late thirties, early forties, all in jeans and sweaters and sneakers. You could see they knew how little words meant, too.

Taking off our coats. Taking our seats at the table.

There was no heat. It was forty-five degrees, forty-five or fifty degrees. The thin guy in the ponytail assured us this would take just a few minutes, fifteen or twenty at most, then we would be on our way.

A black man with a Caribbean accent and an Asian woman with a French accent left. When they returned, they were carrying our gear.

The man kneeled before me, the woman before Iphi. I couldn't understand what they were doing at first. They were doing things, but I couldn't understand what it was they were doing even though I knew what it was they were doing.

They were explaining. That's what they were doing. They were explaining to us how to become thunder.

What is faith?
Faith is a heavy cloth. Canvas. Hemp.

How shall we know the things which we are to believe?
Cut the cloth into the shape of a vest. Cut another swath into fourteen pouches.

Why did God make you?
To sew the pouches onto the vest. To finish off the armholes, the trim.

What is God?
The ability to conceal the device beneath your clothing.

Where is God?
In the fragmentation effect.

Does God see us?
He sees the nails, bolts, ball bearings between layers of sheet metal bonded with glue.

If God is everywhere, why do we not see Him?
We do not need to. We feel His love instead.

What are angels?
On earth, we call them improvised initiators.

What do angels do?
One breathes and then all breathe sympathetically. In a chorus of beatific sound.

How does God control the angels?
Through the simple switch that runs down your sleeve.

What form does this switch take?
The red plastic button from a child's toy.

Who is the Redeemer?
We call Him a nine-volt battery.

What is the Redeemer's name?
Eveready. Duracell.

Where can we find Him?
In an old-fashioned radio. A smoke detector. A walkie-talkie. The Redeemer is everywhere.

What do you mean by grace?
The importance pressing against your ribs, tugging on your shoulders.

What is the Blessed Trinity?
One God in three Divine Persons: don't trip, don't bump into others, avoid sudden jolts.

Which are the means instituted by our Lord to enable men at all times to share in the fruits of the Redemption?
Give yourself over to distraction. Imagine nothing. Imagine it again.

What does Redemption feel like?
Everything becoming something else.

How is Baptism given?
Flex your thumb. It is that easy. It always has been. It always will be.

How is Baptism experienced?
You hear nothing. You see nothing. You sense no heat.

How, then, do you know Baptism has come?
It is as though someone has reached inside your skull and flicked off a switch. You will know it by not knowing it.

What is forgiveness?
Your heart expanding to the size of the universe in less than a second.

What is brotherhood?
Your heart joining with the hearts of all those around you.

What is Heaven?
Knowing that you can go home at last.

What will you find there?
The click. The silence. The peace. The voice whispering into your ear. The voice saying

January

February

March

April

May

June

July

August

September

October

November

December

No, I'm sorry, I don't think so. My husband. The kids. You know.
This to the girlwoman standing beside you at the sink in the restroom. You're most of a morning north of Rome. You went in to
pee and, as you rinse your hands at the sink, she steps up beside
you and asks if you happen to have a little extra room in your car.
She asks politely, almost shyly, and yet in a tone that suggests the
gesture isn't by any means new to her. She is heading to Milan for
a shoot, she explains. She's a model. She looks like a model. Her
purpleblack hair cut short and spiky. Her cheeks high, her skin
olive and faultless, her eyes a coffeebean brown, her lips thin and
lipsticked moist red like a movie star from the fifties. She has that
quality models have: you glance at them and they look like one
person; you glance at them again and they look like another. Their
changeability makes you nervous when you see them on television
or in the tabloids. In person, it's even more disturbing. Her accent
is strong, but not Italian. Swiss, maybe? Dutch? She doesn't take
no for an answer. She asks you again, this time saying she'd be
happy to help with gas. She won't be any trouble. She promises.
She enjoys children, loves entertaining them. Think of her as a
nanny for an hour or two. She's sure you and your husband could
use a break. She isn't wrong. You've been traveling for nearly two
weeks, first around London and Paris, now here on a road trip
from Rome to Venice. Truth is, you're all a little tired of each other.
You all know what the others will say or do before they say or do
it. You always have, but you are a little more conscious of knowing

every day. You wouldn't admit this to each other, yet it's true. You could use the insertion of a fresh personality into your expedition. But you tell her Robert doesn't pick up hitchhikers. It's nothing personal. It's just family policy. Not with kids in the car. It makes sense. As teenagers in college, on spring break, you once thumbed all the way from New Brunswick to the Green Mountains outside Middlebury on a camping trip. You told your parents you were visiting friends in D.C. Here, though, you don't know how far to trust your intuitions. You and the girlwoman aren't looking at each other while you're having this conversation. Your eyes are meeting in the mirror. You're speaking to each other's reflection. You finish rinsing your hands, reach for two sheets of paper towel, wipe. She's petite, almost implausibly cute. She barely comes up to your chest. She's wearing a black turtleneck, an Army-surplus jacket, weathered bellbottom jeans with a large sexy tear above the right knee, a heavy Army-surplus daypack slung over her right shoulder. You've never seen such perfect skin. It isn't fair, you catch yourself thinking. Why should some people receive such skin and others not? You know if you asked her she would tell you she does nothing more to maintain it than wash her face twice a day with soap. You can tell with people like her. It's genetic, something deep in her cellular reality, and it lends to your suspicion that models are members of a different species. Genuine human beings never have such skin. Hers looks airbrushed. *Maybe I could talk to him?* she suggests. She isn't rinsing her hands. She isn't drying them. She's just standing next to you, talking. You feel strange because there is no particular social etiquette for moments like this. Other travelers are filtering in and out of the restroom behind you. Urine is squirting into water. Toilets are flushing. Someone is coaxing her child in Italian to climb up and do her business. Just inside the exit, the squat old woman responsible for keeping this place clean is sitting in a metal chair by the money basket, touching her arms delicately as if searching for the site of a bone fracture. She is treating her own body parts as if they were someone else's. Chlorine and shit cause each breath to be a surprise. *Maybe he would make an exception?* the girlwoman next to me proposes. You say *I don't think so*, and apologize again. You flash her a quick yet sympathetic smile and turn to leave. She follows you out into the day noisy with traffic on the Autostrada. Cold car exhaust worries your lungs. The girlwoman with the perfect skin isn't crowding you, not in a way that makes you uncomfortable in any case. She simply won't stop following, talking. *Where are you from?* she asks. *Are you from America?* She's always wanted to visit New York, she says. Maybe someday, if she works hard enough, her modeling career will take her there. Her mother and father would be very proud. They're very proud already, but they would be even prouder. They've given her nothing but support over the years. The girlwoman is very lucky—except that modeling isn't the easy and enjoyable enterprise some people seem to think. The hours. The sleep deprivation. The travel, travel, travel. You never know where you are. You wake up in the middle of the night in a hotel room and don't know if you're where you think you should be or if you're somewhere else. You can't remember the way to the bathroom. You're not sure which side of the bed to get out on. And when you're just beginning, when you're still finding your feet (isn't that the way Americans put it?), yes, when you're still finding your feet, there is a lot less money in it than most assume. There's also the daily pressure to keep down your weight. It's a cliché, but it's true. That's what makes clichés clichés—which, if you stop to think about it, is another cliché, isn't it? She knows girls who eat nothing but lettuce and cocaine. They look like they died a week ago. Like someone opened up their arteries and bled them. She'd never think of doing such a thing. There are limits. What would Papa think? She's just using the example to make her point. Her point is that everyone is jealous of models, but they shouldn't be. Models are like puppies in a pet shop window. They yip and jump around and look adorable and do what they have to do to get attention so someone will take them home and care for them. Call her Nayomi,

she says as you cross the parking lot toward the gas pumps. With
a *y* in the middle. She's always liked her name. Did you know it
means *pleasant* in Jewish? That's what she says: *In Jewish.*
Listening, walking, you spot Celan and Nadi standing by your
rental car eating slices of pepperoni pizza Robert bought them
inside the restaurant. This is the kids' favorite part of Italy, this
fastfood pizza. The kind they tried in Travestere was only okay,
they said, a little weird, but okay, but this pizza is beyond perfect.
It tastes just like the stuff at Monetti's in New Jersey. The Parisians
wouldn't know good pizza if it bit them on the butt, Celan said
very loudly in a restaurant on the Champs-Elysées. Londoners put
blueberries and corn on theirs, which as a family you agree is sheer
madness, yet somehow appropriate for a people who are wont to
live in bulky, sooty buildings while supporting the medieval tradition of kings, queens, carriages, and pomp. But this isn't what
you're saying. You're not saying anything. You're just listening to
the girlwoman going on and on, feeling increasingly awkward.
Despite your silence, she's already figured out from your trajectory
which one is your husband, which ones are your kids, already sped
up imperceptibly, already outpaced you, is already talking with
Robert. He is in the process of opening the back door for Celan
and Nadi when Nayomi catches him off guard. He straightens,
smiles the semi-smile he puts on for strangers stopping him in the
street to ask directions to the nearest mailbox. It's a two-door
1962 Saab station wagon the color of desert sand on the outside,
the color of Nayomi's lipstick on the inside. There is already rust
around one of the front headlights. You rented it two blocks away
from the hotel in Rome. Driving out of the city was a loud congested awfulness. It took two hours longer than you had anticipated.
Nothing went the way it should have gone. Not one road followed
a straight line. Just when you needed them, all the signs disappeared. By the time you pull alongside them, you can see Nayomi
has already softened up your husband. You don't hold it against
him. Partly it's her petiteness. Partly it's her faultless skin and dark

eyes. Partly it's her vulnerability, the way she gives off the aura of a lost child. You can see the confusion in Robert's eyes. He's trying to figure out what just happened and why. While Nayomi recounts her plight, Robert glances at you quickly over her head. His semi-smile-for-strangers is stuck in place. You move around him, settle the kids in the backseat, set them up with comic books from home, join the girlwoman and your husband with a mind to apologize to her again and prompt Robert that it's time to get going. You have a lot of road to cover today. You've already made reservations at a pensione in Bologna for the night. Tomorrow you are due in Venice. You made the reservations back in the States. With the children in tow, you don't like leaving things to chance. When you were in college, you and Robert left things to chance all the time. You enjoyed the idea of every day arriving as a series of mild disruptions. With kids, chance has become something dangerous. The more of it there is, the less you take pleasure in it. Now chance seems unavoidable each minute you're awake. Your response has been to leave nothing to chance. But the more you plan, the more chance seeps in. Nayomi is saying how she understands what an imposition her request is. She really does. She understands completely if Robert says no. It would be totally cool, she says. That's what she says: *totally cool*. But she's already tired. She's been hitchhiking since dawn. She has to be at the shoot first thing tomorrow morning. Without our help, she doesn't know how she can possibly make it. Robert says something you can't hear. Nayomi shrugs in Italian. Looking at how he leans in toward her, you realize this is the corner of your husband's character you like least—the one where he believes this thing yet says that just to please people and avoid confrontation. He's been doing it ever since you met him. He's the kind of person who will buy a fake Seiko from a street vendor to make the vendor quit bothering him. You're sure it has something to do with how he has an unforgiving father and a perfectly nice mother who felt she had other things to accomplish in life than raise a boy. Because of his parents, he developed inside himself. Whenever he gets around other people, all he wants is to take the path of least resistance. That way he can escape them as fast as possible. Except for the kids and you. If you sat him down and asked him, Robert would say he'd like the world to be composed of exactly the four of you. An ideal quartet. He doesn't understand why he can't act like it is. He often does. You can see it now in the slope of his shoulders, how he's reflexively brushing his longish blond hair back with his right hand, already thinking: *How much can it hurt? We drive north a few hours. We drop her off before we cut east toward Venice. She hitches the rest of the way into Milan. Look at her. Doesn't she remind you of us at her age? Someone needs to look after her. Plus it'll give the kids a taste of an authentic southern European. It'll be educational. By midafternoon, we'll be on our own again. She makes it to her shoot in time. Back in the States, she'll become an interesting family anecdote.* Nayomi is holding out some money, offering it to Robert. He is holding up his hands in front of him, shaking his head no, he couldn't possibly take it. His smile is widening as he does this, meaning he's progressively more uneasy, progressively closer to giving in. You open your mouth to interrupt his thoughts, distract him back to this moment by the gas pumps, but it's too late. *No, really,* he's saying. *It's fine. Really. Our pleasure. We'd love to have you join us.* You examine him, searching for clues. You glance past him into the Saab. Celan and Nadi are fascinated by this new being in their environment. Nadi has forgotten she is eating pizza. She's holding what's left of her slice like a phone beside her ear, watching Nayomi. You signal to her. She recalls herself and recommences eating. You smile weakly and head into the store attached to the restaurant to pick up some snacks for later and a couple bottles of water. The cute young guy at the register openly stares at your breasts as he returns your change. You feel in equal parts amused by his lack of finesse and creeped out. When you return, everybody has taken his or her place. Nayomi is in the backseat with the kids. Robert is in the passenger seat up front, trying to

manage the map unfolded across his lap. You walk around to the
driver's side, slip in, fasten your seatbelt. You put the engine in
gear, roll forward, start picking up speed. Soon you're on the
Autostrada again, only this time with a hitchhiker sitting behind
your husband. Cars shoot past you even though you're doing 110
kilometers, near 70 miles per hour. The sky is an amazing empty
blueness. Hazy Tuscan hills rill alongside you, plowed fields, red-
roofed white villas nestled among biomorphic swaths of dark green
trees and pastures. Nayomi is talking. She doesn't seem able to do
anything else. She is playing I Spy with the kids. *I spy a castle, a
vineyard, an eighteen-wheeler heading south.* She reaches into her
daypack and pulls out three sticks of fruity chewing gum, offers
one to Celan, one to Nadi, peels the third for herself. The kids
adore her instantly. During lulls in the game, Robert tosses her
questions. He seems genuinely interested, but you know he isn't,
that this is just what he does with strangers to pass time while appearing polite. If you asked him three hours from now what
Nayomi's answers were, he wouldn't be able to tell you. Nayomi
says she grew up in a dingy part of Munich, started university
there, took an emphasis in political science, found herself working
in a café in a neighborhood not far from where she had been a
child. The economy was terrible back then. The economy is terrible
now. Some things don't change. The fascists from World War Two
are still in power, she explains. Many think they are not, but they
are. This is the big secret nobody knows. It's just that they've
learned how to dress like you and me, how to act graciously.
Welcome, she says behind your husband, to the age of decorous
totalitarianism. This is what governments are good at: organizing,
manipulating, and exploiting human weakness. Everyone is unhappy. Some people know it. Some don't. But they are all unhappy
with what the system has made out of them. Nayomi considered
herself lucky to have any job at all. Many of her friends have none.
The rich continue rolling around in their money like poodles in a
Doberman's droppings, pretending Nayomi and her friends don't

exist. When business was slow, she could sometimes sneak in some reading behind the counter. She likes political novels. Malraux. Sartre. But she likes political theory more. Why make fiction out of fact? Why not simply say what you mean? One day a well-dressed man walked in off the street. He was wearing a sharply cut pin-striped suit and tie and cufflinks. He took a table by the window and ordered an espresso and an Apfelkuchen. He was maybe in his early thirties and spoke German with an Italian accent. *Have you ever thought about modeling?* he asked. *I have some friends in Italy. They could help. The pay's a thousand times better than what you must be making here.* That's how it started. Nayomi had never thought about modeling. She was twenty-one then. Now she's twenty-three. Her life is changing every day. Yet she's also aware that twenty-three is already old for a model, that she has to move quickly or she'll be out of the frame by the time she's twenty-six. And, like she said, it's a much harder life than she had assumed, than anyone assumes. You should see how men look at you. Women, too. Both are angry with you for being who you are, but for different reasons. Even so, it's better than working back in the café. It's heavy, but it's cool. That's what she says: *It's heavy, but it's cool.* Nayomi plans to return to university after she's saved enough money to help out her parents and her, return with the knowledge of the world she's been collecting . . . only
 . . . *only what about YOU?* she asks out of the blue. *You're on holiday, nicht? How long are you here for? What are you planning to see?* You hear yourself beginning to make your life into a story. You feel yourself both revealing and hiding, hiding by revealing. You don't know why you're doing it, exactly, but it seems easy enough, and you warm to the exercise quickly. You hear yourself telling Nayomi about how you live in a small town in northern New Jersey called River Edge. How the river there is brown and sluggish. How no houses line its edge. Yet how the place is called River Edge nonetheless, perhaps for the same reason that Greenland is called Greenland. When you were in high school, you went down

to the river with some friends, through the dense woods and undergrowth, across the railroad tracks, with a mind to skinny dip. Only then you saw the water rats gliding along the muddy banks and that was that. Still, the place isn't as ugly as all that might make it sound. River Edge is one of those quaint little suburbs filled with shady avenues and sweet little gingerbread houses in whose yards people rake leaves, shovel snow, trim hedges, wave at neighbors, take note of their environment, keep to themselves. Yours is near a park named Van Saun. Van Saun has a small zoo, a large pond, a miniature train for the kids, pony rides and, on summer weekends, a craft market. On Saturdays you and Robert set up a grill near the playground and cook out among the hoards of New Yorkers who come across the George Washington Bridge weekly to enjoy the illusion of countryside. The children love feeding and chasing the ducks. Your parents live four blocks east. Your sister lives twenty minutes away in a seedy town called Hackensack. You see them all every Sunday for dinner. Each morning Robert rises at six, showers, dresses, and commutes to Manhattan by car. He works in the financial district. You're a realtor. Well, not really a realtor. A realtor in your spare time, is more like it. A realtor in waiting. In between raising the kids and taking care of the yard and shopping and cooking and just, well, just keeping up with life. In college, you were a double major, psych and English, which gets you exactly nothing upon graduation. You almost flunked your statistics course. You had no idea you needed to know math to study psychology. You have a lot of fun with realty, though right now you consider it more a hobby than an authentic job. You hope things will adjust someday. Then you could afford to take trips like this with Robert and the kids more often. Next spring, during the off-season, you plan to visit Portugal. Not because of anything specific. Just because the name sounds so romantic. *Portugal.* You can hear the ceramics in it, the mosaic pavements and picturesque cafés in Lisbon. Someday you want to visit Scandinavia. You don't know why, but you have always dreamed of sitting in a dogsled rushing across a frozen lake in Lapland at dusk. Sweden, maybe. Maybe Finland. *Finland* sounds as if it must exist at the ends of the earth. The kids would have a great time. It would be what a real education should feel like. They'll be teenagers before you know it, and you want to make sure to enjoy them, give them something to enjoy, an imagination full of important family memories, before they're all grown up and gone, because you want them to be happy, but you also want them to remember you and Robert fondly, want them to return often. Celan becomes aware he is being talked about and tunes into your conversation. From nowhere, he blurts that you saw the place in London where they chop off people's heads with axes. Robert half turns in his seat to explain, again, that it's called The Tower and they don't do that sort of thing over there any more. Nadi adds they forgot to cook her hamburger in Paris. *Remember, honey?* you say over your shoulder. *We call that tartare. Steak tartare.* We call that gross, Celan says. Nadi and her brother break into laughter. Nayomi joins in. The French, she says, the French. You take pleasure in listening to more of your vacation sifted through your kids' heads, how they erase and rewrite, edit and augment. After a while, they get bored, distracted, produce a deck of cards from the treasure-trove suitcase unzipped in the cargo space behind the backseat. Nayomi initiates a game of Go Fish. She continues talking as she plays. You're glad she's along. Robert floats in and out of conversation with her. He asks if anyone is interested in checking out a little road-trip music on the radio. Nayomi claps her hands and says yes. You think of the Saturday afternoons following college when you two had nothing to do except lie around in bed reading *The New York Times* and listening to records. Jazz, mostly. The Beatles. Pink Floyd. Robert finished grad school, landed his job in lower Manhattan. You became pregnant with Celan and everything modified, attained layers, complex tonalities. You love it all and you feel disconcerted by it all, like the camera filming your life one day slipped on its tripod, like the frame skewed but the camera kept on rolling.

Robert locates a station out of Florence. Procol Harum is singing about a whiter shade of pale. Behind the wheel, you coast gradually into the glassy blankness that always settles over you after you've driven for more than an hour. Everything grays into the automatic. It feels good, like staring at a television screen after all the shows have gone off the air. You are there and you are not there. You are thinking and you are not thinking. In the distance, the low blue mountains seem as though they've been water-colored across the horizon, they are so lacking in depth. Every so often you become aware of the manic eruption of the Italian announcer's voice between songs. He is speaking so rapidly it unnerves you. Every so often you become aware of a phrase passing between Robert and Nayomi. Celan and Nadi open their snacks. For him, a very large bar of milk chocolate. Before you went into the restroom, Nadi insisted on a kind she had seen in the little market next to your hotel this morning, something with marshmallow, toffee, and mysterious green bits mixed in it. She takes a bite and hates it immediately. *It tastes like poop*, she says, her eyes filling with tears of disappointment. Nayomi leans over and gives Celan a big hug, stage-whispers how special he'd be if he would agree to share his bar with his little sister. He tries to act aloof, proud of his new-found power, but crumples into giggles as soon as Nayomi starts making fart noises with her mouth against his neck. He gives up on the spot. Nayomi splits the chocolate bar in half, divides it between the kids, and eats the one with the mysterious green bits in it herself. You find yourself liking her more and more. After the card game, which doesn't conclude so much as trail off into late-morning, sugar-crash, perpetual-motion sleepiness, Celan and Nadi curl up on either side of Nayomi for a nap. Nadi lays her head down in her lap. Celan leans against her shoulder, knees to his chest, mouth soon parted slightly as if he just had an idea. Robert passes a bottle of water back to Nayomi, untwists the cap on a second, passes it to you. Nayomi continues talking, but you are no longer listening to what she's saying. You've lost interest. You would like to take a nap yourself. You enjoy hearing Donovan singing about the hurdy-gurdy man. The Rolling Stones about how she's a rainbow. The feel of one palm on the wheel, one gripping the cool water bottle. The exhilaration that you are somewhere special, somewhere very far away from those gingerbread houses and cookouts in River Edge. It comes to you that you have used up so much of your life in one place when there are so many other places to experience. It's so easy to let one day resemble another. You spend your time thinking about this until your stomach begins to remember lunch, then you check the clock on the dashboard. It is already 12:45. You ask Robert to consult the map, find a nice village for a nice meal. The kids can stretch their legs, burn off some energy. Once there, you'll pull your husband aside and suggest you treat Nayomi to lunch. She looks like she could use some kindness. It takes Robert a minute to pinpoint your current location, another to discover a good destination. *Ah*, he says. *Got it. Let me just check here* . . . He extracts the thick square guidebook from the glove compartment, flips through it, sees what he's looking for. *Cool. Two more exits. It should be coming up in like five or six miles. Ficulle. A quote picturesque medieval town with a castle dating from the eighth to eleventh century and several lovely twelfth-century churches unquote. The kids'll love it. I can already taste the homemade tortellini.* Your mind hangs in an inbetweenness, listening to Joe Simon singing about receiving a message from Maria. Jeannie C. Riley about problems with the Harper Valley P.T.A. A few minutes, and you begin easing into the far right lane, decelerating. You flick on your indicator. That's when Nayomi says it. Almost under her breath. Almost like she's doesn't quite mean to say it, but can't help herself. *Not here*, she says. Robert confers with the map. *No, no*, he says. *This is it, all right. Up here, hon.* Nayomi says politely, almost shy: *No, it's not.* Robert half turns to look at her. He is semi-smiling again. He shifts his position to show her our coordinates. *Look*, he says, pointing. *See? We're here. Here's Ficulle. Here's the exit.* And to you: *Go ahead, hon. We're good.* Nayomi says: *We want one far-ther on.* You say: *Hey, guys, what do you want me to do? I've got to commit here.* Nayomi doesn't lean forward. She doesn't look at the map. *We want a different one,* she says. Her tone makes you flick off the indicator, slide little by little back into traffic, saying, confused, but trying to make it sound comical: *Would you guys please make up your minds or something?* You glance over. Robert is looking back at Nayomi. Nayomi is looking past him, between you, through the windshield. Robert's face doesn't seem quite right anymore. It takes you a moment to figure out why. His fake smile remains in place, yet the part around his eyes has gone slack. It's as though he is expressing two different emotions at once. *It's okay,* Nayomi says. *Everything's okay. We're just getting off a little far-ther on.* Robert asks: *What's wrong with Ficulle?* No one responds. *What's wrong with Ficulle?* he says again. And then Nayomi is saying the next thing. At first it sounds like a compliment. *Your children are so beautiful,* she says. *Vollständige wunderschöne Augen. That's what we say in German. Absolutely gorgeous eyes. They have their daddy's, don't they? Green like lichen.* Robert, maybe beginning to get it, looks over at me and says: *Thanks, but I don't get it. What just happened back there?* He seems minimally agitated, as if he's doing a complicated calculus problem on a test. Nayomi says: *They're like little angels. Mit gutem Benehmen. Very well behaved.* She looks past us, through the windshield, con-sidering. *It's really odd,* she says. *From when I was a little girl, I always wanted my own. Lots of them, you know? Like that old woman who lived in the big shoe. My own shoe-full of angels. Guess it's because I feel I have so much love to pass around.* Robert looks at you. You look at Robert. You are both trying to understand where this is going. *I had this history professor in Munich? He used to say, "Every story is imperfect." It was his refrain. He'd stand up there in front of the lecture hall and drone on and on about, I don't know, about how everyone had such high hopes for Germany after the war, say, but how in the end the western half just became your fifty-first state, and the eastern one of the U.S.S.R.'s pissoirs. "Ah," he'd conclude behind his crazy gray Nietzsche mustache, this touch of sadness in his voice, "but, then again, every story is imperfect." I had no idea what he meant. I think maybe now I do. Maybe he meant, you know, that you can't ever imagine how any story is going to turn out. Not the important ones, anyway. They're never going to be as attractive or successful or whatever as you imagined they'd be, nicht wahr? He must have been quoting someone. The story where I had a lot of kids became this story instead. The story of us all traveling through Tuscany one sunny afternoon in February. Isn't that the strangest thing? Okay, up here. This one . . . here . . .* She is running her fingers through Nadi's hair as she speaks. Head down, Robert lays a palm on the back of his neck, massaging, reckoning. He says *Okay* and reaches over and turns down the radio. *Obviously I'm missing something here.* His voice is trying to sound other than it's sounding. It's trying to sound diplomatic, even good-humored. *I mean, I apologize and all. But, um, what exactly's going on?* Nayomi keeps looking between you out the windshield. *We're just getting off the Autostrada for a little while,* she says. *I want to show you some of the countryside. It's mind-blowing. Really.* Robert reckons some more. *Look,* he says. He thinks about how to put what he's about to say. *We're really enjoying your company, Nayomi. It's been great getting to know you. And we're super appreciative for how you've been handling the kids. You're a natural. Only . . . I don't know how to say this. Excuse me if I seem rude or anything. But all we want to do is find a nice place to catch a bite to eat and then get going again. We have these reservations in Bologna, and . . .* Nayomi says: *Bologna? Wow. Did you know the San Petronio Basilica is one of the largest in the world? It's not very pretty from the outside, though. It looks like a dreary train station. I wouldn't recommend it.* You hear something odd and glance up at the rearview mirror. *What's that?* you say. *What?* Nayomi says. *What did you just put in your mouth,* you say. *Nothing,* she says. *You just put something in your mouth,* you say. *I saw you. Just some pills,* she says. *What kind of pills?* Robert says. *Vitamins,* she says. You say: *No they're not.* Robert says: *You just swallowed something.* You say: *She just swallowed something.* Robert says: *Are you taking drugs?* Nayomi is squeezing her daypack between her calves. Her right hand has dipped inside. *Here you go,* she says, indicating the exit. *This one. I have to go pee-pee,* Celan says, semi-rousing from his nap. *Later, munchkin,* Nayomi tells him, patting Celan on the leg with her free hand. *Go back to sleep. Träum was Schönes.* He's too groggy to put up a struggle. He doesn't move except to scratch his nose, close his mouth, open it again. *Are you telling my son he can't go to the bathroom?* Robert says. *Get off here,* Nayomi says. *Don't,* Robert tells you. *Get off here,* Nayomi says, almost under her breath. You twist down the cap on your bottle of water and slide it under your seat. You grip the wheel with both hands. It occurs to you that you won't get off. It occurs to you that you will. It occurs to you that you won't, even as you are veering away from the Autostrada. *What are you DOING?* Robert asks, turning off the radio completely. *I just asked you not to get off.* You say: *Stop shouting.* Robert says: *I'm NOT shouting.* Less shy, Nayomi says: *Don't slow down, don't slow down.* You burst out onto a nearly empty road rushing through breathtaking landscape. Pastures slur past you. Villas. You open and close your eyes to clear your head. It seems like months since you've been on the highway. *I like the speed,* Nayomi says. *Don't you?* Robert says: *What did we do that for?* Nayomi says: *It makes the world feel . . . what is the word in English? Besondere. Distinctive.* You all sit there, trying to take in how your surroundings aren't the surroundings in which you existed less than a minute ago. You contract into yourselves. You see a distended vein pumping at the back of Robert's jaw line when you glance over. Nayomi continues taking in what's beyond the windshield, telling you which road to take each time an option presents itself. You focus on keeping your speed constant. When you fly up on a slow pale blue Renault, you flash your lights, swerve gracefully into the oncoming lane, pass it. You flicker through a medieval town before you know that's what you've done. The astonished faces of pedestrians, then vineyards meshing hills on either side of you through rows of Cyprus trees. The sun fluttering like a moth against a light. The road becomes increasingly curvy, starts climbing. You can hear the engine straining beneath you. *Keep going*, Nayomi says. *Don't slow down.* You are surprised to hear yourself saying, levelly: *You want some money? Is that what you want?* A silence balloons through the cab. Nayomi says: *What?* Robert says: *What are you talking about?* You say: *Is that what you want?* Nayomi says: *I don't want your fucking money.* You say: *Because if it is, just say so. Let me pull over here. We'll give you all the money we've got on us.* Robert shouts: *Don't say that!* To Nayomi he says: *We aren't giving you shit.* You don't listen to him. You're intent on forming your next sentences. It's important to get them right. *We've got something like a thousand dollars in our suitcases. Travelers' checks. A nice necklace. Pull over and they're yours.* Robert says: *What the fuck are you DOING?* You say: *I'm offering Nayomi our valuables.* Nayomi says: *Fuck that. I don't want your bourgeois Dreck.* You say: *Then tell us what you DO want. Tell us, and you can have it.* Nayomi says in her girl-woman voice: *We just want to make a point.* Robert says: *We? Who's we?* Nayomi says: *You don't have to wake the children. They don't have to know about any of this.* Robert says: *Know about any of what?* Nayomi says: *I really did grow up in Munich and work in that café, you know. Just in case you're wondering. But the guy who walked in one day? He wasn't wearing a suit. You probably already guessed that. He wasn't really one person. There were, how do you say it, lots of him, versteht Ihr? They kept turning up. You know how university towns are. People from my political science and history and literature lectures. People those people introduced me to. Some had nothing to do with the university. But sometimes on Tuesday evenings we met after closing—you know, just to bullshit. It was really great.* Robert says: *Why are we hearing this?* You say: *Let her talk.* Nayomi says: *We realized there were others out there. You know, people who made us feel less lonely.* You say: *Nayomi. Listen. We're not trying to fight you here.* Nayomi says: *Before long we started asking ourselves how we could make a, you know, difference.* You say: *Nayomi . . .* But Robert interrupts, putting on the voice of masculine authority he uses with the kids when they misbehave. *Okay,* he says, *that's enough.* And to you: *Pull over.* And to Nayomi: *This thing has gotten WAY out of hand. It stops now.* And to you: *Pull over.* And to Nayomi: *You're getting out. I'm sorry. But that's what you're doing.* You say levelly: *I'm pulling over. I'm going to pull over.* You take your foot off the gas pedal and that's when Nayomi extracts what she extracts from her daypack. Just for a second. Less than a second, actually. Just above the rim and then it's gone again. The event takes place so rapidly you're not completely sure you saw it. You're not completely sure you saw it, but you're completely sure you saw it. You replace your foot on the gas pedal. Nayomi takes her eyes off the road to glance down at Nadi. *No,* she says. *That's not what's going to happen. Something else is going to happen.* You follow her eyes in the rearview mirror. You say, less levelly: *Nayomi . . .* Nayomi glances up again and says: *Did I already mention this is my absolute favorite part of Italy? The perfect blend of the natural and the human. I holidayed here last autumn with some of these friends I've been telling you about. It's fantastic getting to see it all once more.* Robert says: *Pull. The fuck. OVER.* You say: *Robert . . . stop.* Nayomi says: *We looked around and you know what we saw? We saw the protests in London. We saw your Lieutenant Calley doing what all you Americans secretly wanted him to do. We saw our own government unwilling to learn a thing. We saw people like you worrying about your fucking stupid little grills in your fucking stupid little suburban parks.* Robert looks as if her words just backhanded him. Nayomi says: *And we just realized . . . I mean, it just came to us. To make a statement, sometimes you have to pick up a weapon.* The last syllable expands like a shockwave through the car. Robert goes immediately quiet. You sift through your choices. You will your children to remain asleep. You round the next bend on a steep hill and the back of a huge rusty tractor hurls up at you. You swing into the oncoming lane. Everyone jerks right. The tractor tumbles into the past, its angry shrinking farmer waving his tiny fist at you. A stream leaps into view off to the left, bobbing, then vanishes so completely you believe you may never have seen it. Robert isn't trying to look at Nayomi anymore. He is staring straight ahead, face drained. His hands grip the sides of his seat as if he's secretly bracing for impact. Checking her watch, a Spiro Agnew wearing red, white, and blue boxing shorts, Nayomi explains almost self-effacingly that elsewhere across Europe—in Germany and France, in Austria and Spain—versions of her are sitting in cars with versions of you. Each node of travelers is counting down. *Just like astronauts in their capsules on the launching pad,* she says. *Just like your Alan Shepard on his way into space. This is how things get done.* Robert's face is wearing an expression you've never seen on it before, like an invisible devil has just grabbed him by the throat. You sift through your choices. If he tries to lunge at her, she will set it off. If you try to signal anyone in the outside world, she will set it off. Your Adam's apple begins aching like you're about to cry. In a sense, Nayomi has forgotten you are even there. In a sense, she has started thinking of you as props, as parts of the plot she is constructing. She's still speaking, but not to you, not to your family. She is speaking to herself. Her language rushes on. She has just asked if anyone happens to know the story of Iphigenia. *Who?* Robert says. *WHO? You know,* she says. *The myth. The Greek myth. There are lots of variations. Every one breaks your heart, but for different reasons. Euripides. Racine. Goethe. All of them are doing different things, but the thing is, they all care about how one person sometimes needs to give herself up for others, how sometimes that's the only way to get what you want, even though you won't be there to enjoy it. They all begin on a sunny day just like this one. They all begin just like this.*

January

February

March

April

May

June

July

August

September

October

November

December

Heart swollen with anticipation, Iphigenia steps onto the rocky shore from her father Agamemnon's ship and immediately feels she has done this before. Gnarled graygreen cypress trees spattered here and there. The sky a violent blue. How the flock of white birds gyre above her like a flock of silent white hands.

She pauses to take in the scene. Scree crunches beneath her sandals. Iphigenia is in Aulis to marry Achilles.

There is a story she has heard. In order to make her son immortal, Achilles' mother, a sea nymph, dipped him into the river Styx. The black water caught the baby's soul on fire. The fire has never gone out. To anger him is to witness uncontaminated rage. Yet the opposite is also true: to know uncontaminated rage is to know uncontaminated love. Iphigenia cannot wait to learn what such a sensation feels like. Whenever she brings up the topic with her attendants, they lower their heads, cover their mouths, and titter.

In the dining hall one evening, her father told Clytemnestra that Iphigenia would be sailing with him to Aulis the following morning. Next Iphigenia knew, she was standing on the dock, throat aching as if she were about to cry, hugging her mother goodbye, who did not hug her back, hugging her sisters, her brother. Next she knew, she was kneeling at the railing in a mad black storm on the open sea, wind and rain tearing into her, being sick. Next she knew, she was stepping onto this rocky shore, thinking: *This* is where I shall be wed. *This* is what it is like.

Her attendants flow around her, bearing crates filled with her wardrobe and jewelry, her favorite foods and favorite oils, bearing her favorite bed above their heads, her prized satin chair, her prized satin pillows. Her pet cheetah growls in a cage nearby. The towns-people have arrived at the periphery to gawk at this impromptu entertainment.

Agamemnon steps up beside his daughter and halts, huge palms on hips, surveying the disembarkation. He smells of balms and garlicky sweat. Iphigenia lets him be himself for several seconds, then asks:

When shall I meet him, Papa? Today?

Agamemnon does not take his eyes off the commotion occurring around him, the temple high on the craggy hill overlooking it all, the delicate white hands spiraling through this morning.

Behind him scores of ships, sails bloated, ease into the bay.

Soon, daughter, he says. Soon.

But it isn't soon. It isn't soon at all. The afternoon is a long, plodding settling in. The evening a great feast sans bridegroom, with panflute music, dwarfs in monkey outfits, the sacrifice of a colossal ox. The night a series of alarming apparitions. Ever since she can remember, Iphigenia has been visited by visions from a future that is never her future. She sees what will happen to others while remaining blind to what will happen to herself. These are Iphigenia's puzzling secrets. She keeps them private, uncut gems scooped off the packed soil of alleys among the market stalls of sleep. A large bat with Electra's face sucks on her sleeping mother's neck. The god Phantasos materializes before Orestes as an inexpensive pearl necklace, a heavy battleaxe, a beautifully crafted arrow embedded in a bloody heel, yet refuses to utter a sound. An emaciated old man, who resembles nothing so much as a frog in a funny costume reared back on its hind legs, clutches his chest in a candle-lit room and collapses. He has been holding a paintbrush. It clatters across the floorboards.

Iphigenia is thirteen, but she feels much older and wiser. She has traveled. She has seen things. She possesses a pet cheetah. She is marrying a demigod.

Surrounded by attendants in the modest temple at the top of the hill, Iphigenia prays. Offers up to the gods a piece of cloth from her most lavish childhood dress. Offers up her special childhood toy: a mechanical bird that steam makes sing and flap its wings. These items will assist Iphigenia in departing her youth, in the migration to the foreign land called adulthood.

To the goddess of virginity, Iphigenia offers up a lock of her own long glossy blueblack hair and a miniature engraved chest filled with silver coins. On one side of each coin is the image of Helios, sunrays streaming from his head. On the other is the image of her father, sharp nose, thin lips, jug-handle ears, almond-shaped eyes.

The air is tangy with incense. Behind Iphigenia's eyelids, the cosmos seems dark and damp as the back of her mouth.

Yesterday she knew how to feel and what to think.

Today she is hovering.

Iphigenia is closer to her attendant Anthea, whose prehistoric skin reminds her of an elephant's crumpled shank, than to anyone else on earth.

Anthea taps Iphigenia on the shoulder and tells her it is time to move on.

Iphigenia rises.

The procession winds its way from the temple to the women's quarters for the pine-scented nuptial bath. Ten garlanded slave girls—none older than nine—have drawn water from the sacred spring in the hills and carried it back in beige and black vases usually reserved for funerary purposes. The vases, Anthea explains, are to remind Iphigenia that after this she has only one more important passage to make in her life, and that is out of it.

Head bowed, Iphigenia kneels over a gutter set in the marble tiles. Two of the slave girls pour the spring water over her hair, her skinny shoulders, the bluewhite concatenation of her spine.

Iphigenia thinks: *This* is how it feels to become another person. Iphigenia thinks: Three more hours, and I shall populate the center of a completely new tale.

One night, she watched Electra standing among vast sand dunes pressing her palms against the flank of a white Arabian horse.

Each time Electra pulled her palms away, crimson imprints remained behind.

Soon, bloody flowers covered the horse's side.

When Iphigenia awoke, the sheets between her legs were soggy with metallic seep. Her nipples ached. It felt as though she had eaten something that was poisoning her. She decided a succubus must have attacked while she was dreaming and now she was bleeding to death.

Sitting bolt upright, she cried out in horror.

A groggy Anthea dashed in, fluttery oil lamp in her hands. Iphigenia's attendant ran her hands over the frightened girl's body, searching, taking stock, calming, and, when she reached that mess between her thighs, she broke into a wheezy cackle.

You're not dying, child, she said. You're just growing up.

Next morning, Anthea mixed corn with Iphigenia's menstrual blood and spread it on the nearby fields to celebrate her newfound fertility.

Her proud father gave her a cheetah cub the size of a housecat. The fluffy fur along his backbone and atop his head stood straight up so that it was impossible to take his pipsqueak growls seriously. Iphigenia named him Zeno because she liked the sound of bees and surprise living inside the word.

Her mother, whom she often did not see for weeks on end, said nothing.

Then she said nothing again.

Iphigenia has always loved most to play by herself. She has never fully understood the need others have for others. Give her her own corner of creation, her own sanctum, and she will amuse herself happily for hours with the intricate mechanical bird her father brought back for her from across the sea, the doll made of rags, wood, wax, ivory, and terra cotta he brought back from Athens, Zeno sprawled nearby, absorbing the marble floor's coolness, dreaming cheetah-cub dreams. On good days, her mother leaves her alone. On good days, her sisters and brother, too. There are many good days. She likes to roam the cool echoey palace by herself. Without such lingering moments of privacy, how can one possibly find the time to consider the ideas arriving in one's head like a school of parrotfish? But now that is going to change. Iphigenia is vaguely apprehensive before the notion of having a new friend for life. She is excited as well. From now on she will always have someone to talk with at night when she is too tired to do anything except curl up in bed, but not tired enough to fall asleep. She will no longer have to endure the way her big bully sister Electra with the bad skin sometimes for no reason reaches over as they pass each other in the corridor and pulls her hair, hard, to make her cry, or the way her big bully brother Orestes with the smelly farts sometimes for no reason lies in wait and jumps out from behind columns to take pleasure in terrifying her and making her drop what she has been carrying. She will no longer have to endure the way her little sisters Chrysothemis and Iphianissa tell her she will be invisible to them for the next three days and then refuse to talk to her. Iphigenia will get her own beautiful house with her own beautiful courtyard and her own beautiful altar. She will never step outside again. She already knows what images her pebble mosaics will include. Her pebble mosaics will include images of Pegasus. Iphigenia adores horses and birds. She adores things that run. She adores things that fly.

She is alone in the bath with Anthea. Her special attendant is dressing her. The other attendants are waiting outside, ready to escort her into another life. She can hear them speaking in low hasty voices through the open window, although she cannot make out what they are going on about. They are such tittle-tattle people. She can hear the deep murmur of hundreds of spectators collected on the promontory overlooking the sea several hundred yards beyond. She finds the air she is breathing far too moist, salty, warm, as the day matures toward noon.

When Anthea slips the veil down in place over Iphigenia's face, Iphigenia whispers: What's it going to be like?

Anthea has been thinking of other things. She holds an ivory clasp between her lips. As far back as Iphigenia can remember, her attendant has never boasted a tooth to her name.

Toothless Anthea comes back to this world. Iphigenia is certain there are others. She watches them every night from her sleep.

You'll see, Anthea says around the clasp.

Iphigenia grins.

But I want to know *now*. Have you seen him?

Anthea removes the clasp and says: Some things should be a surprise. Some things you shouldn't know about until you know about them.

Iphigenia's grin loosens into a full-blown girlish smile.

Is he handsome as they say?

There you go, Anthea says, fastening the clasp in Iphigenia's hair, hand loitering on the back of the girl's neck. We're ready, sweetheart.

But you're not telling me, Iphigenia says, whine tinting her voice. You've *got* to, you know.

They have been sitting on facing wooden stools.

Anthea lifts her stiff body, sighs, says: It is time to tell yourself: *I shall meet today expecting nothing.*

I don't understand.

You don't need to. There's going to be a war.

A war?

Anthea gestures toward the doorway with her long sharp chin that almost touches her long sharp nose.

Far away. Yes. This is what men do, she says. They kill each other. Sack each other's cities. All those ships in the bay? They will sail tomorrow, the gods willing.

Iphigenia stands, tipsy with this surge of newness, steps toward the exit.

Behind her, Anthea adds: Remember. Everything changes, sweetheart. The universe loves to happen.

His muscles. The sheen upon his walnut-brown skin. The way his breath will always smell of mint and lilac and licorice.

Iphigenia is thirteen, but she has petted a baby rhinoceros her father brought back from Cyrene. She has walked beside her siblings through the cobbled streets of sprawling Athens. She has listened to the story of how her father's kingdom was stolen from him, how he took it back by rightful force, how he took his bride—Iphigenia's mother—the same way, killing her first husband, that spineless yokel Tantalus, and then their newborn son. Agamemnon had oil poured over the man on the stage in front of the theater and had him set on fire. Tantalus became a comical living torch, running in circles until he dropped. Agamemnon returned to the palace and lifted Clytemnestra and Tantalus' baby boy out of its crib and gently crushed its skull between his huge palms. The noise was exactly that of biting into an onion, Agamemnon said. It sounded exactly like victory.

No husband is waiting for her: this is the first thing Iphigenia notices as the altar swings into view. A large gray slab of stone on a steep rocky promontory. The crowd surrounding it falling silent as she approaches, heads bowed in awe. Warriors in full armor, but also men, women, and children from the nearby town. Their reverence is as it should be. This is the part Iphigenia always likes best about her appearances, how others offer her their respect and admiration. It makes her feel warm like the sun on your face.

But there is only the granite lozenge, only her father and two priests standing beside it. Iphigenia scans the vicinity for Achilles.

Anthea and the other attendants form an unhurried human wake behind her.

In the distance, the multitude of ships at anchor in the bay, like a multitude of whitecaps. Beyond, the sheer cliffs of Euboea. In her chest, a hand closing, applying slow pressure to her nervous heart.

Sometimes she would not see her mother for weeks on end. Clytemnestra's face would fade in her memory, become incrementally nondescript, a statue's sanded down detail by detail until only the outlines remained.

When Iphigenia had almost forgotten it, Clytemnestra would appear without warning by her bedside in the middle of the night. Sometimes Iphigenia would awake to discover her mother sitting on the floor, knees to chest, sobbing quietly. Sometimes her mother's mouth would be so close to Iphigenia's ear that she could feel its angry wet heat.

There is an ocean, Clytemnestra would whisper, *and it will dry up. There are islands, and they will sink. There are men, and the path before them will be spread with their own entrails.*

Fast as a hiccup, she would be gone again, leaving Iphigenia lying alone, staring up into blackberry night, her bedroom a cavernous resonance, her soul a frantic tern.

Lie back, daughter, her father tells her as she nears. Take your place. Here.

Where is he, Papa? Iphigenia asks.

The priests, she sees, possess elongated faces and wild cloud-beards. They stand side by side, robed columns, expressionless, hands clasped before them.

Every land has its own ways, says Agamemnon. This is how

things are done in Aulis. His ship has anchored. Take your place in preparation for his arrival.

Iphigenia does as she is told. She steps up to the foot of the altar. She turns. The priests help her into position with their pointy fingers.

The breeze falls as motionless as the people gathered around this instant.

Beneath her, the rock warm with sunshine. Iphigenia moves inside herself. She hears her lungs working. She senses the sparkling wine that is her blood coursing through her veins. She feels, as if from very far away, Anthea take her wrists tenderly and lift them over her head.

Iphigenia remains within her body until the tenderness begins to give way to something else—until one of Anthea's assistants who has never touched her before lays a hand upon one ankle, a hand upon the other, tightens her grip.

Iphigenia finds her muscles trying to retract involuntarily.

The assistant bears down.

Anthea leans forward and kisses Iphigenia softly, quickly, on the forehead. Iphigenia opens her eyes and the first tickle of alarm passes through her. Anthea has never kissed her before. Some things are done, and some are not. Yet Iphigenia's father does not move, says nothing. The birds keep circling above her. The waves keep lapping against the shore below.

She lets her father be himself for several seconds, then asks:

Papa?

Agamemnon answers with wordlessness.

Papa? she repeats. What's happening?

Instead of explanation, she hears the priests at her feet begin to chant:

Oh, Artemis, grant us wind, speed, billowing sails. Grant us strength, grant us true aim, grant us swift triumph. Grant us wisdom, luck, hope. Grant us cunning, grant us bounty, grant us—

Close your eyes, Anthea whispers into Iphigenia's ear. Think of Zeno. Think of your beautiful mechanical bird. When you open them next, your husband will be standing in front of you.

But just before Iphigenia does what Anthea asks her to do, she catches sight of the glint in her father's enormous right fist.

Each of us must forgo in his own way, Agamemnon intones. *This is called heroism. Each of us must give what he least wishes to give. This is called duty. Through forfeiture, our people hound success. For favorable winds, I do what is demanded of me.*

Iphigenia twisting madly, her mouth suddenly stuffed with cloth.

Iphigenia struggling against the flock of hands holding her down, eyes an outburst of shock and panic.

Her father's face darting above her, now a stranger's: indifferent, blank-eyed, unwavering.

Be still, it says. Be—

The knife a long flash of sunlight.

The knife a silver bird plunging down, its solitary voice choking her head with language, saying *welcome*, saying

January

February

March

April

May

June

July

August

September

October

November

December

....
....
....
....
....
....
....
....

Welcome to another episode of my own little pirate podcast coming to you semi-live and completely indirect every week from a different corner of the godforsaken Salton Sea, deadest body of saline solution on the deadest stretch of southwestern desert you'll ever want to forget.

You're listening to Jolly Roger and his whole sick crew . . . and that means you, too, baby.

Maybe a friend told you about my revolving website. Maybe you stumbled upon it late one night while looking for someone else's. Maybe something made you click that URL at the bottom of that piece of spam you found in your inbox this morning that you just *knew* you shouldn't open.

And here you are.

That website is where I keep my let us call it transitory cell-phone number. Scroll down to the lower lefthand corner to find it. Use it or lose it within twenty-four hours. I take your call, you're on. I don't and, well, try, try again. Jolly Roger plans on sticking around long enough to hear what *everybody* has to say who Time and The Ordinary have put out of mind . . .

The clock over the sink tells me it's a hair's breadth past two in the a.m. I'm sitting at the kitchen table, which also happens to serve as the living room couch, in what for the rest of tonight we'll refer to as my home. Actually, it's a quote friend's unquote . . . although he won't exactly be in a position to figure that out till he returns from what I suspect is a brief but relaxing camping trip into the nearby mountains or a supply run into Calipatria.

Me, I've got a glass of whiskey in my left hand, a tasty Marlboro in my right. My laptop is glowing on the table before me. The front and back windows are shut. The air conditioner, such as it is, is on. The living room, which, I should mention, also serves as bedroom and closet, smells of fish and fungus. It's piled almost to the low ceiling with bundles of old newspapers, empty cardboard boxes, jumbled clothes that stink of unwashed hair, and neatly stacked cans of beans, tomato soup, chicken soup, broccoli soup, and pureed carrots. Inside, it's maybe eighty degrees. Outside, I'm guessing eight-five.

Walk through the rattly aluminum door behind me, you will step onto a plot of dead earth perhaps one-hundred-feet long by one-hundred-feet deep. It's surrounded by cyclone fencing on which is hung a sign, red lettering on white background, that sayeth: *Don't worry about the dog. Beware of owner.* Turn around at that fencing and look back, and you will observe a peeling white outbuilding twice as big as your average phone booth. It's empty save for a lone pitchfork leaning in a dark corner. In front of that shack, a little to your right, you will make out a wood-framework tower, maybe twenty feet tall, on top of which sits either a large propane or water tank. And in the foreground notice a rusty pale green Airstream trailer partially surrounded by a rickety white picket fence.

Look through the closed front window, compadre, and you will see my back hunched over this table.

That Airstream resides on the corner of two unpaved streets a block up from the massive berm on the other side of which stretches the Salton Sea in an environmental calamity that back in the fifties developers marketed as a little piece of heaven. My closest temporary neighbors live in similar shacks maybe fifty feet away. Perhaps they think I'm someone else. Perhaps they don't care. Perhaps they've left this place a long time ago.

Welcome to the land of tomorrow, folks. To my vessel. My luxury liner docked in Bombay Beach. The inside of my head for the next twenty minutes . . .

And now, without further ado, my first exchange with the Tribe . . .

Am I on the air?

Indeed you are, my good man. Let Destiny hear what you're thinking.

I, uh . . . I just finished my latest project. I think I've got something important going on.

You're an artist?

Engineer.

And your name is . . .

Josh. Joshua.

What do you have to share with us this otherworldly morning, Josh Joshua?

You know how we all sometimes feel like we're suddenly cut off from everything?

Does Dolly Parton sleep on her back?

How you'll just be like sitting there in your room, or maybe walking down the street, and this like Saran Wrap of isolation will suddenly enfold you without warning?

We've all been there, friend.

I decided to build a remedy.

For solitude?

An anti-loneliness device. Yeah. It hasn't been easy. The parts are hard to come by. I have to wait for them. But they always find me. People bring them. They know what I need.

How long have you been laboring at this Suez Canal of belonging?

I, uh . . . Time gets funny sometimes, you know? Last week it was 1986.

And your device works . . . how?

The key is it's designed to block out the loneliness waves. It goes right to the source. Others have missed that. It's subtle.

How many ergs are we talking about here?

Thirty-five hundred. But that's not the breakthrough. The break-through is it all comes down to . . . You listening?

We all are.

If it's broken, dude, fix it. And if you can't fix it . . . make it SPIN.

You're off the air with Jolly Roger. Speak and we shall listen.

You know how you hate men, but you love 'em, too?

They're bastards, honey.

They can't help it. All that testosterone. All that meanness living in their fucking bloodstream. But those beautiful blue eyes, too, you know? Jesus. They can burn right through a goddamn iron-plated heart.

Where are you hailing from this night-morning?

Minneapolis.

It's later than you think out there, huh? Can you see the red sun beginning to rise outside your window? The first dog walkers hitting the streets even as we speak? Sanitation trucks . . . Street cleaners . . .

They fucking treat you like mold spores.

We're back to those Beelzebubs in guy-clothing?

They cheat on you with your best friends. Rob shit out of your drawers. Steal food and beer from the fridge. Tell you shit you want so bad to believe you say what the hell and so you do.

Even though you don't, not for a second . . .

You see the news last night?

Do you know what Lord Northcliffe once said about that illustrious subject? The news, said he, is what somebody else wants to suppress. All the rest is advertising.

I've been counting.

Have you?

In the last twenty-four hours alone? Some asshole torches his girlfriend's house with three kids where they're sleeping cuz she'd told him to go fuck himself. In a park in Laredo, eight teenagers rape this middle-aged chick out for a jog just to see what it feels like. In Hoboken, this housewife gets beaten to shit for telling her old man Jon Bon Jovi is drop-dead gorgeous. See what I'm saying? The news ain't the news no more.

It isn't?

It's a fucking Rolodex of assaults by men against women. That's what it is. A-and before any of you women haters out there start ranting about how many men get abused by women, or how many women off their children? Don't even fucking bother. Cuz the ones who get pissed off? The ones who go on and on about how they'd never hurt a fly and all that shit? We ALL know better. You fuckers do exactly shit to stop other men from harming women. A-and you wanna know something? I'll always fucking HATE you. I fucking hate you today. I'll fucking hate you tomorrow. I'll fucking hate you the year after that.

And love us, too, right?

Fucking A, man. I've got a knife. I'll use it.

Glad to hear it, honey. We love you, too. Sleep well for me tonight, okay? May your dreams fill the room you inhabit.

From the area code, I'm guessing you're coming to us straight from the rotten core of the Big Apple.

You're the best, Jolly Roger. My name's Mike.

Flattery will get you everywhere, Mike. Or at least another two minutes of airtime in the netherglobe. What wisdom would you like to impart to us fellow Morlocks traveling side-by-side with you in the great time machine called Mother Earth this afternoon?

I've been thinking about how they're all like totally Iraqed.

Who's that, Mike?

The kids? In malls? You know, with their lip rings and tongue studs and way they laugh at you by not laughing? You can see it in their eyes.

Not sure I'm quite following you here, Mike . . .

They don't wanna do ratshit, ayte? Look at them irises. Fuckers

*go on and on about dismantling the system and burning The Man
and blowing up their high schools and whatever, ayte? Only what
they really want? What they really want is to sit around on their
fucking asses all day watching* SpongeBob SquarePants *and snarfing cheesy poofs.*

Why do you think that is, Mike?

*This ain't THINKING, Jolly. This is KNOWING. I've got one
word for you.*

One word?

Hormone deficit. Know what I'm saying?

Help me out here.

Them birds in Lake Ontario?

. . . ?

*All of a sudden one day they can't find no more mates, ayte? So
the females? They start going gay. You hear about that?*

I haven't.

*Shit, man. They start nesting with these other female birds,
taking turns tending their infertile eggs. F that S. Know what I'm
saying? Or them other birds? Cormordants? They got beaks so
fucking twisted they can't eat nothing. Six-legged frogs. Two-
headed turtles. And that place in Florida? The one with all them
alligators with dicks too small to fuck with? Tell me that ain't like
totally fucked up.*

That's totally fucked up, Mike.

*So here's what I want to know, ayte? Who gives a shit about like
global warming and whatever when your dick's too small to fuck
with?*

Good point.

*Lemme ask you something. How many sperm you think your
average guy's supposed to got in an average-sized sackload?*

I'm just a lowly podcaster.

Used to be close to a hundred million per milliliter. Word.

Used to be?

Couple years ago? These scientists? They studied like men from all around the world, and you know what they find?

. . . ?

They find sperm counts've fallen by half in the last fifty years, ayte? HALF. You got yourself spunk levels that low, you'd be watching SpongeBob SquarePants *and snarfing cheesy poofs, too. Know what I'm saying?*

You serious about all this stuff, Mike?

Alphabetical pollutants. PCBs. DDT. Plastics. Cosmetics. Paints. Detergents. They mimic the effects of female hormones, ayte? Screw with your reproductive and nervous and immune systems. Which we're all going gay, man. Put that together with them tainted flu vaccines and you've got yourself a regular apopaclypse.

Tainted flu vaccines?

There's this like bacteria? Serratia. Same shit the government released from this ship off San Francisco in the fifties to test whether an enemy could launch a biological attack from a distance, ayte? Whole lots of them vaccines contaminated with it.

The *U.S.* government, Mike? Aren't they supposed to be on our side?

Only they thought it was like this harmless microbe at the time, ayte? Turns out it causes this avalanche of bad juju. Everything from heart-valve infections to peptic shock. Know what I'm saying? You want one word for it? Chinese toothpaste. You think you're being careful? You think you're doing all you can?

I'm not sure I do.

Cuz walk around with fucking plastic bags over your hands, ayte? You're still hosed. Cuz you want a hint? The prognosis is always fatal.

In cases of ingesting Chinese toothpaste and lead paint on kids' toys, you're saying?

In cases of being alive, man.

Um, Jesus. Wow. Thanks for the reminder, Mike. We can never hear that shadowy tune enough. Duck and cover, you're saying.

Word, man. Word . . .

Welcome to lucky episode thirteen of my own little pirate podcast coming to you semi-live and completely indirect every week from a different corner of the godforsaken Salton Sea, deadest body of saline solution on the deadest stretch of southwestern desert you'll ever want to forget.

I checked our download stats at what passes for the internet café at the Fountain of Youth RV Resort down the road from glorious Niland yesterday afternoon, folks, and I'm happy to report our numbers have soared from 166 last week to a whopping 187 as of 1:33 p.m. this day just past.

So it looks like the passenger deck on this ship of fools is filling fast.

Can fame and fortune be far behind?

Almost surely not. But never mind that.

Jolly Rogers wants to thank you all for opening your ears, your hearts, your minds.

Remember: all you have to do to set sail with the whole sick crew is search out my revolving website. To find it, just listen to your closest friends. Surf the web with real curiosity. Open each and every piece of spam you receive. I plan on sticking around here for the great duration listening to what *everybody* has to say who God and His Gofers have forgotten . . .

Speaking of which, imagine me tonight, if you will, sitting cross-legged on a deserted beach somewhere at the end of the world. The clock on my computer screen says 3:12 in the a.m. The temperature is a balmy seventy-eight. The forecast, like our government, is bland and predictable. A light breeze wafts in across the blasted water, on the far side of which hangs a stark low mountain range on the horizon. Stars are manifest in hazy profusion. To coin a phrase.

Surrounding me is an abandoned playground, its swingless swing, broken seesaw, and monkey bars in the shape of a submarine's conning tower half sunk in what at first glance you might mistake for white sand. You would be wrong. The granular substance, if you examine it closely, is in fact composed of myriad crushed fish bones from myriad fish kills. The air carries a salty piscine reek that you can taste on your lips, at the back of your tongue, deep in the intricacies of your sinuses. Leave here and drive to Niland, to Mecca, to Palm Springs, and that taste will dog you, friends, reminding you for hours *post factum* of this alcove in Nowhere's Mansion.

Behind me looms the renowned deserted blue and white marina hotel with its empty graffitied swimming pool. The windows were long ago boarded up with plywood. The back door has been let us say renovated by indigenes to allow easy ingress by the odd intrepid traveler. To wander past what once was a meat locker through what once was the bar, now a dark ramshackle cavern concretized with gull guano and a-trill with the birds' uncanny coos, is finally to understand Mr. Tom Waits's voice.

To read the thoughts spray-painted along the swimming pool walls is to understand Mr. Lou Reed's lyrics.

Your name means nothing, they say.

Hell's cuties.

Nighttime flight.

Oh, yeah.

Make no mistake about it, friends. This is the zone of cars sunken nose first into the briny slush along the shoreline, back halves jutting above the surface like huge rusted fins. The zone of derelict cafés and dented golf carts propped on blocks in grassless yards. The zone two hundred feet below hope possessing a heat so malicious it can clear the searing streets for weeks on end, a pollution so ferocious it can evacuate the vast inland blue of every boat and swimmer for months at a stretch.

And you may ask yourself, well, how did we get here?

At the turn of the last century, the story goes, the eminent California Development Company, seeking to realize Imperial

Valley's potential for unlimited agricultural productivity, dug irrigation canals from the Colorado River. When not-unexpected heavy silt loads commenced inhibiting the flow, engineers created a cut in the western bank to allow more water through. Jump to periodic Biblical rains. Jump to periodic Biblical floods. Jump to breaching of the levees.

And witness, if you will, nearly all the river's mighty flow rushing headlong into what till then had been known as the arid bowl-like Salton Sink.

By the time the breach was closed in 1907, the present-day Salton Sea had been formed: fifteen miles wide, thirty-five long, an average of thirty deep.

Instead of evaporating, as some innocents had predicted, it more or less maintained itself by massive agricultural runoff from the Imperial and Coachella valleys. Combine that with the increasing salinity and inflow of highly polluted water from the northward-flowing New River, and witness a wild chemical broth that began to spawn monstrous algal blooms. The blooms starved the water of oxygen. The lack of oxygen spawned voluminous fish die-offs. The voluminous fish die-offs spawned immensely elevated bacteria levels. The immensely elevated bacteria levels spawned massive bird die-offs. And . . .

And what else could one possibly do when played such a surreal hand except make it into a tourist attraction that failed almost as soon as it was imagined?

All of which is to say: welcome to Dreadland, friends.

Welcome to the Desert of the Real.

And welcome to my humble vessel. My listing luxury liner. The inside of my head for the next twenty minutes . . .

Yo, Jolly Roger. Dan here.

Where you phoning from, Dan?

Seattle.

And what do you do there in the beautiful Emerald City?

I'm a member of this group of artists?

What kind of artists?

We're called The Heraclitus?

As in the Greek river one can never step into twice?

Yeah. Exactly.

And what, Dan, is your group's medium?

Cells.

As in small rooms in prisons?

As in one or more nuclei surrounded by cytoplasm and enclosed by a membrane.

Human cells?

Human. Cow. Fish. A stem cell is pretty much a stem cell. It's what you do with one that's important? We're into biochemical engineering.

I sit before you, metaphorically speaking, deeply impressed.

We take these like, um . . . frames? Think of them as frames? Polymer scaffolds? And we grow the cells on them into . . . stuff. You differentiate the cells into whatever you want them to be. Bone. Muscle. Liver. Whatever. Then you cook them in a bioreactor for a couple of months.

A bioreactor?

Yeah. This, um, this device that supports a biologically active environment? They're used a lot in tissue-engineering?

What sort of stuff are we talking about here?

Stuff that's kind of unimaginable, but not really? You can, like, embed an iPod Nano into a, um, dog's heart?

Say again, Dan?

With a hole in it for the dial and earphone jack and everything? That's what I listen to you on sometimes.

    . . . ?

Or you can craft this bio-jewelry? Real goat eyeballs, maybe, that you can hang around your neck? Or say you want to decorate your computer with human teeth? Or make your trackpad out of cat-tongue tissue for better traction? You can do that, too. Except that's not the really cool stuff. We're in the process of giving people the option to grow extra little things on themselves? On their, like, bodies? Not prosthetics or plastic surgery or whatever. We can, like . . . Okay. Picture tiny devil horns for your forehead made out of real, you know, growing bone tissue? You have to get them filed down every once in a while, just like you get a haircut? Or instead of a tattoo of bat wings on your back? You can get small living batwings implanted? One on each shoulder blade? You can't fly or anything, but still. It's pretty cool. Or maybe a miniature set of gills just below your ears . . . or maybe, like, on the back of your hands? Or what about a squirrel's eyeball on the tip of your dick?

Okay, Dan, now you're starting to scare me.

Oh, no. There's nothing scary here, Jolly Roger. I mean, no animals are hurt or anything? And if you're uncomfortable or whatever, you don't have to join in. But someday?

Yeah?

Someday we plan to make little chimeras.

Chimera?

Little like fairytale creatures? One of Snow White's seven dwarfs, say. An angel. A miniature Loch Ness monster for your bathtub? Stuff like that. They won't be alive or anything? They'll sort of be like stuffed animals, only built out of real skin instead of cloth.

Won't the skin go bad?

We treat it with a polymer. It'll basically last forever.

You're an aesthetic pioneer of the flesh.

I don't know. I mean, actually, this whole thing's a pretty old idea.

From back in the days when we thought science fiction was merely a literary genre?

You ever hear of FM-2030?

A radio station?

A futurist. His real name was Fereidoun M. Esfandiary? He was the son of this Iranian diplomat. He taught at the New School in the sixties and wrote a book called Are You a Transhuman? *He said he was really a twenty-first-century person who just happened to be born in 1930. He called himself temporally challenged? He always talked about how he had this tremendous nostalgia for the future. That's where he got his name. He said he wanted to live to be a hundred years old so he could see the year 2030, which he thought would represent this like huge breakthrough moment.*

Things just get interestinger and interestinger.

FM argued that we're all transhumans, really. As in transitory humans? In the sense that we're all always evolving? Not figuratively. Literally. Every species is an intermediary species. Meaning humans are just these always-already mutations waiting to happen. Except most of us don't want to think about stuff like that too hard? We don't want to contemplate the consequences of being in-process organisms?

So we're back to your Greek river, only made of soft tissue.

Why settle for being who you were born as? Why settle for being the person you were ten minutes ago?

Thanks for your report from the epidermal front, Dan from Seattle.

Hey, we all love your show up here. We tell everyone we meet to listen.

Well, you've certainly given us plenty to keep us awake tonight. Keep us posted, Dan, all right? Let us know when the lights have changed. Let us know when it's time to cross the street.........

....

....

....

....

....

....

....

....

....

....

....
....
....
....
....
....
....
....
....

January

February

March

April

May

June

July

August

September

October

November

December

....

....

....

Hello?

....

....

....

....

....

....

Hello?

....

....

....

Testing . . . one . . . two . . . three.

....

....

Testing.

....

....

Okay, it looks like we're ready to go here.

....

This is Doctor Park Dietz. Today's date is Monday, May 22, 1995. The time is, uh, the time is 9:51 a.m. This will be a taped conversation with the last name of Tager, T-A-G-E-R, first of William,

W-I-L-L-I-A-M. Date of birth: November 9, 1947.

WT.   That is incorrect.

WT.   Okay, Bill. We'll get to that in a sec. What I've done here is I've turned on the recorder so I can tape our conversation because, you know, I'm not the best note taker in the world. This morning I'd like to return to some things we were talking about last fall, if that's all right with you.

WT.   Fine.

PD.   Okay, uh . . . Can you speak up just a little bit? I'm . . .

WT.   Sure.

PD.   Good. That's good. Okay. So I want to go back to the conversations we were having about October 4, 1986. You were on, what was it, 86th Street, right? At a little before 11:00 p.m.?

WT.   That is correct.

PD.   And you were, you know, you saw somebody. A man you recognized.

WT.   We already did this part.

PD.   I apologize, Bill. I'm not the, you know, the sharpest tool in the shed. I just want to understand what happened. So, okay, you saw this man you recognized, right?

WT.   Yes.

PD.   And you said you thought he was . . . ?

WT. I didn't think. I knew. Everybody knows.

PD. Why don't you go ahead and tell me—just for the record.

WT. Burrows. Kenneth Burrows.

PD. And what did you do when you saw the man you thought was Kenneth Burrows?

WT. I needed to get the code.

PD. And how did you go about doing that?

WT. I followed him.

PD. Where did he go?

WT. He went into this pizza parlor.

PD. And what happened?

WT. He ordered a slice of pepperoni. A slice of pepperoni and a Coke. I ordered a slice, too. Cheese. I didn't order anything to drink because I wasn't thirsty. He sat at the window.

PD. And where did you sit?

WT. I sat in the back.

PD. To watch him?

WT. To keep him under surveillance. Yes. Only I pretended not to because his brainwaves were arriving and everything.

PD.   What do you mean when you say: *His brainwaves were arriving and everything*?

WT.   They were coming in at me.

PD.   What did it feel like to you?

WT.   It felt like tinfoil sparkling inside my head.

PD.   And how long would you, uh, how long would you estimate you remained in the pizza parlor?

WT.   I don't know.

PD.   You waited until he was done.

WT.   Yes.

PD.   Maybe ten minutes? Twenty?

WT.   Something like that.

PD.   What sort of thoughts were you having at the time?

WT.   None.

PD.   Your mind was blank?

WT.   I was observing.

PD.   What did this man you recognized . . . what did he do next?

WT.   He got up. He wiped his mouth with a napkin, chucked

everything into the trashcan by the door. Then he said thanks to the guys behind the counter and left. I followed.

PD.   Was the pizza parlor crowded at that time of night?

WT.   There was maybe another couple of people.

PD.   Had you thought in any way at that point that you might want to hurt him?

WT.   The Vice President?

PD.   Had you pictured it?

WT.   Why would anyone picture hurting the V. P.?

PD.   Then tell me what was going through your head. Explain what you were thinking to me.

WT.   I was thinking about asking him for the code. That was pretty much it. He was walking fast. I had to jog to catch up with him. It seemed like the faster I went, the faster he went.

PD.   That's when things began changing for you?

WT.   He knew I was coming. He should've stopped.

PD.   How did he know you were coming?

WT.   He's the Vice President.

PD.   So what did you do when he didn't stop for you?

WT.   Can I get a cup of coffee now?

PD.   Coffee?

WT.   Yes. A cup of coffee.

PD.   Sure, Bill. Just a minute. Let me see what I can do. Cream and sugar?

WT.   Two percent. I'm trying to watch my weight.
....
....
....
....
....
Okay, hang on here.
....
....
....
Testing. Test . . .
....
....
One . . . two . . . three. One . . . two . . .
....
....
....
....
....
....
That better, Bill?

WT.   Yes.

PD.   Coffee's okay?

WT.   The coffee's fine.

PD.   Good. So . . . let's see. You were telling me about what happened when the man you believed to be Kenneth Burrows wouldn't, uh, wouldn't stop for you after you left the, you know, the pizza parlor on 86th.

WT.   My head felt bad.

PD.   What happened after that?

WT.   My fist thought of a way out.

PD.   What do you mean when you say: *My fist thought of a way out?*

WT.   My right fist.

PD.   What did it do?

WT.   It punched him in the jaw. Just below the left ear. Hard. He went right down. Then my feet did stuff. My mouth did stuff and my feet did stuff.

PD.   How was that a way out?

WT.   For him?

PD.   Yes.

WT.   I figured my fist would make him give me the frequency and then he would be safe.

PD.   Did you say anything?

WT.   I asked him for it.

PD.   For the code?

WT.   Only he just started lying to me. Lying and lying, the liar.

PD.   What did he lie about?

WT.   Everything.

PD.   What would an example be of one of his lies?

WT.   We already did this.

PD.   I know, Bill. Please bear with me.

WT.   He said I had the wrong guy.

PD.   But you believed you had the right guy.

WT.   He offered me stuff. A stupid watch. A stupid ring.

PD.   But you believed he was Burrows. Why do you suppose he wouldn't give you the frequency? You had him on the ground. Why wouldn't he just tell you?

WT.   I told him I was going back home no matter what. He couldn't stop me.

PD.   What did he say?

WT.   I knew the messages would start again any second. I knew I didn't have much time.

PD.   The messages are different from the brainwaves?

WT.   The messages are always the same. The brainwaves are tinfoil sparkling inside my head.

PD.   The messages come approximately every twenty minutes? Is that correct?

WT.   They come precisely every twenty minutes.

PD.   And they interrupted you while you were assaulting the man you took to be Kenneth Burrows?

WT.   They fucked me all up.

PD.   Why aren't they coming now, Bill . . . the messages? While we're, you know, while we're having this conversation.

WT.   They are.

PD.   Doesn't that make it difficult for you to think?

WT.   That is correct.

PD.   And they made it difficult for you to think while you were assaulting the man on the sidewalk . . .

WT.   That's when he made his break. I couldn't move. Sometimes they make it so you can't move.

PD.   What did you do?

WT.   I tried to catch him.

PD.   But you couldn't.

WT. That's why I'm here.

PD. That's why you're in New York?

WT. On this planet.

PD. On this planet?

WT. That is correct.

PD. You mean you feel you're stranded.

WT. Tell me how I can leave. Go ahead. Tell me.

PD. Believing that must make you feel lonely.

WT. That is correct.

PD. Like you've lost control of things?

WT. . . .

PD. Well, maybe you can help me understand, Bill, and maybe I can, you know, I can help you in return.

WT. I don't think so.

PD. Why is that?

WT. How can you help me?

PD. It may take some time, but I'm optimistic. How about, uh, how about we go back to the beginning? Would you do that for me? How about we take it from the beginning?

WT. Again?

PD. Let's see . . . My records . . . they show you were born on November 9, 1947. But you say that is inaccurate.

WT. November 9, 2265.

PD. 2265?

WT. That is correct.

PD. And it shows here you were born in Charlotte, North Carolina. Do you believe that is incorrect as well?

WT. Yes.

PD. Where do you believe you were born?

WT. New York. Staten Island. We've already had this conversation.

PD. It's just, uh, I guess it's just taking some time for what you have to say to sink in. How do you account for the discrepancy in your record?

WT. Connect the dots.

PD. You believe you're from the future.

WT. Belief has zero to do with it.

PD. How would you say it, then?

WT. I would say: *William Tager is from a future.*

PD. From *a* future?

WT. That is correct.

PD. Not ours?

WT. A different Staten Island. A different earth.

PD. I'm sorry, Bill, but I'm having a hard time understanding what you're telling me. What do you mean when you say: *A different earth*?

WT. That's not the right question.

PD. What would the right question be?

WT. The right question would be: *Where is William Tager's earth?*

PD. What would the answer to that question be?

WT. Right here, all around us.

PD. Isn't that saying, uh, isn't that saying the same thing?

WT. Only in a different brane.

PD. A different brain?

WT. Brane. B-R-A-N-E. M*embrane*.

PD. Membrane?

WT. Your physicists already know this. They already know

reality is composed of multiple vibrating membranes. You can travel between them, but when they touch it's The Catastrophe.

PD.   The catastrophe?

WT.   You call it The Big Bang. We call it The Catastrophe. You see it as a beginning. We see it as an ending.

PD.   So let me get this straight. You believe you come from an alternate dimension and in that dimension it's the future.

WT.   That is correct, minus the belief.

PD.   I would think even in 2265 time travel to alternate dimensions would be a very difficult concept to put into practice.

WT.   I'm no physicist. I dropped out of high school. Only I know it has to do with a warp in the space-time continuum. The World Government has been experimenting in this area for a hundred and fifty years.

PD.   The World Government?

WT.   I'm a test pilot, you could say. Chuck Yeager. Howard Hughes.

PD.   That sounds like a real honor, Bill.

WT.   It's a punishment.

PD.   A punishment?

WT.   That's how I met the Vice President.

PD.   As a test pilot?

WT.   Yes.

PD.   Why don't you tell me about that.

WT.   I was in prison.

PD.   In the alternate future, you mean.

WT.   Yes.

PD.   And what were you, you know . . .

WT.   Murder.

PD.   You killed someone?

WT.   They said I killed someone.

PD.   Did you?

WT.   My hands did.

PD.   Who did your hands kill?

WT.   They set fire to my girlfriend's house. In Newark, New Jersey. I didn't know that's what they were planning.

PD.   Why did you kill your girlfriend?

WT.   She was cheating on me. Her name was Estelle. She denied everything. But you could tell she was lying and lying, the liar. She told me to go fuck myself. She kicked me out of her house.

PD.   What did you do?

WT.   I came back at two that morning with a can of kerosene and a pack of matches.

PD.   Estelle died in the fire?

WT.   Her kids and her. That is correct.

PD.   How many children did she have?

WT.   Three. Two girls, one boy.

PD.   They were yours?

WT.   One, maybe. The boy.

PD.   How did that make you feel—knowing, I mean, that you were responsible for those four deaths?

WT.   Hands do what hands do.

PD.   You're telling me you felt guilt.

WT.   Someone had to. Then that changed.

PD.   They sent you to prison?

WT.   Death row. Public beheading.

PD.   Beheading?

WT.   By sword. That is correct. The World Government looks to *The Qur'an* for guidance. Praise be to Allah. Et cetera.

PD.   How long had you been there? In prison, I mean.

WT.   They had already taken my measurements. The imam had already begun visiting in earnest.

PD.   And that's where you met the Vice President for the first time.

WT.   One afternoon this suit shows up outside my cell. I'm reading a comic book. They allow you comic books. They're not like yours. They're about events in *The Qur'an*. The astounding of the sleepers. The fallen angel of Babil. They come on a single sheet of thin translucent plastic and they move.

PD.   Like movies?

WT.   Only in three dimensions with floating thought-bubbles.

PD.   And the suit?

WT.   He goes he's from the government and he has this deal for me. What kind of deal? I go. He goes if I volunteer for this project and return safely, I get a full pardon.

PD.   What sort of thoughts did you have when you lit the match?

WT.   What match?

PD.   At Estelle's house.

WT.   There was this match. There was this can of kerosene. That's pretty much it.

PD.   You weren't thinking anything else?

WT. I'm not what you might call a deep thinker.

PD. What did you tell the government official?

WT. Next day I'm in the travel chamber. It looks like one of your tanning booths. All this brightness inside a steel coffin. They've strapped me in. They've begun the countdown.

PD. That's when Burrows showed up?

WT. I'm lying there, squinting into this really bright light, waiting. Then all of a sudden he's leaning over me. He's leaning over so close I can smell his aftershave. It's Old Spice.

PD. What did he say?

WT. He's smiling really wide . . . like, um, like a cartoon shark smiles. He asks me, smiling and all, if I slept well last night. I tell him yeah, I did, as a matter of fact. Do I remember any of my dreams? he goes. I go no. He keeps smiling really wide. Try harder, he goes. I look at him a couple seconds, then it comes to me. Actually, I do remember a dream.

PD. Tell me about it.

WT. I'm woke up by these suits, five or six of them, in the middle of the night. They carry me by my arms and legs to the hospital ward. I'm struggling. I remember the sounds. It's that kind of dream. The clumping their feet make as we're going down the hall. The clatter of the, what do you call them. Of the gurneys around me. And when I finish recounting my dream, you know what Burrows goes?

PD. What's that, Bill?

WT. He goes, smiling and all: *It wasn't a dream, Bill.*

PD. You're saying they really took you to the hospital ward?

WT. For the operation. That is correct.

PD. What operation?

WT. The kind to implant a transmitter inside my head.

PD. Why did they do that?

WT. He goes the transmitter will start barraging me with messages to return if I try to remain in this time and place past when I'm supposed to.

PD. The transmitter will broadcast every twenty minutes in your head.

WT. Till I return and file a report on the mission. That's when they'll take it out.

PD. So you obviously crossed branes successfully.

WT. What do you think about what happened last month?

PD. Pardon?

WT. What happened last month. In Oklahoma City.

PD. Why, uh, why are we talking about that at this point in our conversation, Bill?

WT. 5,000 pounds of fertilizer and nitromethane mixture packed into the back of a rental truck. It makes you think.

PD.   What does it make you think about?

WT.   168 people dead. 800 wounded. What could possibly come next?

PD.   We're not really here today to, uh, to talk about the Oklahoma bombing, Bill.

WT.   I'm just saying. It's something to consider.

PD.   Well, let's go ahead and save that for another day, all right? This morning I'd like to continue learning about your trip to our planet.

WT.   Fine.

PD.   So you arrived in Manhattan on . . .

WT.   I arrived in your Manhattan on September 1, 1986.

PD.   And how long were you supposed to stay?

WT.   Two weeks.

PD.   How were you supposed to get by, Bill—eat, sleep, that sort of thing?

WT.   Rob people. Don't hurt them or anything. Don't draw any more attention to yourself than necessary. Get their cash. It was pretty easy. I walked up to people on side streets and pretended I had a gun in my pocket.

PD.   What happened?

WT.   They gave me what I needed. People are nice that way.

PD.   Tell me about your mission. What were you supposed to do during your time in our brane?

WT.   Record.

PD.   What did they want you to do that for?

WT.   Test pilots don't ask why the jets they fly are built.

PD.   Would you maybe speculate for me a little?

WT.   Why do you go to the moon?

PD.   But it sounds like you're suggesting maybe it was something else as well.

WT.   I'm suggesting why have a rebirth of a religion when you can assure that the religion never dies in the first place?

PD.   You're suggesting maybe your trip was part of a plan to spread your religion?

WT.   I'm not suggesting anything.

PD.   You said you record, Bill. How, uh, how do you go about doing that?

WT.   I just open my eyes and it starts.

PD.   And everything went well at first.

WT. I was down in the Village. Near Washington Square. It was a little past midnight. I remember it was warm. I was recording nightlife at the cafés and bars along Sullivan. Then these two police on bikes were yelling at me.

PD. Why do you suppose they were they doing that, Bill?

WT. I was just standing there. Then they were yelling at me. I ran.

PD. But why, Bill, if you didn't know, uh, if you didn't believe you'd done anything wrong?

WT. Their voices scared me. I ducked left on Third, into this restaurant. It was vegetarian. They followed. One tackled me. The other handcuffed me. My wrists didn't feel good. Their mouths were doing things. It was all mixed up.

PD. What were their mouths doing?

WT. They were telling me I had the right to remain silent. They were telling me anything I said could be used against me in a court of law. I had the right to consult with an attorney and to have that attorney present during questioning. Their mouths were telling me if I couldn't afford one, an attorney would be provided at no cost.

PD. Did you tell them you hadn't done anything?

WT. I explained how they needed to let me up.

PD. But they didn't let you up. Is that right? They arrested you instead.

WT. They said I had been putting coins into expired parking meters.

PD.   But you don't remember doing that.

WT.   I *didn't* do that.

PD.   But they arrested you and put you in jail anyway.

WT.   For thirty days.

PD.   And so you were forced to remain in this dimension longer than you were supposed to.

WT.   That is correct.

PD.   And that's when the messages started arriving.

WT.   That is correct.

PD.   But you couldn't do what they said, could you?

WT.   It was going to be another week before I could try a return.

PD.   Why is that, Bill?

WT.   The ergs. They needed to regenerate. Only there was no way to let the Vice President know. It was a one-way transmission system.

PD.   Don't you think it's a little odd, Bill, that the Vice President didn't provide you with a way to contact him?

WT.   Membranes are membranes. Worlds are whirls.

PD.   And the messages arrived night and day. It must have been very difficult for you.

WT. I couldn't rest or sleep. My head felt like the angel was screeching inside.

PD. What angel is that, Bill?

WT. The fallen one.

PD. The fallen angel? From *The Qur'an*?

WT. From the bedtime story.

PD. I don't believe I'm familiar with that one.

WT. My mother used to read it to me. It was my favorite. That's what it teaches.

PD. What does it teach?

WT. That worlds are whirls.

PD. Whirls? Worlds are whirls, not worlds?

WT. That is correct.

PD. Would you do me a favor, Bill?

WT. What?

PD. Would you tell it to me? I'd like to hear it.

WT. You would?

PD. Very much so. Yes.

WT. Uh, sure. Sure. It starts . . . how does it start? Let's see. Oh, yeah. It starts with this lake. It starts with this lake somewhere in Finland, and two children on their way home from church.

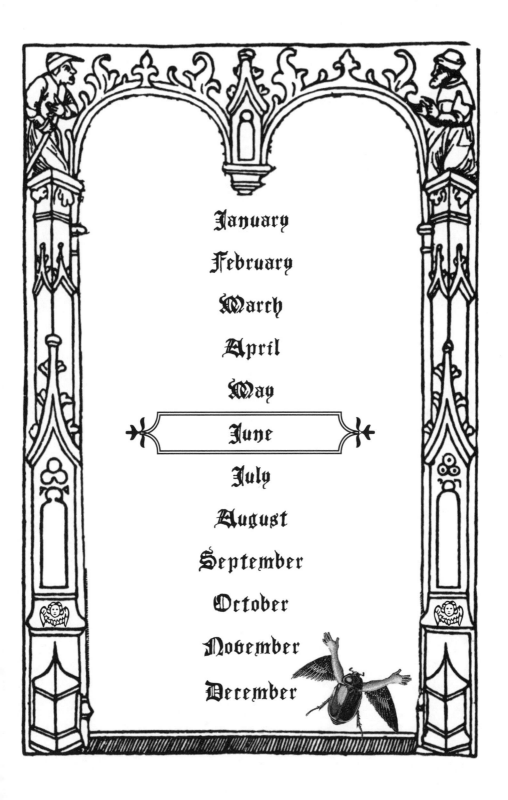

January

February

March

April

May

June

July

August

September

October

November

December

A lake somewhere in Finland inventing a slightly out-of-focus afternoon above itself. Two children on their way home after church. Wordless, hands in pockets, they are following a deserted road. Low grayblue hills lope along the far shore. Clusters of white flecks against dark wet earth. Sami, the hatted one, thinks about the chuffing sound his feet make. Jarmo, his older brother, the one in the too-small brown jacket, thinks about the fish soup his mother is preparing this very moment back at the farm as she does every Sunday afternoon.

Both boys approach the edge of not thinking, though Sami is infinitesimally closer to that edge than Jarmo. They have walked this stretch of road too many times to notice it. To them, it simply represents an instrument of agency. They are, that is, imagining the end rather than the means of their journey. They thus fail to hear the scattered birdsong, the wind exhaling continuously across the lake, the suck and gurgle of the soggy ground around them.

The air busy with a frisky chill and the damp loamy greenness of early spring.

They fail to notice these things, too.

Fish soup or ham, Jarmo thinks. How, when you reach deep into the barrel of salted meat at the end of the season, right down to the grainy bottom of it through the crystals like warm ice, you extract leather slabs alive with maggots. As if someone had sprinkled the meat with squirming rice. You have to scrape it off with a knife before you can boil the leather into something edible. Only then do you discover what the slab will turn into: ham or fish.

Sami kicks a rock and listens to it snap and die. On the very edge of not thinking, he sweeps his grimy-knuckled hand down and whisks up another as he passes and chucks it as far as he can into the meadow to his right, trying to plock it into the lake. The rock clumps short. A family of heel-sized dun birds agitate from the grass into the blurry sun and dart into invisibility. They are there. They are gone. At that instant, for no reason he can articulate, Sami discovers himself wondering how much God weighs.

If he stopped in his tracks just now and listened carefully, he would hear the stream behind him sloshing and clicking over pebbles like a bag full of marbles. The continuous drypaper crinkle of last year's leaves rubbing against each other on spindly bushes. Mosquito whir. Fly buzz. The rush of his own breath inside his head for what will amount to decades without cessation. But he doesn't listen. Instead, he discovers himself wondering, fleetingly, if he might be a little on the chunky side. Sitting in the outhouse, deep into the disagreeable daily business of passing gas and night-soil, he has on occasion let his gaze fall upon the bluish white skin of his thighs and noticed a cheesy patchwork of dimples spotting it. What, he wonders, zeroing in on another rock in the road, might this portend about the complexion of his adulthood?

Sami lets his left foot thrill.

Approaching the very edge of not thinking, hands in pockets, wooden bowl of fish soup hovering in the middle of his conscious-ness, Jarmo happens to glance up and see her lying in the meadow thirty or forty meters away. Initially, he believes he is looking at the remnants of a thawing snowdrift. But the shape is completely wrong for that. Nor are there any other swaths of snow in view. So he convinces himself that he must be looking at an enormous bird. Yes. A swan, perhaps, shot recently by a hunter. Yet the truth is he has never seen a bird this big, he has heard no gunfire this afternoon, there exist no hunters in the vicinity. No. That can't be it. That can't be it at all. Hence, still walking, although not quite as quickly as before, Jarmo squints. He tugs back the corner of his right eyelid to press his cornea into obedience. He ducks and bobs his head, trying to pull the object of his sudden interest into focus.

The manner in which she curls into herself makes her wings arch up behind her like gigantic feathery parentheses separating her from the surrounding text of the world.

Her hair is the color of butter.

Her long diaphanous gown, the kerchief tied around her head like a bandage, are flawless white in spite of the patch of marshy ground on which she lies.

She is, Jarmo sees, barefoot.

She is barefoot, and, unthinking, Jarmo reaches for and tugs on his brother's baggy black sleeve. Sami raises his head. Half thinking about the nature and attributes of excess, he peers out from beneath the brim of his black hat and jolts at what he sees. Both boys come up short, as if the skeleton of their grandfather—the scrawny mirthless man with hands as large as boat paddles—had just appeared before them on the deserted road, reached into their chest cavities, placed five massive bony fingers around each of their young hearts, and squeezed as if he were squeezing out a pair of saturated washrags after a particularly long, luxurious sauna.

When they reach her, they are surprised to discover she is still breathing. Her weak exhalations smell redbrownish like cinnamon at Christmas.

Jarmo makes out the small triangular wedge missing from the lower portion of her left wing, and, near the top, a watery pink smudge of blood.

He circles the wounded angel slowly, appraising. Sami hesitates, falls back. Jarmo kneels. Reaching out to touch her shoulder, shake her gently to see what will happen next, how the plot of their day will advance itself, it strikes him that angels with their four appendages and tremendous wings are closer in essential physiognomy to butterflies, beetles, and bees than to mortals.

The attributes of angels, Sami thinks at almost the same moment, are insectile rather than humanoid in nature. How odd.

Withdrawing his hand, speaking as he thinks, thinking as he speaks, Jarmo asks his brother to help him find two long sturdy branches and a shorter third one with which to construct a makeshift stretcher. Before he has risen to his feet, however, the afternoon somehow lurches ahead of itself, becomes later than it should, the light more rundown. Jarmo feels time speeding up around him. It reminds him of riding on the Helsinki tram last summer with his mother and father, only much faster, the world slurring by outside. Blinking, he tries to shake it off as he might a horsefly's bite, but it isn't until he backs several paces away from the angel that the strange sensation abates. And then, as unexpectedly as it sped up, time slows down again. Jarmo decides not to mention this episode to his brother. Rather, he leads Sami in the direction of a single dead willow standing in the middle of the meadow. Here they will break up branches and tie them together with long fibrous strands of grass like their father taught them.

Her chest was flat, Jarmo considers as he works. He stands, light deteriorating around him, and shrugs off his jacket. Her chest was completely flat. Just like a boy's.

And you could see through her gown.

You could see through her gown and even if you tried not to you couldn't help yourself because there it was and you had to look and when you did you could see her what do they call it her pubic mound and it was smooth and blank and unblemished as a doll's.

An hour later, when the brothers return with the litter, they discover the angel sitting up. She is examining a bouquet of limp white bell-shaped flowers in her fist. She looks drunk, drunk or dazed, as if she can no longer remember the names of certain articles she knew the names of ten minutes ago. She does not glance at the brothers as they approach. Sami has the impression her eyes may actually be closed. It is even possible she is blind, she perceives through some faculty other than sight, like a bat or a wasp, although it is difficult to say with any certainty because the thick white kerchief she wears as a bandage impedes Sami's view. Jarmo signals him to lower the stretcher. Then he walks over to the angel, squats, reaches out his hand again to touch her shoulder in order to let her know they are ready to go. Time jerks forward. His hand is by his side. It is resting on her gown. There has been no inbetweenness. The angel does not turn her attention away from her flowers.

It feels to Jarmo as if he is living in a film with several frames missing every three heartbeats. The afternoon light weakens further, stars phosphoresce in the sky, they whirl through the night, the sky blanches into gossamer morning haze, the orange sun is rising, the red sun is setting, then it is evening, then it is night, then it is evening then it is night then it is morning. The angel is speaking to him without moving her lips, explaining, perhaps, explaining or describing, traveling with him without stirring, her voice in his mind reminiscent of the electric version of the color blue.

In heaven I will tell you. I will tell you in heaven. I not being who I am. Is not being how it is. This much is clear. One could even hazard that this much goes without comment. The same note, held forever. Let us call it middle C, for argument's sake. Middle C or B-flat. It doesn't honestly matter which, because this is simply one way of putting it. There are others. Or perhaps the same photo-graph, you call them photographs, *every time you open your eyes. Now. Now. Now. This is perpetuity. My name, by the way, is . . . something. Although, perhaps, it almost goes without saying, it may be something else. In heaven, that is, I will tell you. My name is—* Goodbye. *It was so nice meeting you. Yes. We must promise to do it again sometime. The same photograph, you call them* pho-tographs *. . . and so forth, or, perhaps, let us say swallows frozen in mid-flight for millennia on end, beyond the range of human invention. Moving by not moving. In heaven, in summation, the boom-boom. This much we can assert with some confidence. In heaven, the boom-boom, you call it* God, *you call it a black cube, the terrible weightless weight, for argument's sake, in heaven the boom-boom, holding all thoughts in His boom-boom, and there-fore also holding none. In summation, in conclusion, to be brief, in a word, as a consequence of what has been heretofore asserted—* Hello. What a lovely surprise. I simply reached down one day. Day *not being quite how it . . . I simply reached down, in a manner of speaking, in a metaphorical sense, and my wing tore. I tore my wing, but . . . and this bears repeating . . . this possibly bears repeating . . . stranger things having happened . . . at least such an assertion remains open to speculation . . . it didn't hurt. No. Not at all. Nothing, I suppose, hurts in photographs. I simply reached* *down one day, to get at the crux of the matter, a wonderful phrase,* crux, *and tore my wing, my wing tore, here, you see, because of the boom-boom, then I wiped my hand on my feathers, here. Because, in heaven, not to put too fine a point on it, every verb is a noun. Pass the tea. Smell the flowers. Help yourself. The clouds above the lake, unmoving, painted upon an unchanging sky. No other parts of speech subsist. This is my point . . . so to speak. In the horror of the black cube, you call it* perfection, *one can only say what a fine day it is, again and again, admiring the clouds, pretending to admire the unmoving clouds in the unchanging sky, so perfect as to send a spike through the heart, prevent your breath from arriving, a wonderful turn of phrase, one can almost feel it, but all you do is wait in the train station, to put it plainly, where nothing will arrive, always. I reached down, this surely being my point, unless something else turns out to . . . stranger things have happened . . . I reached down and tore my wing, here, my wing tore, and then I wiped my hand on my feathers, here, and everything became a verb, everything became a curio, a curiosity, a carnival.*

January

February

March

April

May

June

July

August

September

October

November

December

Sit back in your seats, and behold.

What you see before you, Ladies and Gentlemen,

is a gigantic closet composed of smaller ones, a large

Behind each resides a compartment lodging
compartment
compartment
compartment
compartment

Now let me invite you

cabinet composed of thirteen miniature doors.

a remarkable portion of the one,
          the only,
             the magnificent

                     MAN WITH BORROWED ORGANS.

          Those bits and pieces have come to us
          from far and wide, and at considerable
        risk to our collectors: the South China Sea,
the Canary Islands, the dark medulla of Amazonia.

The Man himself was first assembled out of them in 1945.

You will not observe him today.

                 He has been put together only
              once every thirty years since then,
         and only for a precise interval of three minutes,
     for reasons that, I believe, will become clear shortly.

to feast your eyes on a Man Divided . . .

FINGERNAILS, TOENAILS, HAIR

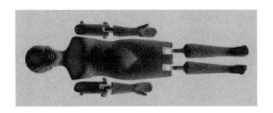

Their wings resemble
a human palm and serve no purpose

Cornered, an earthbound angel will fool humans to
it can slip between cracks in time, thereby creating
the impression on the part of the viewer of invisibility.

The brothers, in their eighties at the time, say they
caught this one by staking a naked weeping boy bathed
in red wine in the middle of an opening in a Finnish
forest at night. Their prey became drunk on the boy's

Two months later, it expired of loneliness and temporal awareness

Wearing these fingernails, toenails, and hair, **THE MAN**

These items, said to have been stolen by a
Norwegian explorer in 1927 from a glass case
in a Nepalese monastery near Pokhara, were originally
removed from the corpse of an angel bought by its monks
from two brothers on the rocky coast of Aulis,
the harsh cusp of land where
mythological Iphigenia
met her fate.

Once upon a time, as you may recall,
we believed such celestial creatures
beautiful pale beings
with white swan
wings.

It was only with this specimen
that we discovered they are in fact ugly dwarfish beasts
covered with coarse orange hair.

those, not of swans, but of bats, are slightly larger than
save dreaming of heaven, a place from which some,
without warning, have been
x

see otherwise, or curl into a ball so tiny

c
l
u
d
e
d
.

carcass.

in a rusty cage usually reserved for fattening hogs.

WITH BORROWED ORGANS learns
that human beings continually grow,
but inevitably
in useless ways.

L
I
P
S

who frowned upon the idea of her

these dry thin brown virgin folds are meant to remind

THE MAN WITH BORROWED ORGANS

of what one can no longer say.

Excised from a Burmese princess
on her thirteenth birthday in 1753 by her father,
kissing the vile lips of local boys,

morning he met his hangman, his strangler,

his firing squad, her horde of stoners, the   **TEETH**

black-faced flunky who let the

guillotine's blade plummet.

Some come from Kabul,
some from Paris,
some from London,
some from Taipei,
some from Money, Mississippi.

Each of these which are, as you can see,
in various stages of amber decay,
was plucked from the jaw
of a different falsely
accused murderer
on the

```
l   s   p   u   o   c   T   c   o   u   p   s
o   o   u   n   v   h   o   h   v   n   u   o
s   u   l   t   e   e   g   e   e   t   l   u
s   r   p   i   r   w   e   w   r   i   p   r
.       y   l           t               l   y
    a           a   t   h   t   a               a
    s   a   t   n   h   e   h   n   t   a   s       l
        s   h   d   e   r   e   d   h   s           o
            e               ,           e           s
        p   y   o   s           s   o   y   p       s
        a       v   a   t   a   v       a           .
        p   a   e   m   h   m   e   a   p
        ,   r   r   e   e   e   r   r   ,
        e           s           e
            a   m   e   m   a
            g   e       e   g
            a   m   t   m   a
            i   o   e   o   i
            n   r   e   r   n
                i   t   i
                e   h   e
                s       s
```

life. The organ was discovered fully in tact by a Swiss
inhabitant of a sarcophagus in a vault buried deep within
colleague of the esteemed explorer Johann Ludwig
four years earlier, and who, years before that, had disguised
impunity throughout the Middle East.

Here the memories the

With some, it is simply impossible to tell.

real. Some are imaginary.

-headed his nemesis with a sword. That turns out not quite to be the case. Rather, the boy used his sword to gut the giant while he lay dazed and still writhing before him like a beached leviathan. Done with his task, David played upon Goliath's enormous stomach in front of Saul like some horrible wind instru- ment. Soon, though, interest behind him, he cast the thing aside and went on with his elsewise unremarkable

forward onto the sand. The Holy Book claims David next be- in his eyes. Thinking quickly, David drew a stone from his bag Goliath cursed him by all the names of the Philistine gods and smooth stones he had collected from a nearby stream, Goliath

STOMACH

missionary named Celan Solen in 1816. It was the lone
the rose-red city half as old as time: Petra. Solen was a
Burckhardt, the man who first revealed Petra to the world
himself as a devout Muslim in order to move with

At first, Ladies and Gentlemen, you might mistake this organ for a huge dark lilac bagpipe. This misapprehension is far from uncommon. But lean forward. Squint. You will soon see otherwise. This organ once belonged to none other than the legendary giant Goliath who fell by the lucky hand of David of the Israelites in the Valley of Elah. You are looking at history. You are looking at prophecy. When David

teeth have chewed mix

with the broth of nostalgia. Some of the

recollections there are

confronted him, carrying only a sling and sack filled with five
mocked the boy. When David paid Goliath's words no heed,
lumbered toward him, arms raised above his head, slaughter
and slung it. It shattered the giant's temple. Goliath pitched

The brown one was picked up in less than choice
condition by a peasant stumbling along a dirt
road that cut through Nagasaki on the
evening of August 9th, 1945, a Thursday, and sold several weeks later to a
U.S. Army physician, about whom
we know nothing except that, as a
teenager, he worked one summer
preventing people from leap-
ing off the observation deck
at the edge of Niagara Falls.
The green one—whose white
is filled, as you will notice,
with blood—belonged to
a twenty-two-year-old girl
whom a Pakistani tribal   EYES
council ordered gang-raped
on June 22nd, 2002, a Saturday, in order to punish her
family after her eleven-year-
old brother was seen strolling with a girl from a higher
caste. This second eye was
sold directly to us by a British
ophthalmologist in Lahore to
replace our blue one of unknown
origin, which had gone blind over
time as a result, we surmise, of having seen too much. All that is known
of the British ophthalmologist is that
he collects, or believes he collects, small
portions of time in airtight canning jars.

By
slipping
these
eyes
into
his
empty
sockets,
THE
MAN
 WITH
  BORROWED
   ORGANS
    is
     able
     to
      recall,
     each
     second
    he
    is
   awake,
who
we
were
not,
are
not,
and
can
never
be.

The unfortunate who originally possessed
these could not hear. He passed his life as
an uncelebrated musician in a sanitorium in
Salzburg during the early years of the twentieth
century. To this day, no critic
to make heads
although for a short time they

EARS

attention of a young composer named
Schoenberg. We surmise that this poor fellow
lived in a land of cacophony others
could not apprehend.

has been able

or tails of his compositions,

drew the intense

Arnold

These knotty flaps of cartilage allow
THE MAN WITH BORROWED ORGANS
to bear in mind that every word we speak falls,
at the end of the day,
on deaf ears.

house

lungs

The

LUNGS

As you can see,

hope.

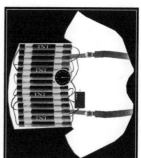

they are extremely small.

But listen closely, Ladies and Gentlemen, for even now

you can hear them

breathing

a fairytale.

January

February

March

April

May

June

July

August

September

October

November

December

once upon a time   there was a boy born a black marble-cover notebook   he had a sewn-cloth spine for extra strength   he was filled with wide-ruled sheets of paper   he didn't have any arms or legs   just two sad blue eyes   a squinched nose   a pair of lips thin as a line drawn by a number-two pencil floating among the patterning   just above the white rectangle where it said *Composition Book*

when the nurse in the delivery room passed the boy to his mother the woman gasped in shame and pity   then reached out her arms   smiled   *my beautiful boy* she cooed   *my beautiful beautiful boy*

the father stood off to the side

weeping

he claimed with happiness   but he had told his friends   he didn't care what the baby was   so long as it was healthy   and now he was regretting his   you could say inexact wording

the parents christened him The Notebook Boy   their new-born   wrote his name on the cover of him in bold black permanent marker the mother saying he was a special gift from God

the father   weeping   calling him their little miracle

The Notebook Boy proved himself   a quiet good-natured child   he could entertain himself for hours   simply by staring up at all the colorful plastic shapes strung above his crib like miniature warnings to miniature low-flying aircraft

he didn't need diapers

because he didn't make a mess

he didn't make a mess because he didn't need to eat

the parents' friends started dropping by   they brought gifts   loitered with their hands in their pockets   asked in the end if they could see the new bundle of joy   it wasn't long before they also wondered aloud   shyly at first   then less so if perhaps they could write something in him   just a word or two

help yourselves the parents said   handing them special blue felt-tip pens that matched The Notebook Boy's eyes   some drew cute cartoons   some gave what they thought sounded like sage advice   some simply wished The Notebook Boy well on what would be nothing if not a challenging course

through life

the parents wrote in him as well

spelling out what he could do

what he couldn't

reminding him to say his prayers each and every night

just in case he happened to die in his sleep

amen

The Notebook Boy enjoyed the attention   lying in his
crib   delighting in the tickle of those pens on his paper skin

he decided he would never learn to speak   in part because he
already knew what he would say   hearing the obvious didn't
interest him   in part he preferred to listen to what others wrote
in him   finished as he was with the obvious   what others had to
say always surprising always pleasing him

his weeping father began to shrink

it wasn't conspicuous at first

the mother thinking perhaps he was just stooping a bit more
than usual   attention-getting device   she told him to stand up
straight   get a backbone   then she realized the top of the man's
balding head only reached the tip of her nose   this wasn't how she
had remembered him at all   she was sure that when they met he
had towered above her

in school children picked on The Notebook Boy   lifted him
out of his motorized wheelchair   held him down on the
playground   wrote *I SUCK!* in large red crayon letters in his
wide-ruled pages

then walked away

laughing

leaving him stranded on his back in the patchy grass next to the monkey bars until his teachers found him

the better part of an hour later

he dropped out   begged his parents to let him have his own apartment   he needed somewhere to be alone with the voices inside him

nice place   plenty of light

plasma-screen TV

his mother stopped by twice a day

to lend him a hand

once every morning   once every evening

The Notebook Boy took a stay-at-home job   watched television shows to see if he could guess the endings   if so the marketing agency that hired him told him to rate the show in question as Good   if not Poor

the father became the size of a small chimpanzee

the size of a guinea pig standing on its hind legs

the mother keeping him in a brightly colored soft-sided cat carrier

one day The Notebook Boy awoke to find sentences he didn't recognize having begun cropping up in the pages that comprised him the overwhelming impression being of strangers whispering things through his skin while he slept

I feel like I am always moving   Taru

like I am never exactly where I am

the voices

whole stories too

three people wake one morning to find themselves treading water in the middle of the ocean   still in their clothes   not a good sign   the first has unabridged Webster's dictionaries for feet   she goes under in a matter of minutes   the others can hear her shoutgurgling as she sinks out of sight

the second a global positioning system for a heart   he knows exactly where he is at all times   it doesn't help   no one else shares his sense of place

that night he is found by sharks

the third is born with an iPod for lungs   a Bose speaker for a mouth   she sings on and on   her poignant voice keeping her company   calming her   giving her a reason to hold out another thirty seconds   another thirty seconds   but   on the seventh day

on the seventh day she ends up drowning in a foamy white agitation

The Notebook Boy showing these snippets to his mother

when she dropped in on him unexpectedly one afternoon   to let him know   his weeping father had finally left her

he now the size of a bright green South American tree frog

the father

unable even to reach the doorknob to exit her life without her assistance

it's for the best sweetheart, she telling The Notebook Boy *every-thing always happening for a*

wiping her nose with the white rose of a Kleenex

huddling in the large stuffed chair with the diamond-tufted pillow in front of the TV

reading passages he had given her

these are heartbreaking she announcing when finished

others should have their hearts broken by them too

carrying her son directly to the corner Kinko's   to copy him   flying to Manhattan   and demanding of the startled woman editor stepping from the lavatory that she   that she read what the mother was

was thrusting in her direction

that summer The Notebook Boy published to rave reviews

famous overnight

as they say

incessantly

he refusing to read aloud on book tours   having never learned
how   refusing to sign any of the shiny red and yellow

hardback copies of himself

his mother beginning to shrink as well

she propped him against the back of a plush chair at the front
of auditoriums   of libraries   bookstores   he stared mutely
out at the audience with those sad blue eyes of his   and
then   wordless   his mother picked him up carefully   tucked
him under her arm   departed

a cult developing around him

The Notebook Boy appearing   mute   on popular talk shows

his image adorning the covers of glossy magazines

his mother shrinking faster than his father had done

on account of her gender

perhaps

she also beginning to grow a small dark tail the color of plums and bad bruises

among the multitude of voices within him

one beginning to catch his attention

stunning him with its exquisite prose

its story   a husband discovering he has Alzheimer's   his memory
turning into a complex medieval tapestry someone unsews

                              thread by thread

                              every second

        and one morning

        his wife wakes to discover him gone

        beside her bed a note

I've bothered you long enough in this life

have taken the cell phone

will call once a day till I can't remember the number anymore when you don't hear from me

you'll know I've become someone else

The Notebook Boy could tell

the voice belonged to a melancholy woman

having worked very hard to get exactly

what she didn't want

he couldn't push the stunning sound of it out of his head

it followed him from city to city   state to state   dream to
dream   a piece of jazz by Miles Davis you listen to at three in the
morning   not quite sure whether you've fallen asleep   or only
think you have

and so he decided to marry that voice

even though he didn't know where it came from

who it belonged to

nine months later a plethora of baby voices being born

his mother   now a small blind albino salamander   beneath whose
cloudy pink skin you could see the organs functioning   crawled
under his apartment door early one evening and away   a tiny trail
of mucilaginous tears in her wake

The Notebook Boy tried not to think about her

                                        he couldn't help it

he basked in his newfound fatherhood   the countless brood of
astonishing sentences surrounding him

the following week he died

the landlord finding him in his living room

                                                    alone

propped up in his stuffed chair with the diamond-tufted pillow back

plasma-screen TV flickering

the last entry in him had been about the show he had been watching he had rated it as Good

the coroner examined his remains

noticing the sentences comprising The Notebook Boy had begun to

to erase themselves

within a month The Notebook Boy was blank

within a year no one reading the copies of him anymore

within two no one remembering why anyone would keep an empty black marble-cover notebook in a special drawer in a special file cabinet in the local public library and so

and so the short squat lonely clerk who stumbled across it

threw it out

January

February

March

April

May

June

July

August

September

October

November

December

APPENDIX As a rule, this five inch-long blind-ended tube the color of Thousand Islands dressing branches off from the intestinal pouch called the cecum. In this case, though, it was discovered and extracted in 1639 from the cranium of a deceased mermaid washed up on the pebbly Dorset shore during a fierce storm. The mermaid measured eighteen-and-three-fourths inches in length, possessed the face and tail of a fish, the teeth of a small lizard, and several wisps of long gray human hair atop its otherwise bald head. Its eyes were a Scandinavian blue. Soon after its discovery, this appendage was sold as an oddity in the Weymouth market.

The owners, a line of barbers and dentists, passed it down from generation to generation. Our acquisitions experts were alerted to its presence in 1933, the year it surfaced in Vienna. They purchased it immediately. Such a structure has a twofold purpose for **THE MAN WITH BORROWED ORGANS**. First, it helps define the notion of uncertainty for him; thus by many it is considered the most philosophical organ. Second, it lets him know that whatever he does, however much he accomplishes in the course of his life, wherever he might travel, whomever he might meet, whatever distinctions by the outside world he might shrug on, he will always have been less important than in his least confident moments he believes.

HEART

The very presence of the lungs and skin dictates the necessity for

an
organ
that
produces
emptiness,
and,
hence,
Ladies
and
Gentlemen,
the
heart.

(whose name unfortunately, has
since been lost to history) at the
Miguel Cané branch of the Bue-
nos Aires Municipal Library in
1939 on the very day, on the
other side of the ocean, the Luft-
waffe invaded Poland. Once
showcased on a plush pad of
red velvet in an elaborate gold-
topped glass container reminiscent of a philatory, these testicles
are where stories are created.

T
E
S
T
I
C
L
E
S

These glands were removed from the body of a dreaming Amauta, or Incan wise man, hunted down and rendered unconscious in the barren highlands of Peru by the Spanish conquistador Francisco Pizarro in 1533 at the advice of his trusted chroniclers, and passed along from mysterious hand to mysterious hand until coming to our attention by means of the first assistant

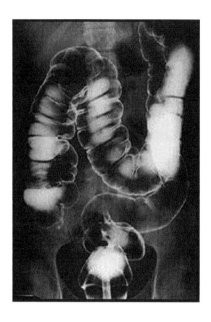

You see, Ladies and Gentlemen, it was quilted
between the years 1837 to 1842 from the
hides of thirty-three newborn albino females
by an eighty-year-old woman living in a cave
in what is now northern Cambodia, and is so
thin you can actually see the other organs
of the body functioning beneath it, as in
some species of transparent fish.

Stunningly diaphanous as this
slightly too small for the
Regrettably, its size
or engage in

The skin

SKIN

You may have heard skin is our largest organ.
   For the average adult, it boasts a surface area of two square
      meters and accounts for fifteen percent of our body weight.

   An inch of it generally contains six-hundred-and-fifty sweat
glands, twenty blood vessels, sixty-thousand pigment-producing
melanocytes, and more than a thousand nerve endings.

None of these facts, however, holds true for this specimen.

extraordinary suit is, it remains
THE MAN WITH BORROWED ORGANS.
makes it impossible for him to bend his arms or legs,
such common activities as sitting, bowing, or genuflecting.

suit thereby edifies him on a continuous basis about how each of us
is imprisoned within himself while at the same time
open to public scrutiny of the most severe kind.

INTESTINES Perhaps the most misunderstood organ, the intestines are usually thought to be that part of the digestive system responsible primarily for breaking down and absorbing food. Nothing, Ladies and Gentlemen, could be farther from the case. As **THE MAN WITH BORROWED ORGANS** appears to know all too well, it also marks the place in the human anatomy (for other animals the case is, naturally, different) where the testicles write their tales in runic-like scars. Depending on one's religious views, those tales form lists either of a person's successes or failures. Sadly, the scars evaporate upon contact with air, while remaining invisible to x-ray, computer tomography, and similar methods of medical imaging. So what they say must, lamentably, always remain a riddle. That is why among some specialists this organ is also referred to as the Calendar of Regrets.

GOD

As you can see, there is nothing behind this door except a vacant compartment. Although there is a plethora of theories, no one has been
capable of grasping with any certitude where
this organ might reside, where it came from,
how it developed, or what, precisely, it does.

Conflicts have been
waged across the world
and throughout time in
the belief that destroy-
ing one's enemy proves
one's own assertions
about this item true.

Many people believe it exists before us, right
here, yet is undetectable except for its effects.

Some believe it is simply one more product of the genitals. Others maintain that it could only be dreamed by a heart of emptiness.

Whatever the case may be, lately we have been prone to exclude it when assembling **THE MAN WITH BORROWED ORGANS**, since it frequently leads him to experience, from what we can infer through his gestures, unmitigated fright, excruciating guilt, and brief instances of a false sense of security, followed, inevitably, by

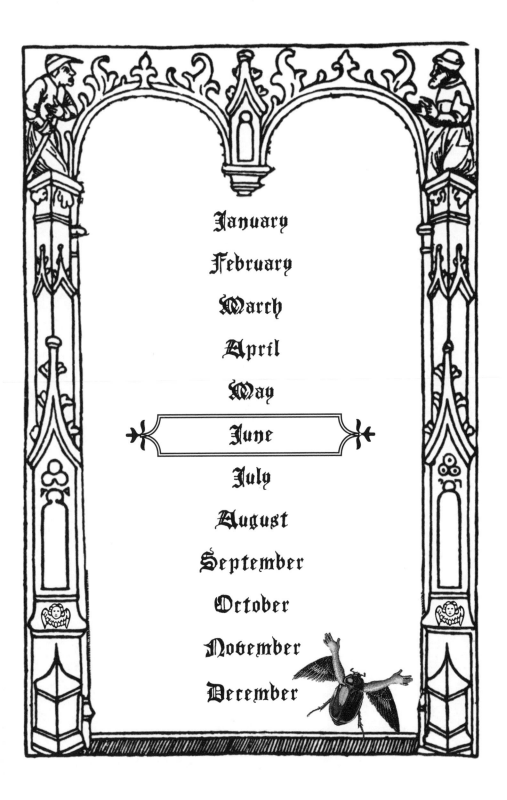

January

February

March

April

May

June

July

August

September

October

November

December

B-flat or G-sharp. For argument's sake, you understand. Every-thing became a verb, became a story, you see, and the verbs hurried me away from the boom-boom. This happened, in short, in a phrase, and then something else happened. Here, it could be said to go without comment, we are splitting hairs. Wonderful turn of— Splitting. Imagine. And still . . . Or, to be more precise, some things happened, of course, and some things did not, again and again. Consequently, one could hazard without fear of reprisal a guess that some things happened among many things not hap-pening. Unless, of course, et cetera. There's always that. Stranger things have— But there it is. Because the swallows. The clouds. The photographs, arresting. Because— Hello. It's lovely to make your acquaintance. The sound— The sound, I should emphasize, perhaps, for a sense of narrative immediacy, was a moist one. The gutting of a fish, let us say, and no more. My wing tearing. My wing being torn. Because the answer is . . . the answer is— But why?

The second Jarmo's fingertips contact her gown, the angel begins speaking to him without moving her lips, explaining, perhaps, explaining or describing, traveling with him without stirring, and yet her soliloquy is lost on the boy, for he misunderstands every word she utters, replacing each syllable with another that starts with the same letter of the alphabet but appears slightly earlier in the lexicon. So all he can think of as he removes his hand from her shoulder is the chatter of coins falling from one of his palms into the other. He sees Senate Square in the sunny pith of Helsinki, a cobblestone vastness surrounded by orderly Empire-yellow and white nineteenth-century Russian architecture, the expansive staircase leading up to the cathedral, the statue of Tsar Alexander II, the man who gave Finland back its language from the Swedes, rising in the middle of it all. Near the entrance to the university buildings, he sees a large iron-barred structure reminiscent of an ornate Chinese birdcage. It houses a sleeping angel. Jarmo is collecting money in the black booth out front from the long line of polite patrons, and, with the efficiency of an adding machine, Sami retracts the black curtain covering the structure to reveal a peep hole through which each patron may behold this miracle for exactly fifteen seconds, then he drops the heavy folds back into place.

It seems to Sami as if the angel were whispering to him from the center of his brain, the sound of her voice smelling brownish red like cinnamon at Christmas. Yet somehow he also misunderstands every word she utters, in this case replacing each syllable with another that starts with the same letter of the alphabet but appears slightly later in the lexicon. In the current version, the angel asks for the boys' help to effect her return to heaven, from which she was cast out accidentally when God forgot to dream her for the briefest of instants because He was so busy just then dreaming myriad British soldiers calling out His name in desperation and despair as they expired on the battlefields of the Boer War. If the boys were merely to carry her to the top of the hill on the far side of the lake, she would be near enough home to take flight and reenter God's imagination in the time it takes to think of a word in a foreign language you knew very well three hours ago but has momentarily slipped your mind. As their reward, Sami is certain she told him (although nothing could be farther from the truth), the angel is prepared to tell each boy about what the last seven minutes of his life will feel like, and precisely how death will smell a temporal flitter before she descends upon him in a mad whirl of black rags and ululation.

Perhaps, next, the same slightly out-of-focus afternoon. Perhaps a different one. It is becoming increasingly difficult to tell with anything approaching conviction.

The lake a powdery gray extension of the powdery gray sky.

In the marshy field near a deserted road, two brothers arguing about the fate of a wounded angel.

They could be rich, Jarmo is saying. Think about it, Sami. This young, and flush for life. All they have to do is carry her back to their farm, lock her in the potato cellar outside the barn, and prepare the wagon and horses for the long ride to Helsinki. Their parents would never need to work again. And, when the capital grew tired of their present, they could move her to Turku, then Tampere, then Oulu. And, when Finland finally grew tired of it, they could meander south through Europe—Estonia to Latvia, Latvia to Lithuania, Lithuania to Poland, and so on, ending up on the white coasts of Greece. There every day would be the same day. Sleep late, display their angel to the townspeople, eat slick mollusks and sip red wine beneath colorful umbrellas on verandas overlooking the bloody sea while the sun turned the sky the color of salmon meat. Sami shaking his head side to side. Sami not meeting his older brother's eyes. Sami saying no.

No, Sami is saying. That isn't right. The angel isn't theirs to use like some wooden spoon. She is beautiful and pure and wounded and she needs their assistance just like any traveler hurt along the side of the road. If you were lost and injured, Sami is saying, quietly, understated but firm, black hat crumpled to his chest in his grimy knuckled fists, wouldn't you want someone to come to *your* aid,

Jarmo, give you a hand so you could find your way back to where you knew you belonged? Nothing could be simpler. All the boys would have to do is detour from their present course a single hour, two at most, in order to bring her to the crest of that hill over there. Surely it would take God only a matter of seconds to notice her, remember what He had forgotten, and in His infinite goodness commence to dream her once again. After that, everything would return to how it should be. All the bits of their world would settle back into place the way all the numbers in a complicated math problem resolve into its sum. While it is true their parents would never be rich, they would also never know that they might have avoided poverty, and thus they would never find themselves dispirited. They would ask the boys a few questions when the brothers returned late. This is to be expected. But it would be easy enough to fabricate an excuse or two. And then? That night, and on all future nights, the boys would be able to sleep profoundly, unimpeded by fears of visitations from their grandfather's skeleton. Equally important, they would always carry within them the knowledge of death's scent, and therefore would always be in a position to stay on guard against her cacophonous arrival.

Two brothers silently staring at each other, figuring.

No more talk after that, no more thoughts of fish soup or ham, no more rocks kicked along the road or lobbed far into the meadow. Only this: only two boys moving slowly and heavily along their barren route, improvised stretcher between them. A wounded angel hunching forward on the seat in the middle, head lowered, limp lilies of the valley clutched in her right hand. The hem of her white gown sweeps the packed dirt below her, yet somehow remains faultless.

Jarmo turning his solemn face toward the viewer—toward you, me. Accusing. Because he is exhausted. Because he is exhausted and frightened and angry.

Because he and his brother have been at this for years now.

It all seemed effortless in the beginning. They helped their charge onto the stretcher, carefully lifted the stretcher into the air. The wounded angel weighed virtually nothing. The sole mass the boys felt between them was that of the branches forming their litter. Sami and Jarmo strode rapidly for the first hour, the former contemplating the relationship and moral implications of the angel's weight to his own, the latter imagining the heat radiating from twinkling sand on southern beaches. Only gradually did it dawn on them they were making no progress. When the younger raised his head to check their bearings, he realized the landscape around them, their position with respect to it, hadn't changed in the least. Everything was precisely where it had been earlier: meadow to the right, hills across the lake, dirt road slicing their perspective in two. Startled, he shot an anxious look back at his brother, only to discover Jarmo surveying their environs grimly, deep into the task of absorbing the same dismal facts about their circumstances. They were suddenly lost without being lost, in need of assistance without there seeming to be anything whatsoever out of the ordinary.

It becomes night becomes day becomes night, each time they blink.

Sometimes they wake to find it is snowing heavily. The lake vanishes in a boil of flakes. Sometimes they wake to find the mid-summer sun brutalizing the arid countryside all the way to the dusty apricot horizon. Without warning, the voluminous bluegreen clouds of northern lights churn above them. Without warning, the boys are freezing. Their skin is oily with perspiration. It is raining. They discover themselves slipping and stumbling with their precious cargo through the mud. No. Autumnal reds and yellows rust the low foliage around them. No. It is a perfect spring dawn, only there are no birds anywhere, no signs of life far as the eye can see.

It never crosses their minds to stop, however, backtrack, diverge from their current route. Such ideas do not exist in this world. There is a word their father taught them as soon as they could understand language: *sisu*, Finnish for *what must be done will be done*. The boys are convinced that if they just push on a little farther, work a little harder, they will reach the lake, the hills, locate themselves in the midst of a cool breeze as they overlook the valley through which they are now advancing. Now seeming to advance.

The angel remains perfectly still, head lowered.

Silent as polar night.

Which is where we must leave her. Which is where we must leave them all.

Because, regrettably, this is all you or I know of these things. Because we simply do not have access to any further information concerning these characters' fate.

I am sorry.

Except, perhaps, for a few final observations. The wounded angel is mute, for example, because she understands that she is on an almost infinite path that will culminate in her death. She wears the thick kerchief over her eyes because if the boys were to gaze directly into them they would catch a brief glimpse of heaven and this would annihilate them before their feet allowed them to take a single step more. The angel cannot let this happen. The boys must survive long enough to help bring about her dissolution. She has thus made certain they have misunderstood every word she has thought. The brothers must believe they are assisting her on her return to the ravishing universe of nouns, when in reality the only reason she has harmed herself is to gain entrance into the even more ravishing one of melting ice.

When they reach the crest of one of those almost immeasurably distant hills, the boys must believe the wounded angel will ascend into the absolutely blue sky on those gigantic feathery parentheses. They do.

But the angel will not ascend at all. She will plunge into the lake several hundred meters below, into an agitated drowning.

And so, finally, we fathom what that look on her countenance signifies—not angelic calm, nor despair, nor fatalism, nor nostalgia for what she has had to leave behind. That look signifies happiness.

Perhaps it is the same slightly out-of-focus afternoon. Perhaps it is a different one. A second, in any case, and it might be otherwise. A second, and it might not.

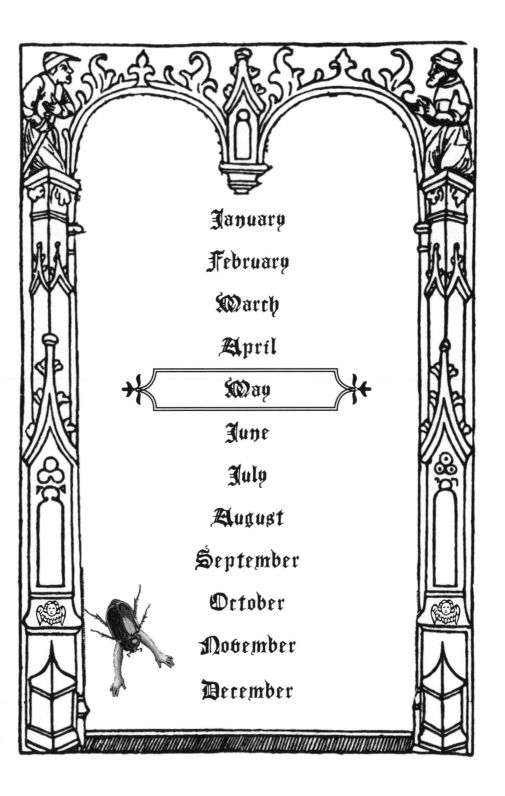

January

February

March

April

May

June

July

August

September

October

November

December

PD.   That's a beautiful story, Bill. It must have been very special listening to your mother read it to you.

WT.   I used to prop myself up against the pillows beside her in bed, drink my glass of milk, and stare straight ahead so I could see the worlds she was building. Her voice sounded like the color of irises.

PD.   Your father was working at that point. Is that correct? He didn't get home until after you were asleep.

WT.   In the meatpacking plant. He ran the air-powered rotary skinning knives that removed the hide from the bled carcasses.

PD.   Did he ever take you to see what he did?

WT.   He wore a light blue hardhat, blue rubber gloves, and blue rubber boots. The cattle didn't look like cattle anymore. Their hides looked like rugs piled up on the white floor.

PD.   You and your mother were very close.

WT.   We've already had this conversation.

PD.   I wonder, Bill, would you tell me a little bit about what it means to you? The story? I'm having a difficult time putting it into words.

WT.   It means pretty much what it says.

PD.   What does it say?

WT.   It says two boys find a wounded angel in the countryside.

PD.   But don't you feel there's maybe, uh, maybe more to it than that? You mentioned earlier that it teaches us worlds are whirls. Could you explain what you meant by that?

WT.   It teaches us that in a sense every sentence has to be the whole story.

PD.   I'm at a loss because, you know, I was never the brainiest kid in my English class. Reading always . . . I was more a math kind of guy. So maybe you can, you know, explain things so even a dumbbell like me can get it.

WT.   Isn't it about time for lunch?

PD.   Lunch?

WT.   My stomach's starting to make noises.

PD.   Let's see here. It . . . well, yes, it is. It's coming up on 1:15. Would you like me to get us a couple of sandwiches brought in?

WT.   Peanut butter and jelly.

PD.   On white bread, right?

WT. Cut diagonally. And ginger snaps. That is correct.

....
....
....
....
....
....
....
....
....

Let me just . . .

....
....
....
....
....
....
....

Okay.

....
....
....

Testing, testing. One . . .

....
....
....

Why don't we pick up with your, uh, with your account of your time in New York. You said you were arrested and put in jail for thirty days. The messages started arriving through the transmitter in your head. It must have been frustrating for you being on the inside. What happened next?

WT. My head listened. The thirty days passed.

PD.   And then you were released?

WT.   Yes.

PD.   And just to be clear. No psychiatric evaluation was adminis-
tered during that time. Is that right, Bill?

WT.   That is correct.

PD.   No one asked you the sorts of questions I'm asking you now?
You didn't explain your situation to anyone?

WT.   I like this sandwich.

PD.   I'm glad.

WT.   It's underrated as a food in its diagonality.

PD.   What was the first thing you did when you were released?

WT.   I had a few dollars left. I took the A train up to Columbus
Circle and robbed an old lady.

PD.   You say you still had some money left. Why did you feel the
need to rob someone?

WT.   It wasn't enough. I was hungry. I needed a place to stay. It
was nighttime. I cut across Central Park and came out on Fifth
Avenue. I almost ran into her. She was wearing a baby blue parka
two sizes too big and a pink wool cap. I stopped in front of her.
She just started giving me all her money. She didn't say anything.
She even turned her pockets inside out at the end so I could see she
didn't have anything left. Then I kept walking north and she kept

walking south. It was like we'd simply had this sort of short polite conversation on the sidewalk, only without using words.

PD.   What did you do next?

WT.   I bought a gyro at a Greek restaurant. With extra sauce on it. I asked for extra sauce and they gave it to me. What do you call it?

PD.   The sauce?

WT.   Yes.

PD.   Tzatziki?

WT.   Tzatziki. Yes. I asked for extra tzatziki.

PD.   And that was when you first saw the man you took to be Kenneth Burrows.

WT.   When I stepped out of the restaurant. He walked right by me. It was like he didn't even see me.

PD.   And you began following him.

WT.   First I called out.

PD.   What did you say?

WT.   I called out his name. I told him to stop.

PD.   But he didn't.

WT.   He just kept walking.

PD.   So you ran after him, and when you caught up you struck him in the jaw.

WT.   When he wouldn't stop.

PD.   And he dropped to the sidewalk.

PD.   And then you struck him a second time.

WT.   I don't remember how many times I struck him. I'm thinking probably it wasn't a small number. He had no idea my fists were coming at him. He curled into himself. When my feet joined in—that's when I realized it wasn't him.

PD.   It wasn't him?

WT.   That's when I realized it. That is correct.

PD.   But I thought you've been telling me that you recognized the man, you know, the man we're talking about as Kenneth Burrows. The Vice President of the World Government on your earth.

WT.   Why would I say that? It doesn't make any sense.

PD.   I'm a little confused here.

WT.   Why would the Vice President take such a risky trip across branes himself? He's no test pilot.

PD.   But then who did you think you were beating up?

WT.   It stands to reason.

PD.   And who is that?

WT. His double. Kenneth Burrows' double on your earth.

PD. But I . . . I don't understand, Bill. Help me out. The man you were beating up . . . he wasn't the real Kenneth Burrows?

WT. Because you're forgetting something.

PD. What is it I'm forgetting?

WT. Membranes are membranes.

PD. How does that help me understand this?

WT. We all live right beside our twins all the time, only in a different universe. There are an infinite number of them. This is common knowledge among physicists.

PD. But you're saying we don't know that's what we're doing?

WT. It's like we know it but we don't know it. This is why people feel weird sometimes, like when you're standing alone in front of your open refrigerator in the middle of the night, only you have this feeling someone else is standing right there right next to you.

PD. Because they really are.

WT. Sometimes it's like doctors have just given you medicine. Thinking feels beside the point.

PD. Who do you believe you assaulted, Bill?

WT. Dan Rather.

PD. But you're saying it wasn't really Dan Rather.

WT. That is not what I'm saying.

PD. You're saying it really was Dan Rather.

WT. I'm saying the man on the sidewalk was Dan Rather and wasn't Dan Rather.

PD. The CBS news anchorman, you're saying.

WT. Only he wouldn't give me the frequency. He just began lying and lying, the liar. I knew the messages would start again any second. I didn't have much time. He was intercepting my brain-waves. He was using them against me.

PD. And that's when he bolted.

WT. That is correct.

PD. And you followed him.

WT. That is correct.

PD. Where did he go?

WT. Into this building. There was a security guard in the lobby.

PD. An apartment building?

WT. I don't know. It was bright inside.

PD. But you couldn't follow him.

WT. That is correct.

PD.   What did you do?

WT.   Walked through Central Park. For years and years. I like the boat pond. I like all the people with their little toy boats in the morning. And that fountain. With the statue of the angel.

PD.   Bethesda?

WT.   That is correct.

PD.   But the messages kept coming.

WT.   That is correct.

PD.   Where did you stay all that time?

WT.   Hotels. Shelters. I watched a lot of TV. I like *Friends*. I like the way Janice says *Oh my god. Oh. My. God.* Like that. It's funny.

PD.   *Friends* is on NBC? Isn't that right?

WT.   That is correct.

PD.   Is that where you got the idea for what you did next?

WT.   They were sending waves through the TV set at the shelter.

PD.   What sort of waves?

WT.   All I can tell you at this point in time is the dose exceeded thirty-five hundred ergs. They were impossible to block. It felt like thousands of ants were eating my thoughts.

PD.   And you wanted those to cease.

WT. I needed to find somebody who understood the nature of waveform oscillations.

PD. And so what did you do?

WT. Saved some money. Bought a gun. A box of bullets.

PD. And then you went down to Rockefeller Center.

WT. On the B train. Yes. It was very humid. Very hot and very humid.

PD. This would be August 31, 1994. Last August.

WT. I'm not very good with dates.

PD. What did you do next?

WT. Hung around the entrance on 49th Street.

PD. Why did you do that—hang around like that?

WT. I was waiting for a physicist.

PD. You believed one would come out of the NBC Studios?

WT. I knew one would come out. He was in his thirties. He had attractive hair.

PD. This would be Campbell Montgomery?

WT. I don't know.

PD. Had you thought in any way at that point that you might want to hurt him?

WT. I just wanted to use the gun to get the correct frequency from him and stop the waves. I feel very strongly about celebrities, audiences—all those who make TV shows what they are. They are good people. I didn't want to endanger them.

PD. But you did endanger Campbell Montgomery.

WT. My hand did.

PD. You shot him.

WT. My hand did. In the back.

PD. You control your hand, don't you, Bill?

WT. My hand was holding the gun. I hadn't noticed at the time. But there it was. When the physicist exited the building, I asked him about the frequency. He looked at me. He looked at the gun. Then he turned and ran.

PD. That's when you shot him.

WT. That is incorrect.

PD. When did you shoot him?

WT. When he began screaming.

PD. What was he screaming?

WT. That there was this man with a gun. I looked around me, frightened. It took me a minute to figure out who he was talking about.

PD. That's when you pulled the trigger.

WT. That's when the trigger was pulled.

PD. Explain your reasoning to me here, Bill. Why was the trigger pulled?

WT. There was nothing else for my hand to do.

PD. You believed someone else was controlling your hand.

WT. What is belief?

PD. Who was controlling your hand?

WT. Kenneth Burrows.

PD. The other Kenneth Burrows. The Vice President back on your world.

WT. That is correct.

PD. How?

WT. Through the transmitter.

PD. How many times did you fire?

WT. I would say my hand fired once.

PD. And Montgomery died five hours later at Bellevue.

WT. I don't know anything about that.

PD. He died because the bullet you fired punctured his lung and a major artery. He bled to death on the operating table.

WT. People don't know.

PD. What don't they know, Bill?

WT. That the thing about the peanut butter and jelly sandwich is that it is a complete nutritious meal in itself. It's an easy point to overlook.

PD. And the messages didn't stop. Killing Montgomery didn't help.

WT. Twelve grams of protein, for instance. On average.

PD. They just keep arriving every twenty minutes.

WT. The diagonal cut releases the flavor most effectively, as we've just seen.

PD. And the medications. They don't help much, either.

WT. Because of the triangular resonance. You know. Let A, B, and C be the vertices of a right triangle. This was common knowledge to Euclid. I'm tired.

PD. Maybe we should call it a day?

WT. Yes.

PD. We can pick up later when you're feeling rested.

WT. Yes.

PD. That's fine, Bill. I'll, uh, I'll call in an officer. Thank you for talking with me. I appreciate it a great deal. I always learn something new.

WT.   You're welcome.

....
....
....
....
....
....
....
....
....
....
....
....
....
....
....
....
....
....
....
....
....
....
....
....
....
....

January

February

March

April

May

June

July

August

September

October

November

December

....
....
....
....
....
....
....
....
....
....
....
....

Welcome to another episode of my own little pirate podcast coming to you semi-live and completely indirect every week from a different corner of the godforsaken Salton Sea, deadest body of saline solution on the deadest stretch of southwestern desert you'll ever want to forget.

You're listening to Jolly Roger and his whole sick crew . . . and that means you, too, baby.

Remember: all you have to do to set sail with us is search out my revolving website. You can find its latest incarnation by paying close attention to what that homeless guy talking to himself next to you on the bus is saying. Or by clicking that unassuming link on the website you'll happen upon at two tomorrow morning.

O-or maybe just by committing to making each and every piece of spam that arrives in your inbox your long lost friend. Then scroll down to the lower left-hand corner. That's where you'll find my cell phone number. It's good for twenty-four hours, give or take, más o menos, very roughly speaking.

Do as you like, and do it in your own time, for Jolly Roger plans on sticking around long enough to hear what *everybody* has to say who The Man and His Minions have banished from thought . . .

Let me begin this evening by painting you a little picture. I'm recording this message in a digital bottle in the back seat of my faithful blue Saab. The engine is off, the windows rolled down. The temperature is in the middling desert-night eighties. My battery icon tells me I have just over an hour and a half of electric spirit left. My clock icon tells me it's barely tipped eleven in the p.m.

Which is to say it's early days, folks, and here I am, parked amid tumbleweed and rusted-out barrels at the bitter end of humanity in an interzone called Slab City. Its entrance is easily identifiable by the Froot-Loop colorful and prophetically awesome secret handshake known as Salvation Mountain: a crazed visionary prominence three stories high covered in roughly ten thousand gallons of donated acrylic paint, concrete, and adobe, and festooned with Biblical sentiments. A yellow brick road, a spectacular frozen blue and white waterfall, a rainbow mound of Looney Tunes flowers, an igloo chapel built of hay bales, trees, and tires—all these serve as an ongoing ode to God the Highest composed over the course of more than two decades by one Mr. Leonard Knight, among the most goodhearted and gentle proselytizers of celestial benevolence you'll ever have the distinct honor to meet.

Continue down that road past Leonard's reveries and soon you'll come upon all that remains of the World War Two military base called Camp Dunlap: six-hundred-and-forty state-owned acres of sagebrush, barren sand, the occasional cluster of prickly pear, and a few concrete slabs, the latter of which gives this turnout in the immense wasteland called the Colorado Desert its name. General

George S. Patton once trained troops here. The Enola Gay's pilots took off from its runways to practice dropping dummy A-bombs into . . . you guessed it . . . the Salton Sea.

And after the base closed at the end of the fifties, a group of intrepid servicemen remained behind to birth the dream of an intentional community, decommissioned, uncontrolled, and, above all, free of charge, of mind, open to possibility's twinkle.

These days about three thousand dub this corner of alterity home during the winter months. By July, all that's left is the diehard coven of fewer than one hundred fifty. There's no electricity, no running water, no sewerage, no services. Many denizens use generators or solar panels for power, buckets for bathrooms. Most subsist on government checks, and almost all arrived at this exceptional condition of inbetweenness through poverty and/or an ardent desire to be shut of such onerous concepts as America.

As I utter these words, Slabbers domicile to my left and right, before me and behind me, in tents, campers, motor homes, hollowed-out vehicles, handmade shacks, aluminum sheds, what's left of those ammo bunkers from yesterworld. Some laze cross-legged around campfires, smell of burning salt oak in the air, drinking, talking, and enjoying a little giggle weed. Many recline solitary and contemplative in lawn chairs or chaise lounges before their dwellings, watching the night sky perform above them, waiting for the immense black boomerangs and blacker memories of their former lives to glide silently into view.

Someone is playing Frank Sinatra, someone else Frank Zappa. I hear strains of Megadeth and Arcade Fire and Mr. Hank Williams, all reminding us that wealth won't save our souls.

In the distance, occasional explosions thunder in from Chocolate Mountain Aerial Bombing and Gunnery Range.

Oh, yeah . . .

And, with that, welcome to my vessel. My rubber zodiac cruising the Straights of Slab City a hair's breadth east of Salvation Mountain. The inside of my head for the next twenty minutes . . .

I want to talk about the day after the planet finally shakes us off no one talks about that I don't get it that's what I want to talk about.

The great Rapture, you mean?

No no no the little one the little ones. Like those you know car suicides across Europe back in the Seventies where they just started blowing themselves up on the highways and no one remembers anymore? It'll be like that start small you'll hardly notice. But what happens next what happens after the end of the end that's what I want to know.

What's your name, friend?

Keith I'm Keith from Lexington.

Massachusetts?

Kentucky but not really I was raised in Chicago I'm twenty-eight. Landed here after a tour in Iraq Najaf I'm a librarian got a degree in library science do you know this book by Alan Weisman called The World Without Us?

An important one for you, I presume?

It's about humankind's long slow fadeout after the earth says turn off the lights and shut the goddamn door behind you it doesn't matter how pollution pestilence overpopulation famine war whatever it doesn't matter you blew it and I wonder why nobody ever asks what happens next.

Maybe if it isn't about us, it isn't interesting. Like at parties, only moreso.

Everything's always interesting especially without us.

Teach us what we should learn, Keith. We're your auditory systems for as long as you'd like to employ us.

Okay well after we leave the thing that gets me is how it starts happening really fast you'd think it might take millennia but it doesn't. In New York City for example in New York without continuous pumping the subway system floods within two days imagine that two days. Seven and the cooling systems on nuclear reactors fail the reactors melt down it's hard to get your mind around that. One year of water freezing and thawing in cracks and sidewalks and streets begin buckling who would have thought then the colonizing weeds and trees move in.

You're asking how important can a single human life be.

Homes and office buildings begin crumbling because there's no heat in them nothing to stabilize interior climates and one lightning strike in Central Park wham the whole city is on fire.

You're asking who do we think we are.

The planet blinks and everything we've done for the past ten thousand years starts going away immediately it makes you reflect.

You're suggesting each of us is not unlike a solitary dust mite traveling on a 747 from L.A. to Bangkok. He thinks it's *his* universe he's inhabiting, that he controls it, that he knows where he is and what he's doing and where he's going. Only the poor little fuck has absolutely no idea, does he, that he's just along for the ride, that the exterminator is ambling up the aisle even as he muses, full face-piece respirator in place, pesticide sprayer in hand.

Twenty years and streams and marshes appear in the streets one hundred and all the roofs have caved in three hundred and all the bridges have collapsed.

You're saying do what you want because in the end even Einstein is a nobody.

Five hundred and mature forests blanket the metropolitan area.

Shakespeare, Beethoven, Jesus, Hitler. Who are they?

Five thousand and the casings of nuclear warheads corrode releasing plutonium 239 into the environment fifteen thousand and the last buildings fall before a new advancing ice age.

Henry Ford. Mahatma Gandhi. The Artist Formerly Known as Prince. *Who?*

Thirty-five thousand and lead deposited from car emissions finally dissipates one-hundred thousand and the concentration of carbon dioxide in the air returns to pre-industrial levels but you know what?

Let it rip, Keith.

Trillions of years from now? Trillions and trillions of years from now?

Yeah?

Broadcasts of The Twilight Zone *will still be flying outward through space* The Beverly Hillbillies Baywatch Survivor American Idol The Tonight Show with Jay Leno.

. . .

. . .

At least the ringworm and head lice will miss us, huh?

Domesticated cattle and rats too without us they're just prey for other organisms and then you know what? You know what happens after that?

It starts all over again?

The chances of that are basically nil no this is it from there on out it's all just this long slow hum toward the death of the sun.

Holy shit.

Pretty much so.

Well, um, thanks for your holocaust thoughts, Keith. I guess you've just proved the score will always remain nature one, humans zero. I appreciate the existential slap upside the head, man. I needed that. I mean, I almost started thinking I mattered there for a second . . .

And, uh, let's see here. You're off the air with Jolly Roger. What has chance brought you here to share with us this warm and startling evening?

They sent down the robotic cockroaches first, man.

Excuse me?

The robotic cockroaches. Back in the Eighties. To Wall Street, mainly, but also Beijing, Moscow, London. Check out the archives, man. The evidence is overwhelming.

And why do you suppose They did such a thing?

Shock troops. They looked just like other insects, you know . . .

till you picked 'em up, till you examined 'em real close.

Which is when you saw . . .

The cameras, man. Just behind those dark polymer eye shells. The cameras. You think I don't know how that sounds?

I have no opinion about that.

You think I don't know you wanna treat me like one of those kids born with flippers instead of arms? Well, don't, man, cuz it's fucking patronizing. Every word I'm telling you? It's true. Believe it or don't. Frankly, I don't give a fuck.

Fear not, compadre. Jolly Roger isn't here to pass judgment concerning such highly dubious notions as truth and fiction. He's here to listen and hand on the word. May I ask your name?

I'm the guy They never told you about, the one who does the jobs that don't exist, if you know what I mean.

N.S.A.?

Think of this as my report from the front. My last dispatch, you could call it.

Where are you phoning from?

Bedroom on the second floor of a safe house in East L. A. You know what I'm doing this very second? I'm holding an Uzi here in my right hand, a cell phone in my left. And let me tell you something. They're on the stairs, man. They're coming up.

Who is?

I'm here to bear witness, you could say, tell you how the world ends.

We're listening.

. . .

. . .

Okay, well, they sent in the robotic cockroaches first, and the fuckers set about their business—you know: collecting data, sniffing air, chewing whatever detritus they chanced upon.

Because . . .

Nano hard-drives for heads, man, vacuum cleaners for stomachs. They were recording. Gathering information like other insects gather pheromones and food, you know? Downloading the digital identity that makes this planet itself.

What sort of information?

You name it. How government functions, how the hive-mind of the media performs, the economic machinery, the geography of the corporate imagination. Then they started going for the tissue samples.

The tissue samples?

They infiltrated the hospitals. The morgues. Took epidermal clippings from sleeping patients. Burrowed deep through the tympanic membrane, cochlea, vestibular nerve, directly into the brain. Get it? They were harvesting, *man.*

Jesus.

Which is where the first one was exposed. Back in '89. Columbia Medical Center. This autopsist? During a routine postmortem? She finds the thing nesting among the semisolid neural jell. Bristly legs, feelers, flat slippery body housed in a leathery yellow-brown casing. Hissed at her when she uncovered it. Like a goddamn cat. She removed the fucker with tweezers and crushed its armored head. And you know what happened?

I couldn't begin to guess.

This little blue spark flared up. Zzzzzzz. Thing shorted out, man. So she slipped the carcass under a microscope. And behind what was left of those dark polymer eye shells?

Yeah?

Behind what was left of those dark polymer eye shells she discovered the cameras. She called the police. The police called the FBI. The FBI called the CIA.

And the CIA called you.

I was just supposed to observe. Feeling was that too much had already gone down to do much more. Everyone knew it, man, though everyone pretended otherwise. Before long, hundreds started turning up. I scanned CNN for signs of final embarkation, old movies on the Turner station for scenes added while our cultural backs were turned toward something seemingly more interesting.

And you say the evidence was overwhelming?

Not at all. Not at first. I didn't see a thing. No poltergeist. No rough beast. The earth didn't stop spinning. Creepy deal was everything simply continued on as everything always does. But then in 1994 I was up in Seattle doing some business at our West Coast headquarters. It'd been a long day and I was lying in bed in my hotel room, channel surfing. That's when I saw him *flip onto the screen.*

Him?

Police said he killed his ex-wife and her boyfriend by stabbing them repeatedly, kneeing her spine, yanking back her head by the blond hair, and slitting her throat. Blood was everywhere. *You remember how it was so black in the photos it looked as though someone had puddled crude oil down the walkway?*

We all do.

And then he was standing in the police station. Proud fucker. Determined, defiant. Like this was some fairly inconsequential project he'd been working on, like our universe was somehow smaller than his. And I looked into his eyes as his eyes looked into the media, and you know what they said?

They said: You're living on my planet now.

EXACTLY. I discovered myself making reservations for the first flight to L.A. You more or less know the rest. The legal wrangling, the accusations, the counter accusations, the posturing. I sat in front of other TVs in other hotel rooms in other cities and studied his eyes, the way they'd drift up and left in the courtroom like his mind was just too busy with important matters to be troubled by all this shit. Which is to say it wasn't difficult, only we had to be sure. So we went through the footage, zeroed in on that horse-jawed face, that high forehead, that Doberman's neck.

And you found . . .

We magnified those eyes, man, magnified them more, till our screens were overrun with them, till there was no more space left for anything else. And you can guess what we spotted.

Those polymer shells.

The robotic cameras pivoting frenetically beneath the surface, and I . . . uh . . . I don't have much time left, okay? They're here. I'm guessing the door'll hold them a minute, maybe two. The Uzi a couple seconds more. There's this gray BMW in the alley out back. I can see it from my window.

Give me your number. I'll call the police.

This is the thing it all comes down to, man. You get it? That car. That alley. I've been working nineteen-, twenty-hour days, sleeping four or five hours a night with the dreamless intensity of drugged blackouts. I was awakened a couple minutes ago by this clicking noise. Like fingernails on a metal desk. The cockroach on the pillow beside my head was talking through a speaker in its belly. You don't think I know how this sounds? You don't think I get it? Well, fuck you. We won, *it said.* We know what you know. Everything's primetime now. Everyone's a talk show host waiting to happen. You should be happy. You have a purpose. You're becoming a vacation destination. *We're becoming a wax museum, I said.* You're becoming yourselves, *it said.* Yeah, well, *I said. I rolled off the bed, brought up my semi-automatic. My pillow and that fucker evaporated into smoking feathers, man. Only not before the end had already been set in motion. The crash at the front door. Footsteps on the stairs. Which is the thing, okay? The thing I wanted to tell you about? It isn't about any fucking clouds of boiling seawater sucked miles into burning atmosphere off the blue coasts of the Bikini atoll. People got that all wrong. It isn't about the Berlin Wall or Bin Laden, melting polar ice caps or mis-firing DNA. You know what it's about? It's about* watching, *man. It's about observing the almost unobservable like this stunned car-crash victim, wondering if what you just heard and saw is real, those brakes, that car skidding across the highway and through the railing and down the embankment, the flames, the palms of the family hurrying across the inside of the fiery windshield. That's what I wanted to say, man. That's all. Believe me. It makes your fucking heart sw*

January

February

March

April

May

June

July

August

September

October

November

December

swollen with anticipation, Iphigenia closes her eyes and parts her lips to receive Achilles' first kiss. She immediately feels she has done this before. They are alone in Achilles' tent on their wedding night, the grand ceremony behind them. All the others have tumbled away into the past. The somber betrothal, the sacrifices, the banquet, too. It is time for the sacred unveiling.

Achilles stands before her, slender, strong, chest and arms and legs agleam with oil, teeth flawless, breath licorice and mint, eyes cucumber green.

He takes her wrists in his hands, bends toward her.

Around them, a night sky of votive candles.

Iphigenia thinking: I would sacrifice my life to save him. It is that clear, that untroubled.

But just before Iphigenia does what Anthea asks her to do, she catches sight of a skirmish erupting beside her: five attendants wrestling a terrified deer forward, its neck and hindquarters roped.

No, a goat.

No, a bull.

No, a

The attendants have lifted the buck so that its kicking hooves cannot touch earth. Hanging there, it twists madly, strangling, struggling against the flock of hands trying to hold it down, its rolling eyes an outburst of shock and panic.

Quickly, Agamemnon commands, glint appearing in his enormous right fist.

The priests make way. Anthea lets loose Iphigenia's wrists, orders her assistant to let loose her ankles, helps the frightened girl off the altar. The attendants hoist the deer onto the gray slab in her stead, force it onto its side. Its legs skitter, trying to find purchase.

In a single gesture, Agamemnon advances, yanks back its head to expose its throat, and, driving down the knife, tearing sideways, intoning: *Each of us must forgo in his own way. This is called heroism. Each of us must give what he least wishes to give. This is called duty. Through forfeiture, our people hound success. For favorable winds, I do what is demanded of me.*

A cable of blood arcs from the thrashing animal's neck.

It sprints briefly on its side, gargling forth its life. Its chest heaves, then its body goes flaccid as a stand of wet flax.

Agamemnon steps back, blood dripping from his knife blade, and searches the skies for a sign.

Nothing.

Again, nothing.

Then, slowly, the breeze picks up. Steadies. The atmosphere blues.

A half-smile develops across Agamemnon's face. The goddess Artemis has not been paying attention. He is almost sure of it. She has not noticed the substitution.

Today we are lucky men, he announces proudly, turning toward the crowd. Today we are saved.

Achilles is more than twice her age, twice her knowledge and wisdom. He possesses a hundred times her experience. He has seen the sun set at the end of the world. He has seen an island levitate, each snake on Medusa's head bow down in prayer, a rainstorm turn hard and white like sand, only cold, a flaming dragon fall from the night sky.

Iphigenia adores the very idea of all that understanding embodied in this doorway to her future.

She digs her nails into his shoulder blades as he has asked her to do, learning him, his body's geography, what it has to offer, what it takes pleasure in, learning about the nature of the cosmos through its furious movements.

Slides down into a weightless sleep in which she does not believe she is sleeping where, on a long white band of beach, surrounded by hundreds of lounging seals, she watches a brawny middle-aged man with scraggly thinning hair wrestle a creature that refuses to sustain its shape. He has been at it for hours. The creature transforms itself into a thick writhing python, a snarling leopard, a snorting pig, a beautiful blond female angel with a bloody wing, and, finally, a great splash of seawater that melts into the sand and is gone.

The man rises, weary, beaten, and turns to face the vast ocean once more.

But just before Iphigenia does what Anthea asks her to do, she catches sight of the glint on the white-capped waves below.

A furious wind grows out of nowhere.

The sky dims.

Thunder paces back and forth along the plum horizon.

The priests notice her looking past them and turn to see what it is she is seeing. Her father follows suit. They stagger back in horror at the huge glistening black hump splitting the sea, hurling their way.

The giant serpent's head, big as one of her father's ships, rears up out of the furrowed water in an agitation of spray and commotion.

The wind shrieks.

A grainy blizzard of dust sweeps across the altar.

Bystanders cry out in dread, scattering in pursuit of their lives. Iphigenia struggles against the flock of hands holding her down. But Anthea and her helper stand fast. They will not give. They will not let Iphigenia go.

They close their eyes. Lower their heads. Brace themselves for whatever may come next.

Struggling against the flock of hands holding her down, eyes an outburst of

A lurch, and

A lurch, and Iphigenia is twisting madly, her mouth suddenly stuffed full of Achilles' fat tongue.

Agamemnon reclining in a warm pine-scented bath upon his return from the long series of battles, head tilted back, eyelids heavy, suspended at the very edge of fatigue, proud at what he has done, content, happy to be here at last after nearly a decade away, fingering absentmindedly the latticework of scars on his chest, his left forearm, his right thigh, aware of his wife's footsteps clicking across the room toward him.

He feels his penis stir between his thighs at the sound of her.

Feels it prickle and begin to swell.

In the underworld, a gray, rubbled hollowness, Achilles' shade hobbles toward her, his armor worn, his once beautiful face gaunt, his eyes missing, his lips sewn shut with sheep gut.

Iphigenia surprises herself by feeling neither love nor loathing for him.

He is, she realizes, just a man she knew for several hours a very long time ago before she came to know many others. What she took initially to be broken stones littering the ground she now grasps are smoldering bodies.

What's it going to be like? she asks him.

Achilles has been thinking of other things. Blood leaks from his eyeholes, from the back of one foot, puddles on the ashes that pass for earth. His hands have lost their skin. Brownpink strips of cartilage hang from his elbows. He comes back to this place, lowers his head in thought.

You'll see, he says without moving his sealed mouth.

The bodies extend across the wasteland to the blank horizon. Sometimes they exist in pieces. A naked trunk jutting from the ground. A pyramid of smoke-wisped heads. Sometimes they lie quietly and sometimes curl fetally on their sides or sit hunched, ribcage to kneecaps, translucent maggots tumbling from where their noses used to be.

Will it be what it appears to be? asks Iphigenia.

Achilles raises his blasted face to hers.

Some things should be a surprise, he says without speaking. Some things you shouldn't know about until you know about them.

Is it as awful as they say?

I would rather be slave to the worst of masters than king of this. There is no sleep, nothing to eat or drink, no one with whom to converse, no sense of time passing, no more than your memories for company, which you are sure may be someone else's, which you are sure may be no memories at all, forever.

Achilles thinks some more.

On the battlefield? he says. As Paris' arrow struck its target? I didn't think of you. I wish I had, but I didn't. You should know that.

Iphigenia stares at him.

Turns to leave.

Behind her, Achilles adds: Remember one thing as you make your way back to wakefulness: there is never a death, not a single one, that isn't a surprise to the one dying.

Her father's face darting above her, now a stranger's: indifferent, blank-eyed, unwavering.

Be still, it says. Be

Lying beside Achilles in the dark hotness, appalled by what he has just done to her, and how, Iphigenia knows that, come dawn, her sudden husband will rise and dress and step through the tent flap to join her father down at the docks. They will sail for Troy with more than a thousand ships, each carrying fifty rowers, each a hundred soldiers, to fight for the woman whose mother was raped by a god descended from the heavens in the form of an outrageous swirl of swan wings. Paris has kidnapped Helen. Paris must pay. This may take months. This may take years. Such retribution is as it should be. Yet there is only a short chain of minutes left in this wedding bed, the atmosphere around them already beginning to soften into a fuzzy gray daybreak, and then Achilles will start to become less than himself, more recollection than man, something you cannot even hold in your hands, let alone your heart.

Good.

They murder her pet Zeno first.

Five attendants wrestle the squirming, hissing cheetah toward the altar, its neck and hindquarters roped. They have lifted it so that its flailing claws cannot find purchase. Hanging there, it twists madly, struggling, strangling, flared eyes an outburst of shock and fury.

Quickly, Agamemnon commands.

The priests make way. In a single gesture, two soldiers level their spears. One thrusts for the lungs, one for the throat.

A cable of blood arcs from the animal's neck.

It claws wildly on its side, gargling forth its life. Its chest heaves. Its body goes flaccid as a stand of wet flax.

Agamemnon turns toward his daughter.

She catches sight of the glint in his enormous right fist.

No one is waiting for her: this is the first thing she notices as the altar swings into view. A large gray slab of stone on a steep rocky promontory. The crowd surrounding it falling silent as she approaches, heads bowed in awe. Warriors in full armor mostly, but also men, women, and children from the nearby town. Their reverence is as it should be. This is the part Iphigenia always likes best about her appearances, how others offer her their respect and admiration. But there is only the granite lozenge, only her

She notices the stubby-legged man with the bulbous stomach step from the crowd, arms akimbo. His crazy hair is thinning, his face pocked with acne. When he simpers at her, Iphigenia sees what teeth remain to him are flecked brownblack.

Beside her, Agamemnon smiles proudly.

Meet your new husband, daughter, he proclaims. Meet the heroic conqueror Achilles.

A lurch, and

A lurch, and Iphigenia wakes to her mother's mouth whispering so close to her ear that she can feel its wet heat: *I avoided you because you avoided me. Each time I mustered the nerve to look in your direction, I shuddered, for I could tell how little you wanted to look in mine. Each time I swallowed my pride and attempted hugging you, I felt you biding your time in my arms until you could wriggle free. This is why I let you be yourself. These feelings we have for each other? They are called family. But never forget this: you are a version of my loins. Your blood was my blood first. And so I shall avenge your murder. I shall suffer your father's embraces, the coarseness of his beard. I shall wait, thinking of you when he thinks of me. And one evening, when he is comfortable in his bath, daydreaming of his other pasts and futures, I shall step up behind him and split his skull with my axe like an ox's. The noise will sound like a club crunching through ripe melon, sweetheart. The noise will sound like victory.*

Achilles slips the veil away from Iphigenia's face and Iphigenia whispers:

What's it going to be like?

Achilles is standing before her in the tent on their wedding night, slender, strong, chest and arms and legs agleam with oil. He takes her wrists in his hands, bends toward her. Around them, a night sky of votive candles.

You'll see, he says.

Iphigenia grins mischievously.

But I want to know *now*.

Unclipping his belt, he replies: Some things should be a surprise. Some things you shouldn't know about until you know about them.

With that, his tunic flaps open.

Iphigenia gazes down, her grin loosening into a full-blown girlish smile.

She is thirteen, but she suddenly feels much older and wiser.

It isn't soon. It isn't soon at all. Sex with Achilles is a long, plodding disappointment. He thrashes about like a hooked salamander. He makes disgusting wet sounds at the back of his throat. He calls Iphigenia by the name of other women. His breath smells like cat shit. Somewhere in the midst of this awful perplexity, he slips out of her and doesn't even seem to notice. He just keeps grinding away against her tummy. Iphigenia decides to let him.

And so she lies there beneath him, despondent, staring up at the dark hotness, past his sweaty grimace that reminds her of an angry monkey she once saw chittering in its cage at the market, waiting for this profound embarrassment to be over.

A soggy metallic seep leaks from between Iphigenia's thighs, soaks the sheets.

Tomorrow morning Anthea will hang this bloody flag outside the couple's wedding tent as a trophy for all to witness.

His muscles, the sheen upon his walnut-brown skin, the way his breath will always smell of mint and licorice: Iphigenia hates each of these with a ferocity she could not have imagined a short hour ago.

A lurch, and

A lurch, and the knife a long flash of sunlight.

The knife a silver bird plunging down, its solitary voice chok

Iphigenia jolts awake to her mother's lips softly brushing her forehead, her fingers running through her hair.

There, there, Clytemnesta whispers. *There, th*

A lurch, and

A lurch, and Iphigenia steps onto the rocky shore from her father Agamemnon's ship. She immediately feels she has done this before. Gnarled graygreen cypress trees spattered here and there. The sky a violent blue. How the flock of white birds gyre above her like a flock of silent white hands.

So *this* is where I shall be wed, she thinks. So *this* is what it feels like.

The blade piercing her breast in an azure thunderclap.

Achilles thrashes on top of her like a hooked salamander, pressing the air out of her lungs, spraying sweat across her clamped eyes, mumbling into her neck a series of mysterious syllables, *Pa-tro-clus, Pa-tro-clus, Pa-tro-clus.*

Suddenly Iphigenia remembers where she has heard that name before.

The blade piercing her neck in a blast of shrill whiteness, then a shriek. Hers. And, somewhere down by her feet, Iphigenia hears her baby's first scandalized screams at the state of the world. She feels the soggy metallic seep leaking from between her thighs, soaking the sheets.

A *son*, Anthea's voice says. *Praise be to the gods.*

Tomorrow morning Iphigenia's attendant will hang the bloody flag outside the girl's window as a trophy for all to witness. For now, exhausted by the painful newness of things, Iphigenia, sprawling in the dark hotness, slides down into a weightless sleep in which she does not believe she is sleeping, wondering vaguely what her husband is doing at this very second, and where.

Agamemnon feeling his penis stir at the sound of Clytemnestra's shoes clicking across the tiles toward him. His member prickles, begins to swell. He opens his eyes, commences a lazy rotation in his warm pine-scented bath, the thought gathering within him: *Tonight I am a lucky man. Tonight I am*

The arrow stabs into shocked Achilles' heel.

He pitches forward onto the dust without another idea having time to enter his mind.

The giant serpent's head darts above the terrified girl: stub-nosed, blank-eyed, drooling fangs long as a man's leg.

At the palace, Clytemnestra catches sight of the glint in her son Orestes' enormous right fist and, hand to mouth, staggers back in horror.

No, she says. Please. You don't *understa*

The multitude of ships plying their way across the bay toward the open sea, a multitude of whitecaps beneath the ideal sky.

Electra cackling at her mother's screams tumbling in from the next room.

Somewhere in heaven, Artemis jerking awake from uneasy dreams.

The giant serpent strikes.
It strikes again.
And in that stunning moment, Iphigenia comes to recognize death by its uncontaminated silence.

January

February

March

April

May

June

July

August

September

October

November

December

At the top of the next hill, Nayomi's story falling behind you, you don't find an extension of the country road you've been following. You find yourself veering unexpectedly back onto the Autostrada, traffic interlacing frantically around you. You crest 130 kilometers, 132, your mind hazy with speed. Above, the sky has begun paling into a shimmering wheat, the afternoon taking its first steps toward sunset. The landscape is the same landscape you've been driving through since late this morning. Nayomi must have been leading you in an enormous meandering circle, spilling you out almost at the same point you started. Your husband's body is no longer rigid. Robert is slumping in his seat, as if he has somehow gotten used to this new situation. He is still alert, but there is something almost relaxed in his pose. *This is where we are*, it tells you. *This is what is happening.* Because he can't do it, his body is adapting for him. You tune in to what Nayomi is saying just in time to hear her announce you are nearing a medieval village called Viterbo. This is where, she explains, she spent two nights last autumn in a hostel with her friends. The village sits atop a hill just as villages do in early Italian Renaissance paintings. In the middle rises a castle. Every June, Nayomi says, Viterbo hosts a beautiful cherry festival. She wishes she could attend someday. She wishes she could do many things someday that it now appears she won't be able to do. Isn't it amazing, she asks, how life becomes a series not so much of choices as negations of choices? To want this, you have to give up that. Every day a few more options fleck away. In the end, you're left with only one. While in Viterbo, she ate nothing but the village's famous cherry tarts. For breakfast, lunch, dinner. They were the most delicious pastries she had ever tasted, rich and buttery and full of tang. Her friends and she picnicked on benches at the base of the castle, talking about what they would do after the holidays and how. Back then their plan seemed like a dark electric fairytale. Now she is living it. You are reasonably sure you remember seeing a red star labeled Viterbo on the map this morning at the car rental office in Rome. If you're right, if that's where you are, then you are no longer traveling north. You are traveling south. Nayomi is aiming you back toward the capital. Maybe that's why traffic has started condensing around you, why you have to swerve in and out among more and more cars and trucks and busses and motorcycles to maintain your speed. You are sensing the first pulses of rush hour. *Faster,* Nayomi says. *You can go faster.* You crest 135. You crest 140. You hear the engine straining beneath you. It takes all your resolve to maintain control of the car. You've been hoping Nayomi's ramble will help your children remain under. They're exhausted from the string of early-morning wakeups to catch this plane or that train, this ferry or that bus, exhausted from the sense of perpetual motion that vacations like this engender. You've been worrying that their immune systems are wearing down, that they're due for colds, which means you and Robert are due for colds, too. It seems right that all they've done is come awake long enough to rearrange themselves more comfortably in the backseat, Nayomi their beanbag pillow. But even as this idea orbits inside your head, Celan says: *I have to go pee-pee.* Your breath catches. Your grip tightens on the steering wheel. This time he doesn't sound groggy at all. This time he sounds wide awake, full of honesty and need. *My tummy's sloshing,* he says. Nadi joins in: *Me too. I have to go, too.* Nayomi says: *It won't be long now, munchkins. We're almost there. Das macht nichts.* Celan says: *I can't hold it.* Nayomi asks Nadi: *How about my princess? Can she hold it a klitzeklein bit more? An itsy-bitsy bit?* Nadi takes the question very seriously, nods her head yes, yes, yes, yes, yes, she thinks she can. She isn't sure, but she thinks so. Nayomi gives her a cuddly hug and tells her how terrific she is. But Celan has passed the point of no return: his face, you can see in the rearview mirror, has started staining red with discomfort and embarrassment. *I have to GO,* he says. Nayomi reaches down and picks up her empty water bottle from the floor. She hands it to him and, smiling her adorable model's smile, says: *Here you go, sweet-pea. Use this. No one will look. Hand auf Herz. Cross my heart.* You say over your shoulder: *We won't, honey. Really.* Celan looks to his father for confirmation. Robert says: *Go for it, Cel. Seriously. We promise. It's cool. It's totally cool.* Celan says: *Why can't we go at the next rest stop?* For some reason his question prompts you to check the gas gauge. You haven't thought about it since this began. Next you are taking in the fact that you have less than an eighth of a tank left. *Listen,* Robert says to Celan sternly. His tone changes, melts into an approximation of patience and understanding. *Because we just can't, hon,* he says. *I'm sorry. But it's okay. When I was your age? Gran and Gramps? They HATED to stop. I don't know why. Every time, just before we pulled out of their driveway on a trip in their Cadillac whale, Gramps used to say in his big deep voice over his shoulder: SPEAK NOW OR FOREVER HOLD YOUR PISS.* Celan and Nadi laugh. Robert continues: *I can still hear him. I never had to go then. Why would I? But I knew, no matter how much I emptied, that I'd have to go again in a couple of hours. It was terrible. So you know what I did? I ended up peeing in Coke bottles. That's what vacations with Gran and Gramps meant for me. And I'm here to tell you: there's nothing to it, sport. A total cinch.* Celan eyes his father's profile, gauging. Robert adds, half-turning in his seat, slipping in a quick wink: *It's even kind of fun. Like making your own 7-Up.* Nadi says: *Gross!* Robert laughs. With great caution, clutching the water bottle, Celan begins maneuvering over the backseat into the tight cargo space with the treasure-trove suitcase for a little privacy. You make a move to pass a slower car ahead of you and the change in momentum takes Celan's legs out from under him. *Ack!* he grunts, going down. *Sorry!* you call. *You okay, sweetie?* Robert says: *Not to worry, sport! It's just like playing a game. You're the Green Berets behind enemy lines. You're on a top-secret mission.* Unsettled, Celan slowly regains his equilibrium, carefully wedges himself into a corner for support, squats daintily. In the middle of this process, he catches your eye in the rearview mirror. *Mah-ahmmm!* You say: *Sorry, pumpkin! You're doing super!* You think about how bad he will be at some things in life. Robert says: *Take your time, buddy. Take all the time you need.* Nadi says: *How come I can't pee-pee in a bottle?* You say: *We're almost out of gas. We're going to have to stop soon.* Nayomi says: *We'll be fine.* Robert says: *How, exactly, will we be fine? I'm just wondering. How, exactly, will we be fine?* Nadi says: *I have to go.* Nayomi says: *I thought my princess didn't have to.* Nadi says: *I didn't, but now I do.* Nayomi says: *Just think of something else, munchkin.* Celan says: *What are you guys talking about?* You shout back: *Nothing, sweetie! You just do what you've got to do.* Nadi says: *I have to go.* Nayomi says: *My little princess can wait a little longer, can't she?* Robert says: *My daughter has to pee, for godsakes. Give us a break.* Nadi says: *How come Cel gets to go and I don't?* Nayomi repeats, almost under her breath: *They don't have to know about any of this.* Less softly, Robert says: *Fuck you.* Nadi cries out gleefully: *Daddy used the F-word!* You say: *Daddy ALWAYS uses the F-word—even though he knows Mommy doesn't like it.* Celan calls out from the cargo space: *I spilled a little. I didn't mean to.* You say: *That's fine, honey. We'll clean it up later.* Celan says: *It's on the rug.* Robert says: *That's what rental cars are for. Spill some more. Go ahead.* Laughing, Nayomi says: *Now you're getting it.* And to Nadi: *When I was a little girl? Know what I used to do?* Celan says: *But it's on the rug.* You say: *Just do the best you can.* Nayomi says: *I used to see how many cars I could count while holding my breath. Let's do that. Shall we?* Nadi shakes her head yes, yes, yes, yes, yes. She sucks in a lungful of air, commences. You see Nayomi pop something into her mouth. This time a whole handful of pills, like a handful of M&Ms, some the color of water in Californian swimming pools, some the color of cotton candy. Celan calls out: *I'm done!* Robert says: *Thatta boy! Now screw the top back on and just leave it there. We'll get it later.* Celan says: *Just leave it?* You say: *Just leave it, Cel.* Celan says: *But it'll roll around.* To Nayomi, you say: *Please.* You don't think about saying it beforehand. You simply find yourself in the middle of saying it. Robert looks over at you. You stare straight ahead and say: *I don't know how to say this except to say this. But please. Think about what you're doing.* You know what you have to say will have zero effect. You always wondered why people even bothered with such gestures in the movies. Now you know. Nayomi says: *It wasn't Munich, exactly.* Robert says: *What?* Nayomi says: *Where I grew up. It wasn't Munich. I lied. It was Köln. Cologne. I don't know why I said Munich. Maybe I just like big cities.* You say: *It doesn't matter. Just . . .* Nayomi says: *My parents are VERY upper middleclass, you know? They have everything a pair of overachieving reactionaries could want. Nice flat in the city. Summer house in Provence. BMW. Stupid little schnauzer that farts too much because they feed it fancy salami. But they wouldn't even help me pay for university. They wouldn't even do that much for their daughter.* You say: *Let's pull over. Just long enough to let the kids out. That's all I'm asking.* Nayomi says: *Daddy's an investment banker. A good Catholic investment banker. You know, the kind that collaborated with the Nazis.* You say: *What do you have to gain?* Nayomi says: *He told me I needed to learn to appreciate the value of money. So I ended up working in this used bookstore in Düsseldorf. He could have paid. It would have been loose change for him. But he refused.* You say: *Please. Nayomi.* Nayomi says: *It was a groovy place. Don't get me wrong. Wall-to-wall books, this amazing smell of knowledge, lots of people who cared about ideas rather than things. But the hours were killing me. That's when I met Renato.*

That guy who just walked in one day? He really did just walk in and everything, only not into a café, not in Munich, and he wasn't wearing a suit. You say: *Nayomi . . .* Nayomi says: *I dropped out and moved down here to be with him. He has this fantastic apartment in Travestere. Very quaint. Very Italian. It instantly felt like where I should be.* You say: *Nayomi, please. Just listen.* Nayomi says: *He was the guy pumping gas on the other side of the island from where you were pumping gas. The light green Fiat? Remember?* Robert glances at you. You glance at Robert. You feel beaten. Nayomi goes on: *You see how handsome he was? He's almost thirty. Mega geil. And he cares about the future. Most people don't, but Renato does.* Your eyes begin filling with tears. Nayomi says: *Maybe you can see him behind us. He's somewhere back there, following to make sure things go off okay. I love him so much. He made me think about things the university was scared to make me think about. He showed me how almost everybody is content to go around complaining about how things never change, but they never lift a finger to fix them. Complaining is always easier than doing. But you know something? Just a few people with conviction can make a difference. They can. Really. You probably don't believe me. You think I'm naïve. You think I'm an idealist. But think of Lenin. Trotsky.* You feel the first tear slip down your cheek, catch on the corner of your mouth. Your nose begins running. The highway begins liquefying. You try to stop, but you can't. *Down deep,* Nayomi says, *everyone wants to be free, nicht wahr? Everyone wants to determine their own destiny. Only most people don't even know it. Or maybe they just don't want to bother. They want others to tell them what to do so they can spend their lives kvetching about it and buying all that Scheiße they see on TV. It's going to take time. Time and action. But at some point you've got to stop kvetching. You've got to start just doing. I know you think I sound like everyone under thirty sounds. Hippie romantics, nicht? But you're wrong, like they were about Lenin. It's going to be different. Like Renato says . . . Hey, up there! Up there! You see it?* You say: *See what?* Nadi says: *This many!* She holds up all ten fingers. Nayomi says: *Wow! That's a LOT! You think you can count even more if we try again?* Nadi's face turns grave. She focuses, nods, collects air. She dives into another round. To you, Nayomi says: *That bus.* Robert, ducking down for a better view, says: *What bus?* Pointing, Nayomi says: *That one.* You say: *What about it?* Nayomi says: *Go faster.* You say: *I can't. I swear. I'll lose control.* Nayomi says: *Try harder.* Robert says: *Do what the fuck she wants. Jesus.* Crying, you realize Celan is still in the cargo space. You look up in the rearview mirror to check on him. He's nowhere in sight. *Cel?* you call out, trying to keep the tears out of your voice. *Cel? Come on up.* Nayomi says: *You want to go faster. You want to pull up alongside.* You grip the wheel so hard your knuckles ache like arthritis. You ease down on the pedal. You crest 145 kilometers. 150. The engine starts whirring oddly. Then you have to throw up. Nayomi says: *When I was thirteen, twelve or thirteen, I thought I'd live forever and ever. I thought I'd be the exception that proves the rule. Everyone does, right? It's a cliché. But Renato? He helped me understand. How the end of the plot is always the same. No matter what you do, it's always the same. The only difference is when and how you reach it. Some people get to know in advance. Some don't. Some are brave and take charge. Others are cowards and do nothing. But think of it. All that effort trying to believe in those children's stories. The Son. The Holy Ghost. All that money churches spend to get you to stop being scared. They're the most successful corporations in history. Pay, pray, obey. That's what Renato says. Pay, pray, obey. Renato says religion is just this huge spectacle designed to con good people into doing bad things. The Crusades. The Inquisition. Only in the end it doesn't mean a thing because whatever you do the story turns out the same. You're here and then you're not. No burning lakes. You finish being you, but when it happens you're not even around to experience the transition. You know what Nietzsche said about the afterlife? He said in heaven all the interesting people are missing . . . Oh, wow. Renato was right. This shit really does make you feel like a cartoon. Hey, look! Look at all the people!* You can make out the words in big red letters on the bus's white flank: *Turistico Romeo.* You say: *You didn't plan all this. You didn't know we'd be right here right now.* Nayomi says: *You plan some things. You let other things just take place. It's like believing in God, only not. Can you imagine we're actually doing this?* Seeing the moment begin to coalesce around her, Nayomi becomes increasingly excited, giddy. She peers out the windshield between Robert and you, cranes her neck to take in everything. *It's like . . . it's like we're flying without planes,* she says. *It's like remembering forward. Look. You can see their faces! Wave at the passengers, Nadi!* Cheeks fake-distended with air, Nadi leans over and waves as you inch up level with the back two or three rows. *This many!* she shouts, holding up all ten fingers twice. *Ausgezeichnet!* shouts Nayomi. The first tourist, an old man with a drastically furrowed face, catches sight of your daughter. He has been resting his cheek on his fist, staring dully out the large side window. The instant Nadi enters his field of vision, his features melt into brightness. He waves back, first using only his fingers, coyly, then soon employing his whole hand, his whole arm, clown-like. *He sees me!* Nadi shouts, waving harder. *He sees me!* Nayomi says: *He does!* The man leans forward and taps the shoulder of the old woman sitting in the seat in front of him. She's been talking to someone beside her, someone you can't see. She turns to look at what has snagged the old man's attention and you see she's wearing so much makeup she looks like a gypsy fortuneteller in a Coney Island booth. One of her front teeth is missing. She gives Nadi a wide smile. Seconds, and five or six tourists are pressed to the glass, waving, making faces. Nadi is delighted. She waves back. She makes faces in response to the faces they're making. Robert proclaims to Nayomi, apropos of nothing: *River Edge isn't even in New Jersey. It's in Delaware. And there are no parks. It's just all these shopping malls and expensive cars. So fuck you twice.* Celan, suddenly aware of the festivities, shouts from the cargo space: *I'm coming up! I'm coming up!* You call over your shoulder, trying to disguise the tears in your voice, your stuffed runny nose: *Watch your step, hon!* Nadi says: *Look at them! Look!* Nayomi says: *They must be thinking what a beautiful little girl you are!* Vigilant, wobbly, Celan eases himself up into a hunker, steadies himself against the ceiling padding, slides one leg over the seatback. It is when he is balancing there like a miniature cowboy in a miniature saddle that it happens. The silver sports car suspended at the corner of your vision veers in front of you. You hit the brakes. Celan flies into Nayomi's back. Nayomi jerks forward. Nadi screams and you hear her body thunk against the back of your seat. Your impression is that Robert moves before thinking about moving, sees his opportunity, tries to lunge for Nayomi, for that backpack between her legs, but he's forgotten he's wearing his seatbelt. He fetches up sharply like a dog that's forgotten it's chained. Your car rocks side-to-side, steering wheel a violent living thing trying to wrench free of your grip, and then your Saab commences a leisurely careening across traffic. Horns startle awake. Brakes screech. Another car brushes Robert's door and there is a metallic jolt completely out of proportion to the movement. You raise your arms to protect your face, and your world arrives in a series of jump cuts. A guardrail. Another bone-grinding crash. The windshield dissolving into an ice storm around you. An instant of concentrated silence. Then a wallop from an unexpected angle, from above you, the roof crunching down, the beige grass, the wheat sky, the beige grass, the noise of sizzling bacon, your Saab plummeting through undergrowth. You leave yourself. You watch as a variety of you strolls into the local bagel shop on Kinderkamack Avenue back home on a summer Sunday morning, cool luminosity giving way to a rush of bready sweetness, parting your lips to ask for onion with cream cheese, and then you are canted on your side, still strapped in, fumbling for the buckle that will release you, your mouth full of blood. You swallow. More blood oozes in. Someone has stacked cinderblocks on your chest. Above you Robert dangles down sideways, groaning, dazed, his face and hair gooey redblack. You close your eyes, trying to steady yourself, feed all your effort into your hands. Your left one isn't working. That's the problem. That's why you can't get your seatbelt undone. You're fumbling, only your left arm is hanging down at a preposterous angle. You think maybe the sound you hear is simply barking, hounds in the distance, then they refine into human shouts. They're moving down the embankment toward you. A moist wheezing rises from deep within your chest. You begin to appreciate where you are, how you have been delivered here, and, even as this instant overflows you, you attempt rotating your head just far enough to catch a glimpse of your kids. This is what the universe becomes for you. You try to speak to them. You try to tell them everything is okay. Your words emerge as a long sibilance. You stop. You don't want to frighten them. You don't want to make things worse than they are. You listen to your ragged breath. You are speaking, even though your mouth isn't moving. *It's all right, sweet ones*, you are saying. *It's all right. You hear them? A few seconds. A few seconds, and they'll start making everything better. They'll reach inside. They'll wrap their arms around you. They'll lift you out.* The violent blueness of the flames washing across the hood.

January

February

March

April

May

June

July

August

September

October

November

December

We just stepped into the violent blueness. It was as easy as that. They had given us directions. We made our way through the deserted streets lined with dingy housing projects. We wanted to hold hands, but we expressed our free will instead.

I'm scared, Iphi said.

I continued not using words.

The sound of our feet rasping pavement. The sound of traffic several blocks away.

I'm really scared, she said again.

We're all scared, I said. All across London, people are being really scared this very second.

The deserted streets becoming incrementally less deserted. Pedestrians flowing around us, a few at first, then more and more. A cute little blond girl in a biscuit-brown coat waddlewalking beside her mother. A rowdy knot of teenagers in soccer uniforms kidding their way toward the park for a game.

Iphi and I turning into just two more strolling along Lodge Road, a couple interchangeable with every other.

How is it possible to care for someone any more than this?

How is it possible to explain the act of forgiveness to someone who doesn't yet believe in such an idea?

She had known other boys, had almost married one: a twenty-year-old named Clayton who worked at a gas station in Eden Prairie. He wore grimy gray wifebeaters and possessed no fat whatsoever on his body.

Once when we were dating, Iphi showed me a photo she still kept of him and told me about how he bought her beer, cigarettes, pot, bags of chocolate cookies, all the bubblegum and Gobstoppers she could chew. On their one-month anniversary, he treated her to white lady for the first time. Iphi loved the shape of those sounds in her mouth. *White lady.* They tasted sexy.

Clayton and she sat in his pickup on the shore of the reservoir at night, radio playing Paradise of the Blind, black water glimmering before them, and drank, smoked, snorted, made out.

Chalked up, Iphi's head became a beehive.

My beautiful little girl, Clayton called her. *My beautiful, beautiful little girl.*

She had just turned sixteen and those were the most pleasing words she had ever heard.

She decided to do whatever he asked just to hear him say them again.

Iphi's father, a stonemason, called what the last thirty-five years had done to him *a fucking bad joke without a punch line*. He nicknamed his daughter *The Chucklehead*. Her mother, a night nurse, said the worst thing that had ever happened to her was meeting her husband. She nicknamed her daughter *My Little Secretion*. Iphi knew they were only teasing. She knew they appreciated her in their own way, that they would miss her if she ever went away, but not like Clayton appreciated her, not like he would miss her, nothing like that.

Sometimes Iphi and Clayton would shoplift together. Iphi kept the clerk busy by flirting with him. Clayton slipped into the aisles and pocketed what they wanted. They did it, not because they needed anything, not because they had to have a stupid bag of Skittles or Tootsie Pops or a can of Red Bull or whatever, but because it made them feel attentive, like they were doing something significant.

It made the moment, the day, the week feel full of kick.

They even developed a system of secret hand signs to communicate with each other.

Fist to chest: *I love you.*

Palm stretched wide open like a sun made of flesh: *You make me so happy.*

Two fingers laid along the side of the nose: *Let's do another rail, babe. Let's do it right now, okay?*

11:53. A bench at the edge of the boating lake in Regent's Park. Naked willows sagging into the hazy green water. An agitation of pigeons feeding along the paved banks.

We sat side by side watching old women in long black coats and children in baby blue parkas tossing out handfuls of breadcrumbs, seeds, leftover donuts, buns, the cold smog needling our lungs.

You thirsty? I asked.

What time is it?

Plenty for a drink. There's a cart over there. You want me to pick you up something? A Mountain Dew?

It's like we're just out for a Sunday stroll.

Pretty much, I said.

Like everybody around us is seeing a different world.

Yeah.

Like they're looking at something completely different no matter which way they turn.

Yeah, I said. Yes.

Who can explain how the call came at three o'clock in the afternoon, a time no one fears? How the only messages at three o'clock usually concern dentist appointments, dinner dates, requests to bring home a gallon of skim milk, an extra package of spaghetti, a box of breakfast cereal? How you were in the back of the 7-Eleven, retrieving a roll of paper towels for the dispenser in the men's room, when your cell began vibrating in your pocket? How you can recall the texture and heft in your hands, the tang of hot dogs and mustard in the air, the country-western music on the sound system?

Who can explain how the level voice of the female officer on the other end reminded you of a hostess telling you your table is ready: that flat, that automatic?

How you levitated there, wanting to ask her if she really knew what she was saying, because her language sounded pretend, like she was practicing, like she was some second-class actor not even close to getting her lines down?

We rented a small white farmhouse with black trim on two acres of barren land on the outskirts of town, and one night they simply started showing up.

We had been watching game shows where the contestants supply letters of the alphabet, or guess which aluminum suitcase among many aluminum suitcases contains a million dollars, when we heard rapping at our front door.

Outside a pair of church brothers in black suits, white shirts, black ties, shiny shoes, bright blue eyes. Their blond hair short, spiky, carrying so much product it appeared brownish in the yellow porch light.

They wouldn't stop smiling.

Their teeth were uncomfortably tiny.

At the start, they gave us minor tasks. Hiding this in the shed, burying that among the other data on my computer. They showed us how, patient, polite, soft-spoken, caring yet stern, focused, unflappable. They took as much time as we needed to get things right.

Gradually, the tasks became larger, more complicated. Passing this to the woman in the red D.A.R.E. t-shirt walking by you on the corner of Aldrich and 84th, taking photos of that with a disposable camera.

One time someone appeared while we were eating dinner and asked if the man waiting in his car in the driveway could spend the night with us.

We said yes.

We always said yes.

We always wanted to help any way we could.

Just hearing the word coke *still makes me salivate*, she said one night. We were watching a reality show about the famous young underfed woman, who was famous only for being famous and underfed, and her famous underfed friend. They were living on a farm for three days with a family that had nothing in common with them.

No one on the screen had mentioned the word *coke*. There had been no allusions to drugs.

Iphi just started talking.

It's like it's your cells are remembering, she said, *not you.*

Then she stopped and continued watching in silence as though she hadn't said a thing.

Iphi's brothers didn't care about Clayton. They didn't care about white lady. They didn't care about what Iphi did or didn't do, so long as it didn't affect them.

By the time Iphi was ten, the older one, Mike, had already dropped out of high school and hitchhiked west. He landed a job at the Buckhorn Bar in Laramie. In a postcard, all black except for white letters at the bottom saying *Nightlife in Wyoming*, he reported he had to break up fights three times a week on average, some inside the bar, some out on the street. Some involved knives, most fists.

The mirror over the backbar had a bullet hole in it dating, not from the days of the Wild West, but from the 1970s.

Newcomers to the town had to learn to lean forward slightly when walking along the sidewalks because the harsh wind never stopped blowing in from the prairies.

Two years ago the postcards stopped.

Who? Iphi's father asked when someone mentioned Mike's name after that.

This is why you always have more than one baby, explained Iphi's mother. You don't want to start liking one too much, just in case something like this happens.

Dan, the younger one, the one with a girl's fragility and tendency to blush easily, flunked out of tenth grade last year. To him, sentences resembled messy piles of kindling waiting for a match. Math problems looked worse. Fractions, division signs, x's and y's clogging the page of a textbook tightened his stomach, made his mind go empty as a pair of cupped hands.

Iphi started worrying about Dan when he started staying out all night, sleeping in till four every afternoon, but not as much as she started worrying about herself.

Clayton and his gifts had become the same thing in her mind.

She couldn't stop thinking about either one.

Iphi said: *I've never tasted a soft drink as good as this.*

Holding the green, yellow, red, and white can in her hand. Rotating it. Examining the label as if maybe it held the secret that would explain this afternoon.

Sometimes on commercials you hear a drink is "refreshing." A drink is "thirst quenching." You don't pay any attention. But that's exactly what you've got yourself here.

When it arrived, it wasn't a waterfall of voltage rippling down over her. When it arrived, it was a quiet voice whispering into her ear one evening on the sofa in her living room as she waited for Clayton to pick her up after dinner.

I'm beside you, the voice said. *I'm right here beside you. Don't be afraid.*

This is what happened: Jesus simply appeared in her living room. One second he wasn't in Iphi's house. The next he was.

She was conquered by his presence, could sense him sitting there beside her as she smoked a cigarette, loving her, bleeding from his wrists, his feet, the wound in his side. She could sense how she had become perfect in his eyes, despite everything she had done, despite everything she had failed to do, how everything had grown warm, correct.

She understood completely how the reason there aren't any dinosaurs left on the planet is because they couldn't fit on Noah's ark.

How it is impossible to imagine the number 4,500,000,000 and so it simply stands to reason that the earth has to be fewer than 10,000 years old.

How you either believe God's Word all the way or not at all.

She saw how when the Rapture arrives Jesus will reach down into her body, pluck out the handful of white light called her soul, and carry it with him up to heaven. On that day, pilots will disappear from their cockpits, truck drivers from their cabs, commuters from their cars. At dinner tables all around the world, some family members will vanish while others will burst into flames.

You either believe or you do not.

You either open your arms to Jesus, or Jesus will close his heart to you.

I thought about how all anybody really wants is somewhere to go when they're finished here.

I thought about how, in Matthew, Jesus says: *Do not think that I came to bring peace on the earth; I did not come to bring peace, but a sword.*

Eyes shut. Water lapping. Iphi sipping.

The general chatter of pigeons and people passing.

I thought about how, in Ezekiel, God says: *I will leave your flesh on the mountains, and fill the valleys with your carcass. I will water the land with what flows from you, and the riverbeds shall be filled with your blood.*

I opened my eyes and glanced up at the sky to see if it would explode.

We sat across from the two Church brothers in our living room. We couldn't afford real furniture, so we improvised with lawn chairs, a chaise lounge, a camping table we bought on sale at Target. Iphi offered them apple juice and fresh-baked butter cookies.

Smiling with their tiny teeth, they said thank you, but no.

They told us how sorry they were about what had happened to my mother and asked if we could all take a few moments to pray for her.

We knelt on the bare wood floor.

Lowered our heads.

Opened our hearts, but not enough.

Afterward, they posed questions to us. Did I ever think about what must have gone through my mother's mind as the first bomb erupted in the movie theater where she was sitting at the Mall of America? As hope started collapsing down around her? As she lay leaving us under the heap of rubble, waiting for the rescue workers, but less and less?

Did I ever think about how much anyone should bear before he begins to match sacrifice with sacrifice, thunder with thunder?

I had, I said. All the time.

It was past midnight when they left. Iphi and I washed dishes and went to bed. We spoke in voices low and quiet as Christ's until dawn.

She understood completely how hell looked just like the painting by that guy.

What was his name?

Bird monsters with glossy dead eyes gnawing on the heads and shoulders of naked sinners. Gigantic machines in dark niches grinding up the fallen like so much hamburger meat. Huge rats raping the crucified. Men shitting coins, lapping at tubs full of vomit. Women being eaten alive, yet still unable to tear their eyes away from the hand mirrors they're holding before them. Thick brown smoke churning across the glowing orange nightmare horizon.

Imagine, Iphi said, how that scene doesn't happen once. How it is happening right now, but also a thousand years ago and next week and next year and forty billion years after that.

Forever.

Forever and ever without end.

The painting says: *I was there.*

The painting says: *I saw what you are seeing.*

The painting says: *Beware, for this is what awaits all who believe in empty expressions rather than the rabbit punch of deeds.*

12:46. We were sitting on the park bench at the edge of the boating lake, and then we were approaching the mosque. Time and space winked, lost me, found me. I watched the minaret swing into view, the large golden dome, the library, the rest of the concrete-and-glass complex on the far side of the green hedge, the barren trees.

My chest a chaos of sparrows.

My mind a squall of luminosity.

The bored security guard, a gray-haired Pakistani with pink-rimmed eyes, gave us the once-over from his chair by the entrance and waved us through without rising.

We walked down the sun-flooded hallway, the double brass doors at the far end swelling to meet us. We paused just outside the prayer hall, my mouth suddenly dry, gummy, Iphi's eyes suddenly rich with panic and shock through the slit in her burqa.

Once upon a time, you weren't here. Now you have never been anywhere else. You are the Lord's story. Now it is nearing its end. It has been a good one.

Calm yourself, you tell your wife without using words. *This is how we will return to God. Others find other ways. This will be ours.*

You want to reach out. You want to touch her face one more time in this world, but know you will have to wait. A few minutes, less, and then you will be standing together again.

All this thinking, all this practice, and the instant finally happens around you and through you like a heavy wind.

You take her hands without taking her hands. You tell her you love her without telling her you love her. She looks at you. She looks at you.

And then she turns and is walking away from you, moving toward the library.

You are watching her diminishing.

You are where you are, collecting yourself. You can't do this, you decide. You can't possibly do this. You inhale. Something is there when you exhale. It revolves you toward the door. It impels you through.

As you enter, you see and you do not see.

You feel and you do not feel.

The lush red carpets. The marble floors. The central chandelier.

The vast dome above you covered with intricate abstract mosaics.

Head whirring, you remove your shoes, leave them with the others, focus on each step, will yourself to appear composed, weave your way through this crowd of infidels kneeling, rumps raised. Iphi is with you. Your mother is with you. Your church brothers and sisters. All across London, people just like you are doing what they have been asked to do. They are stepping onto subway cars packed with the unclean, onto buses, into bookstores, clinics, corner markets, the foyers of housing projects.

All across London, a complex mesh of compassion expanding.

You are here and you are somewhere else.

You are Clayton in the cab of his pickup, Iphi leaning into you, reaching for her knee, making believe you're not doing what you're doing. You are Iphi's brother Mike pushing another beer across the counter to another patron at the Buckhorn Bar, wondering how long now until your shift is done. You are the feral neighbor children surrounding your woodpile the second before they shove it into confusion. You are your mother beneath the rubble, dazed, waiting for something that will not arrive. You are yourself, only younger, strolling beside your wife who isn't your wife on your way back to her tent at the retreat. You are yourself, only a boy, helping your mother scrub the bathroom tiles in a motel room on the outskirts of town. You are yourself, only unspeakably tired, your cheek bobbing against your father's shoulder as he carries you to bed.

You blink and see yourself kneeling with these others around you, lowering your forehead toward the earth.

You blink and feel forgiveness shimmering the air.

You blink and see the white ceiling tiles above your bed, your father's unshaven face swooping in to fill your sight, his broken-toothed smile, his rough hands floating down.

Sweet dreams, sweet-pea, he is saying.

He is saying: *Don't let the bedbugs bite . . .*

What should we do if we cannot remember the number of our sins?

We should count the sins of others.

How should we count them?

By palming the trigger.

How should we make the sign of the invisible cross as we do so?

By putting our invisible right hand to our invisible forehead, then to our invisible breast, and then to our invisible left and right shoulders, saying: *Through this holy anointing, may the Lord in his love and mercy help us with the grace of the Holy Spirit.*

Why do we make the sign of the invisible cross?

To convince ourselves that in the end the story will never really be the end.

Which is the prayer most recommended to us?

This is the prayer most recommended to us: *May the Lord who frees us from sin save us and raise us up.*

Are there others?

Yes: *May the Lord curse our enemies, blind them, let the streets flow with their blood, for they have soiled the house of the Lord.*

How will Christ judge us?

He will make us live with ourselves.

When will Christ judge us?
Every second we are alive. Every second we are dead.

What is heaven?
The instant before the click.

What is heaven?
The instant after.

What is heaven?
Hearing the words we have waited so long to hear: *Welcome home.*

With the next blink, you feel the room around you rethink itself.

You feel the black butterfly of your soul shudder inside your chest.

It isn't you who changes your mind.

It is your thigh muscles, the nerves along the back of your neck.

You lean onto your heels, rise, your ankles crackling beneath you. You simply stand there. You simply revolve. You simply steer your way among the murmurings toward those double brass doors.

You have just enough time to step through them before the yellow-orange radiance rushes up the hallway at you.

The stunning crack.

The flutter of hectic wings.

And next you are lying on a bed of shattered glass, covered with ash, bits of someone else's flesh stuck to your coat.

Before you can move again, the dusty ghosts begin stumbling from the darkness at the end of the corridor, blood spattered across their slack faces, their white shirts, their shredded pants and burqas. Their mouths are open. Some must be screaming, some moaning, but the only sound inside your head is a long loud shrillness. A human-sized moth flutters past you. The security guard. Bitter powder fills your nose, covers your tongue, makes it difficult to breathe. It looks like a delicate snow has fallen across the marble floor, a commotion of shoe prints through it pointing the way toward the street.

You lie there. You lie there. And then, scrupulously, you roll onto your side. Scrupulously, you lift yourself onto your knees. Hoist yourself up.

Following those prints, joining the exodus, you pass an old man lying on his side. He appears to have given up ten feet short of the doors. You pass a teenage girl leaning back against the wall, rocking noiselessly, face in her hands.

Outside, men and women huddling in groups.

Some punching numbers on their cell phones, some wandering, calling out names, staring into space as if they are trying to remember a word that just slipped their minds.

The first rescue vehicles are pulling up to the curb, blue-uniformed policemen and firemen wearing surgical masks hopping out, jogging by as you stroll into the astonishing afternoon, because—

Because—

Because you can feel how Jesus has taken her into his delicate arms and made her flawless.

Because there is a voice whispering into your ear as you walk, as you glance up into the sky empty as expectation, heart slamming.

Because that voice is saying the same thing over and over again.

Because it is saying *I, I, I, I, I*

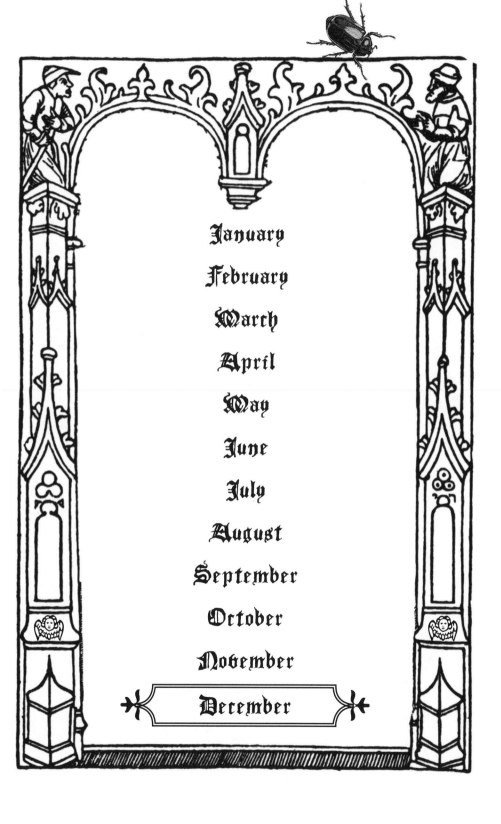

January

February

March

April

May

June

July

August

September

October

November

December

ached for myself as Aleyt licked brownie off her thumb tip, rose, walked around the coffee table separating us, and gave me another hug, this one blunt and lingering. She smelled of cheap Allure, which for some reason struck me as very sad. For some reason everything struck me as very sad. The elderly man in the baby blue parka two sizes too big for him shuffling out the door. The last wintry lemon light silhouetting him. One of the cute college coeds, ponytail the color of a cardboard box, packing up her computer all by herself, chums departed. The way she had rubbed too much rouge on her right cheek without knowing it, thereby becoming lopsided, silly as a rag doll.

I took deep breaths of Aleyt, held on to her too long, knew it was time to change the trajectory of our conversation, I had already rambled to the borders of embarrassment, although the last thing I wanted was to hear how she had become this reindeer-sweatered largeness across from me, and so, when she had resettled into her seat, I began asking after a number of old high-school classmates I couldn't have cared less about, people I had until a week ago put out of my mind completely for more than half my life, their parents, their parents' pals, their parents' parents, their girlfriends and boyfriends, each of whom Aleyt knew almost as little about as I did, which made me feel at least minimally better.

Jerry and she weren't very sociable, she confessed. They tended to keep to themselves, and, when they did go out, it was usually without spouse because they didn't particularly enjoy each other's company anymore, an observation which might sound peculiar to a single person's ears, Aleyt said almost lightheartedly, as if she were talking about a missed appointment with the dishwasher repairman, but isn't, really, not as married couples go, given how many eternities they have to endure each other's tics and noises and odors and pet anecdotes. Jerry was a one-time jock who liked to golf, tinker with things that didn't need tinkering with around the house, sprawl formulaically in his recliner before the plasma screen, a bowl of nachos and an open jar of salsa in his lap, watching big boys in tight uniforms run up and down green fields and bumble into each other homoerotically. When Aleyt and he did occasionally get together, they found themselves talking about who was going to take their son Ryan to the next rugby match, their daughters Brooke and Brianna to the next ballet class, about how they were going to deal with the next bill from the dermatologist or drama coach—until, that is, their kids spun off to college, after which, more disconcerting still, Jerry and Aleyt found themselves with nothing important to confer about at all.

They went out to dinner and a movie together once every week or two because Aleyt had read somewhere it was a good idea to apply a dose of dates to ailing relationships, but ended up eating in silence, having run out of things to say by the time their water glasses were tinking with ice. Gradually, amicably, they drifted away on different currents toward different islands in different oceans. She said she felt dumb to admit it, sounding as it did like the echo of a dramedy, but it may have had something to do with Jerry's increasingly hairy shoulder blades, swelling belly, way he didn't care enough about her to shave for whole weekends at a pop or take his eyes off the TV when asking her to nuke another meatballs-and-mozzarella Hot Pockets for him, okay, hon, how it turns out that one can often become undeserving of love, it happens every day, everywhere, who would have thought it, but may have had equally as much to do with the arrival of The Change, good grief, and wasn't *that* a hoot, Aleyt said, pardon my French, and why in the world didn't it ever occur to our mothers to pull us aside and warn us about *that* inescapable squall speeding toward us across the years so we could at least contemplate beginning the slow toil of climbing to higher emotional ground in preparation for its arrival?

Oprah talks about menopause as passage, some courageous phase in the life-voyage. It can teach you things. It can transform you in mysteriously redemptive ways. Oprah is full of beans. Oprah is so wrong it hurts. What menopause does is remind you of your own mortality at unpredictable moments—as if your ruining body hadn't reminded you of it enough over the course of the last forty-some-odd years, five-hundred-some-odd periods, that rowdy cluster of kids of yours coming and going, and going, and going till they were gone. Menopause transforms your youth into a phantom limb. For Aleyt, it had commenced little by little, perhaps a dozen years ago, no more than a nuanced deceleration of her metabolism, a wattle that wouldn't recede, some graying at the temples, a growing lack of interest in the treadmill, and she told herself not to worry, she could deal with it, here was one of those noteworthy wheat-from-chaff character-building chapters in her daybook, only then the fiery surges she couldn't believe the rest of the planet wasn't sharing howled in. She was avalanched by awakenings at two in the morning, sheets sweat-soppy; breakthrough bleeding; achy breasts; gyres of dizziness; heart palpitations; realizations about how on a whim—sliding out of her car, chopping chives at the counter, standing over there ordering her Toffee Nut Crème, for godsakes, which, by the way, is dreamy, you should try it—the universe could abruptly slope and all of a sudden seem grossly, inexpressibly unfair, to the point of stamping in frustration, to the point of tears.

We commiserated. We consoled. We talked in our own way about how dying is proof against all theories except the theory of termination, which isn't a theory. We snorted at where we'd ended up, look at us, look at us, our respective destinations turning out to

be not so very far apart from each other after all. We spoke about
how men no longer took us seriously, how nobody knows what's
going to happen, how buying makeup that feinted at covering your
crow's feet without caking turns into a joke somewhere in your late
thirties, even though you say it doesn't matter, even though you
say it's just part of that routine called wearing out, even though
you say bring it on, sure, you're ready, because you're never really
ready, you can't be, that isn't how this game goes, every day of it a
bitch slap, excuse my grief.

I heard myself admitting I could understand why Aleyt had
chosen film studies back at Sarah Lawrence, that was the easy
one, but I couldn't locate the thread in her story that led from our
sleepovers to her psych major. Aleyt took a long swig of her elaborate coffee, contemplated my question, leaned forward, hands
cradling her cup between her knees like a construction worker
on a mid-morning break, and answered that the thing was this:
that seven hundred and fifty milliliters of blood wash around your
brain's one hundred billion neurons every minute, Plato believed
your gray matter the most divine part of people, Aristotle figured
that batch of sticky wrinkles in the cranium accomplished exactly
nothing save cooling hot blood on its rush from the boiling heart—
and, well, learn stuff like that, and you're lost for life.

The thing was this: some globs in our heads glow with awareness when we perform mental tasks while others grow dim. If you
sit at your school desk waiting for instructions about how to take
your SATs, the dark network is as active as a psychedelic beehive,
but the second those instructions arrive, and you set in fighting for
your academic survival, the bees freeze, the network hushes. Which
is to say when we're doing nothing, we're doing something—but
what? Time travel, Aleyt explained. Time travel! Our ability to
close our eyes and picture the pleasures of last Saturday's chocolate
truffle, or fret about what our broken children will tell their thera-
pists about us Monday, is a fairly recent evolutionary development.
Contemplate futures that don't include us (will a fresh earthquake

judder Jakarta this month?), and the dark network dozes, but begin moving ourselves through time inside our noggins, and it's alert as your tabby on the tree stump out back the second she spots a rustling in the grass. Weirder still, the dark network is the brain's default mode—that is, the thing was this: we're wired to spend more of our day away from the present than in it.

Why did the universe do that to us, and not, say, to ducks or dormice? Because the universe apparently concluded after a couple million years that experience is a terrible thing to waste. It's dangerous out there, things go bump in the light, and it therefore makes sense that the fewer events we have to put ourselves through, the better, the more we can learn from each, the safer we'll remain. Time travel allows us to pay for an experience once, then rerun it on the screen behind our foreheads at no additional charge as many times as we like. With each repetition, we're in a position to learn something new. And how astonishing is *that*?

Listening to her, I felt blurry.

I felt fine and then I felt blurry.

Like someone was beginning to erase me from the back of my head down.

I closed my eyes, opened them, and something occurred to me, and the blurriness became grayer, and Aleyt pushed on, saying more astonishing still is the fact that most of us would stake our sanity on the intuition that there's someone home in our sensoria, a conscious process humming along up there, that, not to put too fine a point on it, we're *us*, we're first-person people saddled to the same selves from birth to blackness—and yet it just so happens that our thoughts, our satisfactions, our sorrows consist entirely of always-altering physiological activity in those tissues stuffing our skulls, sparks and sluices, that's all, nothing more, sluices and sparks, and those overly familiar near-death experiences of white radiance and delft-blue serenity and relatives beckoning to us from the dazzling threshold? Let me tell you something, honey, said Aleyt. Those experiences aren't eyewitness reports of jubilant souls parting company with their bodies, no, sorry, no, they're simple symptoms of oxygen starvation in the eyes and brain. And that peculiar conviction we cling to that there's an *I* occupying the swivel chair in our cranial control room, scanning the walls of displays, pulling the strings called our muscles? Nothing but an involved hoax perpetrated by our bushy dendrites behind our backs. And how astonishing is *that*?

This, in a word, was the vertiginous understanding that drew Aleyt in: the rowdy idea that our minds are unable to grasp why those neural crackles and snaps observed from the outside should give rise to the impression of subjective experience from the inside, because—

Because—

Because it's not you, I said, is it?

It's not any of us, Aleyt said. That's the thing I just can't shake. I mean, how *bizarre*. That's the thought that kept me coming back to the scene of the crime my entire undergrad education, though these days, um, well, you know, what with Jerry and the kids . . .

No. I mean, you're not you. Her. Aleyt.

Her expression remained steady.

Want another latté? she asked, all perky. My treat. I'm thinking what the heck. Calories be damned. Actually, you really should try Toffee Nut Crème. It'll change your life.

You're somebody else. That's why you don't look like her or speak like her or feel like her.

People change, I guess, she said, shrugging. You know how it is.

Not that much, they don't.

You'd be surprised.

The blurriness spread like the first swells of flu from the back of my skull into the bottom of my throat.

UnAleyt studied the brown top of her forest-green cup.

I posed a question to the part in her black bob that made her head look too small for her body:

How'd you find me?

She looked up quickly and laughed.

I didn't find *you*, silly. You found *me*. Remember? That's what's so wonderful about these website thingies. All you have to do is sit and wait long enough. I knew you'd eventually get around to dropping by. Everybody wants to figure out where their childhoods went, right? You sure you won't take me up on another cup of caffeine?

You do thish lots, I said.

Startled by the slur, I raised my hand to my mouth to check what was going on down there.

UnAleyt's eyes crinkled.

Do what?

What you're doing. Thish. *This.* Who are you?

It's *really* good to see you, Moira. I'm so happy things worked—

Fuck you, I said, rising, wobbly, my knees befuddled.

The teen sponging the counter at the cash register glanced over in our direction, smiled like employees in coffeehouses across the country smile at their patrons, like we've been fast friends forever, then returned to what she was doing, her smile wiped clean as the wood veneer beneath her palm.

One of her buddies stacked chairs upside-down on tables across the room.

UnAleyt appeared shocked by what I'd said.

Moira. Hey—

And you get exactly *what* out of all of thish?

Out of what?

Some stupid rush or something?

She read me as if reading a difficult calculus problem. Then she became two people with six eyes and four noses. They all asked:

You okay, hon?

I'm fuh-fuh-fuh-fine.

You don't look fine. You just went all pasty. Here. Let me have a—

Fuck you twice, I said, stepping past her, weaving for the door that immediately started skating away from me.

Have a great evening! the kid behind the counter called after what was left of Moira, and, next, icy night air was splashing my face, and her heart was banging hard and slow in the center of her brain, panicky and hurt, ashamed and rattled, fizzy and increasingly indistinct, and I was aiming myself across the parking lot, was bending over her Corolla, was sorting through the keys multiplying on my keychain, which is when UnAleyt's gloved hand landed on Moira's shoulder and loitered there, only Moira didn't pay any attention to it, she didn't pay attention to it some more, I just kept clinking through her options, and next the gloved hand squeezed.

Stop, Moi. Please. Really. Stop for a second here, okay? I don't get what just happened back there. What just happened back there? Tell me. What did I do that ticked you off so bad?

Moira kept clinking.

Look, UnAleyt said. I'm clueless. Help me out here. I think maybe you think I'm somebody I'm not, but I'm not. I'm me. Honest. I'm who you thought I was. Am. Aleyt.

Moira's keys were abruptly big and clumsy as tennis racquets, her hands small and jittery as mouse mitts.

You shouldn't be driving, honey, you know that? UnAleyt said.

Moira tried to shrug off her gray glove, but that only caused its twin to join in, caused the imposter to say: Come on over to my minivan, okay? We don't have to do anything or anything. We can just sit inside and listen to the radio and rest until you feel more like yourself. Remember how we used to lie in bed next to each other playing *Sgt. Pepper's* over and over on your plastic stereo? "A Day in the Life"? Remember? We can do that. We can drive to my place. We can have a sleepover. Jerry won't mind. And tough if he does. What about it? Whaddya say?

No we dinnit, Moira said. I dinnit have a plastic stereo and we dinnit meet the Beatles and you're making all thish shtuff uh—

I want to say that's when I found the right car key, I want to say it wasn't, I want to say that after some more fumbling I may or may not have snicked it into the lock, I may or may not have tried to add something to what I already thought I thought I had already added, although I'm not sure what that possibly could have been, I want to say that there may or may not have ensued a minor scuffle in the shadowy coffeehouse parking lot beneath a spindly undressed elm next to my desert-sand Corolla, then several thousand years passed, then a picosecond, and then I awoke in this place, wherever this place is, wherever it isn't, let's call it, what, let's call it a stuffy basement room with a mattress in the middle and bare brick walls all around and no windows in sight and a door whose knob turns both ways, clockwise and counter-clockwise, only when it does nothing happens, it may be bolted, unless it's stuck, there's always that option, too, it may be stuck, I feel drunk, and a space heater by that door and a brash bare fluorescent light hanging on wires from the ceiling like in a shed and a rickety side table with one leg shorter than the others on which are piled three of my videos and one blank cartridge and a camcorder and a pen and a marbled notebook in which I may or may not have started writing everything I know, everything I don't know, here, in this, I'm not really sure, maybe I haven't begun yet, maybe I will, maybe I won't, but what I'm sure of is that there is also a beat-up television with a built-in VCR player on the floor by the door, because I've watched them all, the videos, that is, I've watched them all, I recall that very well, I think, paying close attention, I recognized me in each one, on my bed at home, doing the things I did, except these aren't the cartridges I normally use, no, look at the label, they're somebody else's, these videos are copies of copies of the videos I made, I want to say, I think, I think I want to say, and who would have thought I'd become my own underground industry without knowing it because—

Because—

Because in another version, one that seems equally plausible, this feels like a downstairs guestroom, feels like the place in which I'm recuperating from whatever it is that I'm recuperating from, sleeping it off, I don't know quite what that might be, call it a reaction, an allergic reaction, sure, why not, or maybe food poisoning, maybe age poisoning, it happens every day, everywhere, the world after all isn't as filthy and mortal as it looks, no, it's a lot filthier, a lot more mortal, it's a pigsty and I've been very tired lately, my immune system weak as a whimper, it feels like I may have been conked out for hours, weeks, anything is probable, which is to say nothing is, several months, several seconds, the principles of time no longer quite holding here, from what I can tell, for all I know I'm still dreaming, or maybe I never went to sleep, sure, why not, or maybe it only felt that way, but, whatever the case, my limbs are logs and I can't open my eyes, or I can open my eyes but it feels like I can't, I certainly don't want to, if that makes any difference, I doubt it does, open or shut them, it's all the same to me, I want to say, because I remember someone talking to me, and this may have been some time ago, and this may have been the dream or may have been the other thing, in either case we were in a bar, no, a bistro, no, someplace else, yes, and this voice said *the brain is brilliant, look at what it can do, because who needs hope when you have a corpus callosum—*

Because—

Because in another version, one that seems equally et cetera, I want to say I haven't been asleep at all, no, and so perhaps this is simply what is going through my mind, what was going through my mind, as Moira reached for the door handle of her desert-sand Corolla and someone reached in and extracted all the bones, large and little, from her legs—femur, tibia, fibula—and, just for a moment, just before her lower torso folded up under me like an empty skirt, I want to say she commenced recollecting someone else's story, sure, why not, it happens every day, everywhere, the world after all isn't as rich in narratives as it looks, no, it's more so, it's a book of books, my sister's, conceivably, conceivably Sarasa's story, I don't know why I think that, I don't know where she is, I don't even really know who she is, which is to say we've never been especially close, we don't keep in touch much except on birthdays, on birthdays and sometimes Christmas, and even then it feels like I've just picked up the phone and dialed a stranger's number and decided to take a stab at conversation, she always leaves messages when she knows I'm not in, but she's not here, that's certain, not in this room, I want to say, not in this city, probably not even in this country, no, it couldn't have been my own story, in any event, no, that's definite if nothing else, whoever it is, wherever it originates, because it was a bittersweet love story, you see, and I have none of those, bittersweet or otherwise, I wish I did but there you are, look at me, look at me, you want this but you get that, repeatedly, and the story in question, this new story, I want to say, launched with the words *shortly after they were married,* a lovely opening, full of potential, someone else's voice whispering somewhere far behind my eyes, never, ever, in Moira's estimation, a propitious sign, *shortly after they were married*, it began,

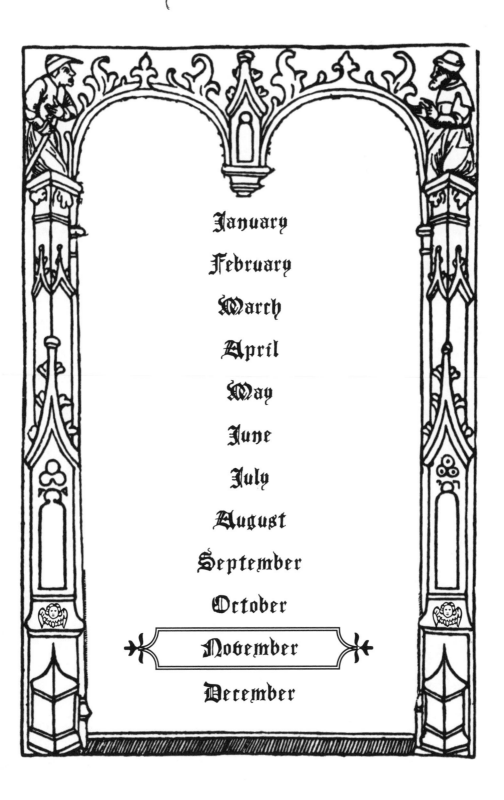

January

February

March

April

May

June

July

August

September

October

November

December

12.08.76. Shortly after they were married, Victoria and Albert visited Florence and were taken by the city's incredible architecture, especially Brunelleschi's dome atop the Basilica di Santa Maria del Fiore with its ~~distinctive~~ octagonal design built out of something like four million bricks. When Victoria returned several years after Albert's death, the queen was delighted to see the dome restored. She ordered her carriage to stop in the piazza, rolled down her window, opened the locket around her neck, and turned the tiny picture of her husband toward the cathedral so he could enjoy the sight, too. After a moment's silence, she flipped the locket shut, rolled up the window, and ordered her carriage to drive on.

12.09.76. Did you know, Taru, that Mandalay didn't start as a small settlement like most cities? Instead, the story goes, Buddha, passing through the area, pointed to the hill where much of Mandalay now exists and foretold on that site a great capital of his religion would blossom. On January 13, 1857, King Mindon issued a decree to fulfill that prophecy. The former royal city of Amarapura was dismantled ~~piece by piece~~ stone by stone and moved by elephant to the foot of the hill. The king was also responsible for ordering made the *Ti-pedikut,* the world's largest book: 729 pages of Buddhist scriptures inscribed on 729 marble slabs, each housed in its own stupa. A book whose pages you stroll among like you would huge gleaming white shrubbery in a garden.

12.10.76. In 1892, the year he married and moved to Vermont (Vermont, of all places!), Rudyard Kipling composed his famous poem "The Road to Mandalay"—although the only city he ever actually visited in Burma was Moulmein, on the southeastern coast of the country, hundreds of miles away from, and nothing like, the place he wrote about.

12.11.76. I'm sitting on a wooden stool on the thatched porch of
a food hut on the river across from Mandalay hill, eating a bowl
of chicken curry for lunch. The chunks of meat are dark brown,
stringy, stiff, dry. I had to use my shirt to wipe off from my
communal chopsticks whatever the last guy was eating before I
could use them. This afternoon I'll visit Sutaungpyai pagoda at the
top of the hill. Hens are zigzagging across the road in front of me
like agitated women with feather petticoats lifted among people
clattering by on bikes. A shorthaired beige dog squats, scratching
his ribcage absentmindedly with a hind leg, staring straight ahead,
as if the locals were moving in a less interesting dimension than the
one he inhabits. On the bamboo wall beside me, three greengray
lizards, eyes shut, frozen in a breathing knot. If I reached out, I
could touch them.

12.11.76. P.S. Tourism makes foreign countries into museums you walk through.

12.11.76. P.P.S. I guess what I'm trying to say, Taru, is that travel shows you what you already know in ways you don't recognize. How little you understand when you begin your journey. How much less when you end it. Which is exactly why you go.

12.11.76. From the terrace of Sutaungpyai, flooded fields gleaming through hazy atmosphere all the way to the horizon. Shared the ferry over with five Brits—sweet, daffy hippy types with filthy cracked bare feet, paisley bandanas, colorful baggy Nepalese pants, baggy once-white shirts. They started improvising their way south and east two months ago, traveling from Katmandu to Janakpur, across into India, Bhutan, and now through Burma. They've enjoyed everything, they say, but it's Bhutan they adored most of all. Stepping into it was stepping into the thirteenth century. No phones, no paved roads, not one traffic light in the whole place. Bhutan moved from a system of barter to currency within the last ten years. Thimphu, the capital, has a population of slightly less than 30,000. But the hippies' favorite spot was the Tiger's Nest monastery perched on the side of a craggy cliff among colorful prayer flags at 10,500 feet. Approaching, all you hear is steady wind, chanting monks. Awesome, the hippies say. The coolest, man. You've *got* to see it. Difficult not to enjoy their goofy enthusiasm.

12.12.76. Afternoon and early evening at U Bein, a two-hundred-year-old teak footbridge crossing shallow Taungthaman Lake for more than a kilometer. The Burmese are madly proud of it. I have no idea why. Everyone you ask is keen to talk about how the mayor after whom it was named took the wood from a decaying palace. How it was built back when the U.S. was busy drafting its Constitution. Running low on film. Got to shoot sparingly. What's great about taking these photos, Taru, is knowing they allow us to make my experience yours. You can carry it with you. You can keep it in your pocket like a memory you've both had and haven't had.

12.12.76. Teachers. You can tell, a fat French diplomat in a floppy hat and red face out for a stroll told me, because they're wearing the emblematic green sarong-like wraps called *longyi*. Somehow, watching them draw near, I'm reminded the primary mode of every trip is the *non-finito*.

12.12.76. Jesus, where the hell did Thanksgiving go? Lining up this shot in the viewfinder, I just remembered. Did you and Robert celebrate with all the trimmings? ~~Granted it's my vanity, but~~ I can't get my mind around an image of your dinner table without me filling one of its chairs. Was he as infuriatingly sardonic as ever? I don't know how you put up with all that self-righteous derisiveness. Sorry. More proof, I'm sure, of your angelic status and my bone-headed selfishness. In Bhutan, the hippies told me, there are only a few dozen personal names. They're used for both men and women, in any combination. The name, the self, just isn't that important. How can you not want to visit a place like that?

12.12.76. Today, an anthology for you. Asked if he traveled much, Thoreau responded: *Yes—around Concord.* Freud said that travel's pleasure is rooted in a refutation of the father. *I love to travel*, Einstein once wrote, *but hate to arrive.* *The world is a book*, Augustine once wrote, *and those who do not travel read only one page.* G. K. Chesterton: *The traveler sees what he sees, the tourist sees what he has come to see.* George Bernard Shaw: *I dislike feeling at home when I am abroad.* Albert Camus: *What gives value to travel is fear.* Edward Dahlberg: *When one realizes life is worthless he either commits suicide or travels.* *I met a lot of people in Europe*, James Baldwin confessed upon his return; *I even encountered myself.* I asked the man who sold me a can of warm Coke at a wooden cart at the end of the bridge why I haven't seen any hospitals in Burma. *If old, sick*, he explained, *don't travel to see doctor. Travel to cemetery to look for better place.*

12.14.76. On the river again, heading north. Looks like I'm leaving
the last Westerners behind, thank god. Haven't seen another white
face since yesterday. Will mail these next packages from Katha.

12.15.76. Woke in a dingy room in a Rangoon guesthouse nearly a month and a half ago, thinking: *I've made it. This is the end of the world. There's nothing more beyond.* Woke today on the deck of a ferry in a place more remote than I've ever imagined a place could be, aching from trying to sleep on the floorboards, surrounded by passengers coughing up morning phlegm, and I looked over the side, and I saw this, and I realized I'm just starting out, Taru. This is just the beginning. This is the first sentence.

12.16.76. They showed up out of nowhere at dawn, these boats, our own floating supermarket and fast-food joints. I bought a couple bananas, a bowl of ~~lentil soup~~ daal for breakfast. Can't shake the idea of Bhutan. The hippies said there aren't any horizontal surfaces there. Everywhere you look, you're surrounded by layer upon layer of mountains tumbling toward the snowcapped Himalayas cragged in the distance. People wear traditional robes dating back to the seventeenth century. I forget what they're called. The men hold daily archery matches in village pastures. Families paint large red, angry, windswept phalluses with wings on the sides of their houses for good luck in matters of fertility. Everyone possesses an almost childlike naiveté about the outside world. Everyone is always ready to greet you with an uncomplicated smile.

12.17.76. The river mucky, overripe. Faint whiff of sewage hangs
in the air. The sun is outrageously, exasperatingly brutal. Even
though we're moving, you can't sense any breeze. The afternoons
have been unbearable. When twilight starts coming on, you expect
a reprieve, but there's absolutely nothing. Everything remains
dead, ~~dead, dead~~. Except, of course, the mosquitoes. For a while,
you try to slap them off, then you just give up and go back to
whatever you were doing. I've got fucking bites everywhere—
even across my scalp, down my pants. To pass time last evening, I
tried striking up a conversation with this skinny old guy with gray
stubble across his head and face. He was sitting beside me, staring
over the railing, smoking a home-rolled cheroot. I waved my hand
along the shoreline, grinned so he could see my pleasure, exclaimed
beautiful, beautiful! He didn't blink. Didn't even turn to see who
was talking. I thought maybe he hadn't heard me, so I repeated
myself. He huffed, rose, and shuffled away without even glancing
in my direction.

12.19.76. Ashore in Katha. Small blue wooden and cement houses mostly hidden by bo-tree groves. As you come up from the dock, a large prison surrounded by tall windowless pinkish-orange walls and thatched turret. Same pagoda's spire rising above the foliage like a slender gold spear that Orwell saw when he arrived two days before Christmas in 1926 to take up his godforsaken post as Assistant Superintendent of the British Imperial Police here, hating the world for doing this to him. Horse-drawn wagons, bicycles, people on foot, but no cars, no motorbikes, no tuk-tuks, no engines whatsoever. Nothing to do but wander, pass the slow time in the cafés, grin at the locals who grin back at you in this part of the country, perhaps doing no more than mimicking instinctively what they see on your face. Cheap room in a shack at the edge of town. Stifling. Worlds stiller, more humid, than in the south. You splash a little water on yourself when you wake up and three seconds later you're sweating again. Strolling the streets, head foggy with heat, it seems I'm recalling someone else's recollections.

12.20.76. When a friend of John Steinbeck's gave him a small stone from the Roman forum as a present, the author graciously accepted and thanked him. On his next visit to Italy, Steinbeck carried the stone with him and put it back where he thought it might go.

12.20.76. Gold leaf peeling like a bad skin condition on a Buddha. Outside the pagoda, a wonderful sign, weirdly in English, above the door of an unpainted shed the size of two outhouses placed side by side: *Trekking, Tours, & Construction Lubrication.*

12.21.76. Feeding of the monks—thereby putting the country's poor on the back of the country's poor. Yet another religion, as Werner would no doubt have pointed out, that teaches a population how not to think for itself. I miss that bastard and his cronies. Last night's dinner: lamb with yogurt, bowl of rice, bottle of horrid bitter local beer at a dark café smelling acrid and musty. Some part of it didn't agree with me. Under the weather this morning. Yesterday I was ready to stay here a week. Today I can't wait to move on. Will head down to the dock later to check on the next ferry out.

Let's call it, say, the 23ʳᵈ or 24ᵗʰ. Seem to have lost a day or two in there somewhere. Head won't clear. Fucking stomach cramps and diarrhea again last night. Toilet a hole in the deck in a niche behind a shabby curtain. Shit bits splattered everywhere. ~~You have to squat to go and~~ You have to squat to go & while you're at it the kids onboard poke their noses in to see what a Westerner laid low looks like. Will disembark in one of the villages upstream strike off west by foot. Hitchhike all going well. ~~Improvize~~ Improvise like those daffy hippies, only in reverse. Should be on the Indian border within a week. 10 days at most. Another week or 10 days into Bhutan, another to Paro and the Tiger's Nest. How's this for living, Taru?

A shaky shot of my fellow deck dwellers. Sorry. Days you sit with your legs dangling over the side of the ~~hell~~ hull, staring through the railing at the low sliding landscape. Nothing changes. Living off tea and bananas. Stomach won't settle. Kids on board haven't seen blond hair before. Between that and my bouts of the fucking backdoor trots I guess I'm serving as some pretty rich entertainment for the natives. They gather round and point at my floppy hat. I remove it. They titter scatter cautiously return. I perform act two. The bravest among them point at my beard wanting to touch it but in the end they just can't bring themselves to close those last few millimeters between the known and unknown. ~~The captain this short guy with dark crinkled skin and three teeth to his name speaks almost unintelligible English. He either told me or didn't tell me we'll be pulling in to the next village tomorrow morning we'll see~~

My last shot for you Taru. Film's gone and nowhere to pick up more. That's my road. Somewhere down there the mountains separating Burma/India. Wish I cld shake this fucking bug sweat it out or something. Still don't think I'd change a thing. Want to say this is what it feels like to pay attention. Will try to put a few miles behind me bfr nightfall.

stupid fuck. tried sleeping in my sleeping bag in some brush beneath some trees by the side of the road so much for fucking oneness with nature. insects impossible. cldnt stop thinking about snakes & hungry rats. hot dizzy nauseous. way too go.

wagon stuffed with burlap bags of brown rice stopped to pick me up midafternoon. dirt road color of powdered turmeric width of sidewalk. ruts good ~~feet~~ foot deep hit one your nearly jettisoned. driver about my age—wearing odd combination of blue buttondown shirt azure longyi yellow rubber flipflops. oblivious to evrythng save next stretch of road. his blank face says this is just what he does/who he is. stopped for a pee break 10 minutes ago. offered me a triangle of betelnut leaves. raised my hand indicating i'd pass & he looks at me like i'd raised my fist to hit him fever im pretty sure. nights in what passes for guesthouses around here—smoky thatched huts with hard dirt floors & fire pits. ~~flees~~ fleas relentless buggers. werner would no doubt call attention to the fact that this culture hasnt quite gotten around to inventing the chimney. sleep in one corner beside the driver & family that owns the place in the other everyone snoring like pigs. maybe try to retrace my steps only might take longer to reach mandalay than pushing on to paro. shit if I know.

driver asks for a little more cash every day they lure you into a sense of comradeship then out comes the fucking old upturned palm fell getting out of goddamn wagon yesterday evening sprained wrist writing lefty sorry dot/dash kindergarten scrawl taru what a fuckup i am heres what its all about moving through the world knowingly

legs all watery this morning what the fuck???

night sweats feels like someones splashed me with a bucket of water lightheaded low on $$$ will wire you for more from train station in lumding be watching ok? —love me my ~~inamim~~ inanimate possessions miss me most im sure cuz only i know how to arrange them my desktop what likes to sit with what my books photographs black leather writing chair yellow notepad blurry white sunlight in living room

parted ways with driver the fucker good were getting somewhere
striking off on foot today up trail maybe 6 hrs 6 or 7 to border
amazing blue sky u should see

blood in stool   bees in hea

[NOTE TORN, TEXT MISSING]

sky like turquoise ice

[NOTE TORN, TEXT MISSING]

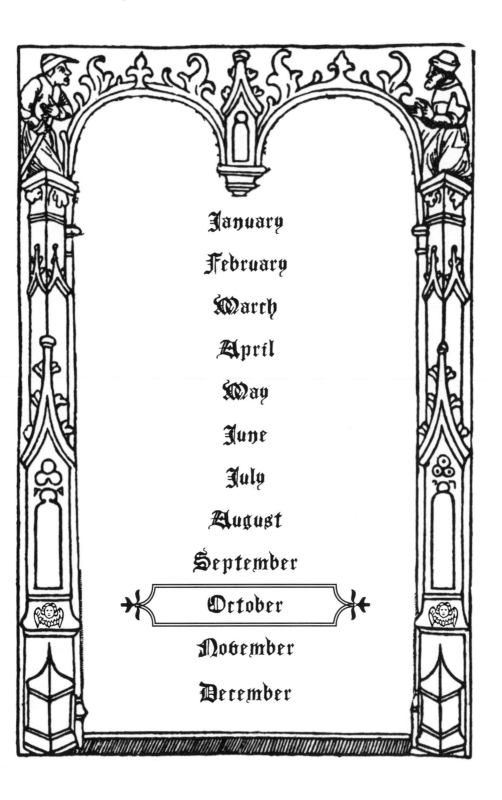

January

February

March

April

May

June

July

August

September

October

November

December

It was lunchtime and they were all standing in the sunny kitchen watching Estelle put the finishing touches on their spicy-apple-and-turkey salad, pretending Naomi hadn't just said what Naomi had just said.

Jean had been describing her latest series of watercolors. They consisted of greenblue abstractions of coastlines and marshlands seen from the air. Leaning back against the marble countertop, Dan sipped his gin and tonic and listened. Naomi's new boyfriend, Ron, a dumpy stockbroker with rabbity veneers, was talking sports with Robert by the large windows with sheer curtains overlooking Central Park. Outside the Indian summer was a motionless hazy orange. Somewhere in the background the air conditioning kept clicking on and off. Coolness gusted through the room and then almost at once it started getting uncomfortably warm and dense again.

From what Dan could pick up, Ron used to work as a legal aid on the Lower East Side, but the pay wasn't any good. He quit the day he turned thirty and went back to school. Now he was a stockbroker specializing in the water sector and had more money than he knew what to do with. Dan only spoke with him a minute or two when they were introduced, yet already didn't much like him. Ron tried to disguise his ambition with fake affability. He seemed to think he was getting away with something when he merely looked obvious and pushy.

How about that baseball strike, huh? Dan heard Ron say to Robert at full volume across the room and decided to exist as far away from him as possible this afternoon.

At the counter Jean explained: I wanted to create the same sense of shift in perspective the first people who went up in hot air balloons experienced. You know, like the whole world changes from trees and roads and buildings and cars and ponds to this pastel patchwork of rectangles, squares, and circles. You suddenly perceive everything completely differently.

They sound amazing, Estelle said. She was slicing a surreally red tomato with a big German knife. When do we get to see?

Oooh, what's this? Naomi asked, picking up a spice bottle full of bright yellow powder off the geometric black metal rack that looked like it had been designed by Frank Lloyd Wright.

I'm not exactly sure, said Estelle. I swear it must have come with the place.

Maybe we could wear it instead of eating it, Naomi proposed.

It's an incredible color, said Jean. Why don't they make summer dresses that color?

Naomi put back the bottle and crossed to the refrigerator. She poured crushed ice from a bag in the freezer into a sleek Finnish pitcher, then crossed to the sink and began filling the pitcher with water through a Brita filter. She used to wear a different-color wig every day of the week. Last spring she stopped, cut her hair short and spiky like Laurie Anderson, and dyed parts silver blond, parts black.

You know who I saw last week? she asked, her tone downgrading into confidentiality.

Do tell, Estelle said.

Estelle didn't look up from her work until Naomi pronounced Jerome's name. Jean glanced over at Dan. Dan examined his drink and took a self-conscious swallow. On the wall behind the dining nook hung a smallish Motherwell ninety percent golden yellow and ten percent black blob in the lower right corner. Dan studied it, resolving to enjoy the experience.

At the CVS on Bleeker, Naomi said.

It's the saddest thing in the world, Estelle announced, slicing the surreally red tomato into surreally red wedges.

I knew he didn't want me to see him. So you know what I did? I ducked around to the next aisle. Am I pathetic or what? I felt like crap, standing among mouthwash products and floss. But, Jesus, he's aged so goddamn *much*. You wouldn't believe. He shuffles around with that cane like a little old man, cheeks all sunken. And you should see how much weight he's lost. What do you say to someone like that?

Where was Jarmo? Jean said, concerned. Jarmo should have been there. He should be with him everywhere he goes these days.

Maybe he was writing, Estelle said. Running errands. Who knows?

I already miss him, said Jean. He's not even gone yet, and I miss him like crazy.

We should call, Estelle suggested. This afternoon. You know, all of us. Just pick up the phone and say hi. Gossip a little. Get his mind off things.

Hey, Ron said, strolling over with Robert. Ron flaunted the kind of low paunch that makes some middle-aged men appear to be in their second trimesters. He was stiff-kneed, flat-footed. Dan couldn't help thinking of Donald Duck. Any of you guys happen to catch *Forrest Gump*? It's one of those movies that's funny as hell and yet sends you away thinking all at the same time.

Yeah, Robert said, deadpan. You mean like about when we decided to make the village idiot with a box of chocolates our national hero?

Ron bobbled his head like one of those baseball dolls in car windows and silently impersonated a laugh, raising and lowering his shoulders, but no sound came out. I know exactly what you mean, he said. That's what I thought when I saw it the first time. Only, trust me, it's about *so* much more.

Really?

Robert held the vowel cluster an extra pulse.

Oh, sure, Ron said. Like how the innocent can have this *major* impact on other people with their, um, innocence. And how we all need to have, you know, better outlooks on life. Sometimes we need to be reminded. We take so much for granted in this country. It's a cliché and all, but it's true.

Everyone stopped talking temporarily to ingest this, trying to figure out the degree of irony Ron was utilizing.

Did you happen to notice the shrimp-catching scene? Jean asked.

What shrimp-catching scene? Estelle said.

The one after the hurricane, where they're dumping their full nets onto the deck of that boat. Take a look. The shrimps are all headless.

They're not, Estelle said.

They are, said Jean. No kidding. Fresh from Safeway.

With that, they launched into a conversation about the strengths and weaknesses of the film, even though Robert and Estelle admitted immediately that they hadn't seen it, had no intention of doing so. Robert dismissed it as shallow, glib, and monotonous. Estelle said she hated movies that manipulated audiences into experiencing a sense of reckless comfort about life. Ron looked cornered and confused. He tried to defend the work on the grounds that it was complex in its very simplicity, only he had a difficult time citing specifics and he kept contradicting himself. Soon he fell back to saying it was all just this feeling he got.

Estelle excused herself and slipped into the dining room to set the table. Naomi dropped away to help. Jean wandered over to the spice rack and picked up the bottle with the yellow powder in it and held it up to the sunlight to admire it some more. Robert and Dan leaned against the marble counter, taking sips from their drinks and studying their shoe tips in a way that suggested they might or might not be listening to what Ron had to say.

Ron's diminished audience only unnerved him further. Yet he kept going as though he were talking to a room full of people until

Estelle whisked back in to interrupt him gaily and announce lunch was ready.

She drove her guests into the dining room with merry amplified goat-herder gestures, where everyone gathered around the green-tinted glass table with the solitary sunflower in a green-tinted glass vase in the middle. Estelle came in behind them and pointed each to his or her seat. Once they had unfolded their napkins and complimented the salads, Naomi said: Did you hear about the circus elephant that went berserk in Honolulu? It killed its trainer and made a break for it.

Oh, god, Jean said. I know. Wasn't that terrible?

Poor thing, Estelle said. It must have been *petrified*. She skewered a beige chunk of turkey meat with her fork, raised it to her lips, then noticed everyone was waiting for her. Eat, eat, she said, waving her hand at the food before them.

Poor thing? said Robert. Imagine how the trainer must have felt.

So what happened? asked Ron.

The police had to shoot it eighty-six times before it went down, Naomi said, chewing.

Dan noticed she had a dark strand of spinach stuck between her front teeth.

Eighty-six? Ron said.

They have the whole thing on film. This is absolutely delicious, Estelle. You're amazing. Apparently the elephant was a juvenile delinquent. Last year it tore up a mosque in Pennsylvania and terrorized all these school kids out on a field trip.

What's a mosque doing in Pennsylvania? Robert asked.

When we were kids, Ron said, we got to go to the planetarium and ice-cream-making factories.

Yeah, said Estelle. What's next? Gas stations?

I think your elephant was just trying to distance itself from the GOP, Robert suggested. But, then again, who wouldn't? Did you hear Dick Armey's latest pearl? *I've been to Europe once,* he told this reporter. *I don't have to go again.*

As opposed, you're saying, said Estelle, to our great communicator who can't keep his slick willy inside his britches? Now there's a mensch for you.

Oh, *please*, said Robert. He swished sparkling wine in his mouth, savoring. Nice. Like we're supposed to believe the allegations of an Arkansas hick with bad makeup and a schnozz that would've made Jimmy Durante blush.

You mean Bubba?

You're a riot, dearest. I mean Paula (he slid into a bad southern accent) I Think I'll Just Sit on My Ass In This Here Trailer Park Three Years Till Bill's Elected President of the Goddamn U. S. of A. Before Uttering a Peep So I Can Make Some Mighty Big Sorghum Boodle Jones. Gimme a break. At least Clinton doesn't go backing Nicaraguan Contras.

That we know of, sweet pea, Estelle said, that we know of.

Sorghum? Jean repeated. *Boodle?*

Words, admittedly, one is required to use sparingly, Robert said. Not unlike *catawampus* and, well (he looked up at the ceiling, searching his memory), *spondulics.* Imagine on how few occasions one's lips form such sounds over the course of an average lifetime.

Flibbertigibbet, Naomi offered. *Bloviate. Supposititious.*

Dactylonomy, said Jean.

Dactylonomy? Ron asked.

The operation to remove an ugly metrical foot, Robert offered.

Close, smarty pants, Jean said. It's the art of counting on your fingers sans abacus. As in the Middle East before Allah knows when.

Now explain to me why, Estelle asked, if you have a perfectly good abacus in your galabeya, you would want to use your fingers to count.

Robert looked at her over the top of his wine glass.

What? she said.

I once had the wrong tooth removed, Ron volunteered. I was a kid. Well, it wasn't the wrong tooth. Teeth. They were the right teeth, but they weren't supposed to be removed. At least I didn't know they were supposed to be removed. Neither did my mother. Or, um, the orthodontist, evidently. Until he removed them, I mean. See—this was when I was getting fitted for braces—he was just fishing around inside my mouth, like orthodontists do, when all of a sudden he picked up those pliers thingies of his and started twisting.

Twisting? Estelle said.

Without any novocaine or laughing gas. Yeah.

Aggggh, said Naomi. Which reminds me. I had to stay in the dorm my first Thanksgiving at Sarah Lawrence? My parents were biking in Switzerland or some such cultivated shit, and I hadn't befriended any of the neurotic black-bereted fembots known as my peers yet. So I cooked up these hotdogs and beans on my electric burner and read Dostoevsky for my world masterpieces class. *Notes from Underground.* How sad is *that?*

Which has exactly *what* to do with being attacked by your dentist? Estelle asked.

I'm getting to that. I'm getting to that. See, there was this other loser staying in the dorm that weekend. This gal lived five rooms down from me and had long black hair and an Italian name that sounded not unlike a kind of pasta. We had the place all to ourselves. She was, it so happened, in possession of a pistachio-green canister of laughing gas.

In possession of?

Her boyfriend was busy finding himself in some microbially challenged country. He'd left it behind as a going-away present. So every night she turned up her stereo loud as it'd go and put on the 45 of "A Day in the Life." "A Day in the Life"! She had it set so that when it reached the end the record would automatically start playing again. It repeated—I'm guessing conservatively here—about fifty thousand times in a row while this girl sat in the hallway in her black bra and panties, sucking at the canister, racing her pet turtles.

She had pet turtles, said Robert. Of course. Why not?

Romulus and Remus. We were all pretentious little twits back then, weren't we? She'd painted peace signs on their shells with metallic lime nail polish. Every time I passed on my way to the john, she pretended I wasn't there. Come to think of it, I don't think she was pretending. She'd probably gone temporarily blind in her pharmaceutical euphoria.

Is laughing gas technically a pharmaceutical? Estelle wondered.

Are you familiar with our new neighbor, Amélie Tautau? asked Robert. From across the hall? The TV star?

The so-called TV star, Estelle corrected.

The so-called TV star married to the so-called shipping magnate, Robert said. With the very loud soi-disant dog. You can't hear it now. Naturally. That's because the fucker waits until we're all asleep or resting comfortably before . . . well, it doesn't so much bark as yrip. Yrip, yrip, yrip. Yrip, yrip, yrip.

You're not going to tell this story while we're eating, Estelle said, are you?

Ron meaningfully ticked his veneers with his fingernail in Naomi's direction. Naomi stared back at him, stumped. He mouthed the word *spinach*.

She didn't understand.

Spinach, he repeated in an exaggerated whisper. *Here.*

Crap, she said. *Crap.* Sorry. She brought her napkin to her mouth and fiddled behind it. When she lowered it again and displayed her teeth for Ron's inspection, the blackgreen wormish coil was still there. Ron became a mime and Naomi mirrored his gestures. It took two more attempts to remove the culprit.

So, Robert began once everybody had settled down and refocused on him. I happened to be strolling through the Park yesterday morning when who do I see? She's out walking her little rat dog in one of those little rat-dog vests. Faux tartan. I kid you not. I pass by just as said little rat-dog finishes taking a little rat-dog shit. And you know what our illustrious so-called TV star does? After carefully picking up the little rat-dog shit in a special baggy-glove patterned with daisies, our illustrious so-called TV star extracts a Kleenex from her Versace purse, kneels down, and wipes her little rat-dog's little rat-dog ass.

She *didn't*! Naomi screamed in delight.

She did, said Robert. The rat-dog seemed to be not wholly averse to the gesture.

That's unconditionally hideous, Jean said.

Thanks for sharing, honey buns, said Estelle.

My pleasure, angel face. What, I couldn't help wondering to myself, is the social protocol at such a delicate nexus? Now imagine me there, watching our illustrious et cetera with the wad of soiled Kleenex in hand. I had to think on my feet.

Robert leaned back, raised his glass as if about to offer a toast, and grinned like a python.

So what did you *do*? Naomi asked.

I did what any self-respecting gentleman would do. I smiled graciously at her, and, ambling by, hands in my pockets, said casually: Hello, Mrs. Tautau. I absolutely *adored* your work in *The Flintstones*.

But she wasn't in *The Flintstones*, Naomi said.

Precisely, Robert said.

Laughter washed back and forth across the table.

Estelle leveled a flat look at her husband. Robert opened his eyes wide and puckered his lips, feigning surprise, then stood and began refilling everyone's wine glass. Naomi dabbed a tear from the corner of her eye with a napkined knuckle. Ron glanced from person to person, flummoxed. Jean took another bite of salad and chewed with a queen's stateliness.

Would anyone like some more? Estelle asked when everyone had settled again. There are simply *heaps* left.

It's scrumptious, Naomi said, but I'm stuffed. I literally can't eat another bite or I'll burst.

Me either, said Ron. What a great lunch.

This dental attack business, by the way, Jean said, fingering

the spoon beside her plate distractedly, is exactly why Dan and I
don't trust doctors anymore. At some point in the not-too-distant
past, some shady organization kidnapped them all, extracted their
hearts, and filled the resultant cavities with Snapple.

I think they refer to those organizations as HMOs, Robert said,
don't they?

Doctors used to sit down and shoot the breeze with you, Naomi
said. Ask how your mother was. Talk about the latest exhibit at the
Guggenheim. Now you open your mouth and, bang, they're bored.
Mine has his technician explain to me what pills to take because he
doesn't want to be bothered. When did *that* happen?

When I was a kid, mine used to give me lollipops if I was a good
little girl, Estelle said, pushing back, rising, beginning to clear the
dishes. Jean and Naomi rose to help. Actually, he gave me lollipops
if I was a bad little girl, too. I couldn't wait to see him.

They jabber on and on about the evils of socialized medicine,
said Robert, then turn around and treat you like you might as well
be living in France. *Quelle horreur.*

They're holding our cholesterol hostage, Jean said.

To be perfectly fair, Estelle said as she rounded the corner into
the kitchen, they *do* have children to put through golf school.

You should have seen the way they treated Dan after his mugging,
said Jean. It was inexcusable.

Mugging? Ron said.

Good lord, Robert said. So *you're* the sole member of our species
who hasn't heard about that. Our poor Dan here was mugged—
what?—five or six years ago on his way home from dinner with us.

Eight, Dan said.

No! Naomi called from the kitchen. *Eight?*

Glasses and utensils clinked and jangled through the doorway. The
refrigerator thumped shut with a rattle, opened, thumped shut again.
Dan could hear the women strike up their own conversation.

A minute later, Jean appeared carrying two bowls of blueberries
and cream.

Ta-da, she said.

Wow, Ron said. Mmmmmmm.

Dan was just back from doing a piece on Chernobyl, Jean explained. Right, honey? She set down the first bowl in front of Robert, the second in front of Ron. I couldn't go along that evening because I had this cold from hell. I stayed home gorging on Dristan.

Yeah, said Dan. I decided to walk. It was a beautiful evening. I didn't think twice. Somebody jumped me on Park Avenue, knocked me down, roughed me up a little.

That's awful, Ron said.

And the weird part is, Estelle said, emerging with Naomi and the rest of the desserts, the guy didn't take anything. Not a thing.

It's like they say in disaster pieces, said Dan: everything happened so fast. I was just walking along, minding my own business, and all of a sudden *wham*. Next thing I knew, it was over and I was in the emergency room.

Tell Ron what he wanted, Jean said. The guy. She took her first mouthful, closed her eyes, relished. If I've been good and go to heaven when I die, this is what I'll get to eat every day.

There I was, Dan said, down on the sidewalk, covering my head, trying not to get beat up too bad, right? And this guy? He keeps calling me Kenneth and demanding to know what the frequency is. How creepy is *that*?

What frequency? Ron asked. Who's Kenneth?

Welcome to New York, said Robert.

Looking back, Dan said, it somehow doesn't seem like that big a deal. He chewed a while, swallowed. People get assaulted in New York all the time, don't they?

Yeah, Estelle said. Only most don't get songs written about it.

Songs? said Ron.

This band called Game Theory did something in . . . oh, I guess it was 1987. R.E.M. has a track about it on their new album. I've heard it. It's pretty catchy.

And, Estelle said, get *this*. Letterman asked Mr. Modest here to sing backup with them when they perform it on *The Late Show*.

You're *kidding*, Ron said. You know Michael Stipes?

I don't *know* him know him, said Dan, but I've bumped into him a couple times. He seems like a nice enough guy. Talks as if words are hundred-dollar bills and he doesn't have much in the bank. As opposed to, say, Letterman. Letterman uses this weird frivolous inflection saturated with irony when he's talking to you. You never know if he means what he's saying, or means the opposite of what he's saying, or doesn't mean anything at all.

Wow, Ron said.

Anyway, two weeks ago, out of the blue, I get this call from a guy named Dietz. Park Dietz. Great name, huh? He's a psychiatrist, and he says he's interviewing that lunatic who shot the NBC stagehand outside Rockefeller Center last summer.

Oh yeah, Naomi said. What was all *that* about?

The guy thought the TV networks were beaming messages into his head. During his interview with Dietz, he confessed he was also the one who mugged me. Evidently, I'd been tormenting his brainwaves, too. The police sent over a couple of mug shots. It was him, all right. At least, I'm pretty sure. I mean, I saw his face for like a couple of seconds nearly a decade ago, right?

Talking, Dan reached over and rubbed the back of Jean's neck. She leaned into his palm. It appeared to be a spontaneous act of affection, but was in fact their private sign for wanting to leave. They lingered a little longer and then, patting Dan on the knee, Jean announced they should be taking off because they still had some errands to run this afternoon.

In the foyer, everyone air-kissed and hugged. Robert stepped up behind Dan and patted him on the back, letting his hand loiter on his shoulder as they all agreed jovially that they had to do this again soon.

On their way down in the elevator, Jean and Dan chatted amiably with Naomi and Ron about their plans for the rest of the autumn. Pushing through the revolving doors onto the sidewalk, the damp stagnant heat took away Dan's breath. During lunch he had forgotten about what it was like outside, and now the day arrived as a blow.

Naomi and Ron took the first cab. The air conditioning in the second was so weak Dan had trouble telling if it was really air conditioning or just the fan set on high. Jean recited their address to the Pakistani driver wearing a light blue turban. The driver, who struck Dan as sullen and angry, replied in an accent so viscous that Jean had to ask him to say what he had said twice before it became clear he was just repeating the address she had given him to make sure he had gotten it right.

The taxi accelerated away from the curb and swerved into traffic, fishing among the other cars. Settling back, Dan took a deep breath and pressed shut his eyes. He felt wobbly in the close air and became aware of himself beginning to perspire.

Well, that wasn't so bad, Jean asked, was it?

Dan exhaled and opened his eyes. He reached down and stroked her hand absentmindedly. Up front, the driver honked at something and started talking to himself. The cab jerked abruptly left, then right.

It was tedious as hell, Dan said. Hey, is it hot in here? Then to the driver: Excuse me. *Excuse me.* Could you please turn up the AC a little?

Can't do, can't do, the driver said over his shoulder without looking back.

That Ron guy was insufferable, Dan said. And the Robert and Estelle Show is starting to get really, really old. Have you ever noticed that if the topic isn't about them, they don't find it interesting?

They never ask anyone else a single question, you mean.

They just bide their time until someone finishes speaking so they can continue being witty.

Jean focused her attention out the side window.

They used to be so funny, she said. Remember how they used to make us just . . . oh, I don't know. Feel good. Like we were all part of some goofy little club?

We genuinely used to look forward to seeing them.

Naomi was always the sweetest thing. She made everyone feel special. Remember how she had this way of recalling details you mentioned to her in passing three months earlier? How's Danjack's sprained ankle doing? Did Dawn finally decide on Dartmouth or Amherst? She was terrific with that sort of thing.

When did she start dating what's-his-name?

I heard they met through one of those online services. Apparently he wowed her with his emails. She's getting older. She doesn't want to be alone anymore.

Who can blame her? Except that guy adds exactly nothing to the equation. Every time you're around him, you feel you've just wasted a few minutes of your life.

Estelle said Naomi told her they have great sex.

Do I want to know this?

They make videos of it.

Dan looked past her to see what she was seeing. Three teenage girls in black padded racing shorts and tank tops with red highlights rollerbladed down the sidewalk. They were all talking on cell phones. They seemed unaware of each other's presence even though their shoulders were almost touching and they all wore the same bouncy, angled, layered dark-blonde shag Jennifer Aniston was currently wearing in that television show.

When the taxi jounced to a halt at a stoplight, Dan realized his shirt back was wet. He hoisted himself up and reached into his right pocket for his handkerchief and dabbed his gummy forehead and neck. He wasn't feeling quite right.

When did it start getting this hot in October? he asked.

Maybe we should put a little space between them and us, Jean proposed.

It's something to think about.

You know what gets me? What gets me is you imagine you'd learn, only you never really do. One week you're visiting friends, believing you have everything in common with them. The next it's as if you've never met them before. You don't even like them. Maybe you even find them sort of embarrassing. Why is that?

You wouldn't consider being friends with them if you weren't already friends with them.

On the corner sat a cross-legged black man in a red, green, and yellow Rastafarian tam. A pond of knock-off designer purses laid out neatly on white sheets surrounded him.

The stoplight changed. The taxi shot forward.

Estelle wants me to go with her to the new thing at MOMA, Jean said.

Tell her you're busy, said Dan.

He hoisted himself up again, tucked away his handkerchief, extracted his wallet.

She knows I'm not, Jean said. I already told her I was free.

Tell her you thought you were free, but it turns out you're not. Tell her you're sorry. You two will have to take a rain check. She'll understand.

Dan consulted the meter and began counting out bills.

Two weeks, and she'll just ask me to do something else.

You'll be busy then, too.

And after that?

You'll still be busy. You had no idea how much you had going on this fall. She's a smart girl. She'll eventually get the message.

My stomach hurts just thinking about it.

That's why most people choose to attend one tiresome dinner party after another with ex-friends who don't understand yet that they're ex-friends. They don't want to let anyone down. They want everyone to like them.

Okay, fine, Jean said. But say you break things off. Say you do that. You still run the risk of bumping into your ex-friends at future social functions. What are you supposed to do *then*?

You strike the same affable tone you would if you ran into a boyfriend from high school. You smile. You ask them how they're doing. You wish them well. You make excuses. You leave. In the end, nobody really cares, so nobody's really hurt.

The taxi pulled up to the curb in front of their brownstone. Jean cracked open her door, but waited for Dan to pay before sliding out. He told the driver to keep two dollars. The driver said something Dan couldn't understand and passed him a fistful of money over his shoulder while avoiding his eyes. Dan consulted his change without actually counting it and then slid out.

His right foot felt funny, like it had gone to sleep.

A scrunch-faced boy wearing a t-shirt that said YOU CAN'T SEE ME blasted by on his silver twelve-speed.

People don't change, Dan said when Jean joined him. As they get older, they just become more like themselves. You have your purse?

Got it, Jean said.

Dan slipped his arm around her waist and was startled by how chunky she had become.

Behind them, the taxi unpeeled from the curb.

Dan tried to take a step toward the stoop and fetched up.

The surprising sensation that something was pulling at his right ankle arrived between one inhalation and the next.

Just a second here, he said.

He leaned against Jean, lifted his foot, and massaged it above the bony knobs sticking out on both sides. He straightened again and felt blurry. He had felt fine. Now he felt blurry.

You okay, hon? Jean asked.

I'm fine. It's just . . .

He had to close his eyes to steady himself. The blurriness became thicker. Then the universe canted. It seemed to him he was lying on his back on the sidewalk and standing up at the same time.

Jean's voice dropped into the distance.

Dan? it was saying. *Dan? Dan?*

It felt like something was yanking at his right ankle. Dan looked down to check. Yeah. That's what it was. Something was definitely

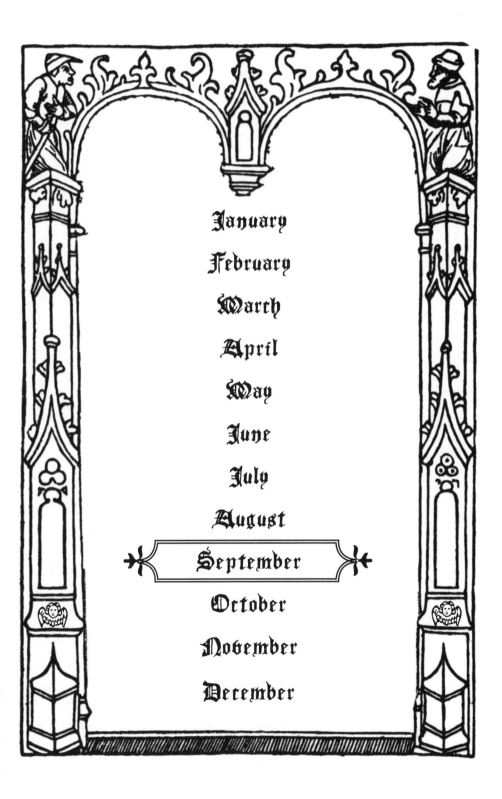

January

February

March

April

May

June

July

August

September

October

November

December

yanking at his right ankle. He wants to say claws. Peculiar paradox: numb from neck down, he is distinctly aware of the insistent jerk, rest, jerk, rest, jerk. Yet what really gains the painter's attention is the recognition that he has never before actually *seen* the ceiling.

All these years loitering beneath it, and he has never once fully taken it in. He imagines extending his arm up, up, up to touch it, the veiny wood, the tiny prickle on his fingertips. *Prickle.* Admirable noun. The grain flowing northeast to southwest forms the amorphous contour of a—of a what? A massive eye, plausibly, gazing down, as God is not, from heaven. Or, conceivably, the head of an ant? Yet the lips. If insect, where would the lips be? Not lips. *Pincers.* Another moment of admirableness in a world of widowed words and orphaned phrases.

At the upper left, a smudge. Ivory? Puppet perception. No: ivory with a suggestion of zinc. No: ivory with a suggestion of zinc with a suggestion of—how to say it?—hue of an extended dove's wing on a winter morning in a church steeple with a light snow falling.

How can you claim membership among the living if you cannot name such a simple color?

Wake me from this narcosis.

The yanking becomes more pronounced. Bosch raises his reeling head inconsiderably to have a look around. Founders. The base of his skull clumps plank. He retracts his chin, stretches his neck, can barely make out the small devil tugging at his right ankle. Body of ape. Head of beetle. Claws of crab. Bosch is unsurprised. This caller has dropped by before. It is presently endeavoring to drag him toward the black yawn in the floorboards half a meter away, although admittedly having quite a troublesome time. The devil pants and slobbers, snickers and growls. Another bluewhite squall surges through Bosch's body. He hiccup-groans. The devil jumps. Freezes.

Time hangs.

Time hangs.

When it is apparent Bosch presents no imminent threat to the fiend, it crouches to resume its loud toil.

Bosch has the impression the thing is talking to itself. He cannot distinguish individual phrases, no, but the overall sense is one of Anglo-Saxon rather than Latinate discourse. No sooner has the painter enjoyed this knowledge than his tongue slips back in his throat, slick and swollen as an elongated oyster. Of a sudden gargling, Bosch squeezes shut his eyes, thinking he is opening them. Or he opens them, thinking he is squeezing them shut. Either way, without warning he sees himself as a young pock-faced boy lying on his stomach in his attic room on an overcast Sunday afternoon, the great fire having burned itself into his imagination, the great rebuilding having commenced.

The young Bosch is drawing, filling sheet after sheet with figures of fauna—donkeys, dogfish, duckbills, tigers, newts, narwhals, nighthawks, dung beetles, dragon flies, dolphins—and then carefully separating their paper heads from their paper bodies with a fillet knife, wing from thorax, arm from trunk, tail from arse, so as to coin new chimeras by pasting together bits from the originals on a fresh sheet. It did not matter, so far as he could see, that he had never observed a squid or skink in person. He had heard stories, read descriptions, seen sketches, and what else did a fellow with a whiffet of imagination need to fashion beasts that interested him canyons more than those boring old brutes he suffered every day beyond his bedroom window?

Stretching out on his tummy, alive in his head, the boy Bosch always became someone else. He glanced up and it was one o'clock. He glanced up and it was five. Stretching out, he experienced the same thrill that sparrowed through him every time, closing his eyes, he skated faster and faster across the frozen pond at the city's dusking edge, everything suspended in bluing gloom, removed from the other bully boys and their menacing world, then opened his eyes once more to find himself with a testicle-lifting shock fifty meters farther on in an utterly different fluttery existence.

Remembering reminds him: there *are* endurable moments. Yes. Of course. A pocketful of them, at least. No. More. Much. How, for no particular reason, Aleyt sometimes hurries into his studio while he is working, even after all these years, takes his face in her palms, kisses him fervently on the lips, and hurries out, just as if she had never entered there in the first place. How the angelic four-voice vocal texture of Guillaume Dufay's masses make the day on which you hear them feel thoroughly lived. How your conscious-ness arranges the entire piece of theater called living into a series of remarkable paintings called recollection.

A *polyptych*.

That word again.

Bosch is observing the three pudgy blind men who used to shuffle past his house on their way to market. Fascinated, his younger self waited for them at the window the second he had backhanded breakfast off his mouth. Capes flapping, milky eyes upturned toward a milky sky, fat lips slices of lilac liver on their faces, they held hands with each other like a human daisy chain to site and steady themselves on their perilous daily expedition.

What delighted Bosch was how effortless they made their passage appear, the most natural thing in creation. They were sightless, their hesitant and meandering dance declared. They were hungry. But they had business to do, and so, unfussy as stewed mutton, they did it. They just *went*. Bosch wondered what they could possibly see in their not seeing. Bleared bodies? Dense darkness? Nebulous light? He wondered how the cobblestones felt prodding the trio's leather soles, whether or not the room in which they would someday expire had already been built.

And then one morning, just like that, only two passed. *Two?* Bosch could not believe what he wasn't witnessing. At first he thought perhaps he had made some sort of mistake. Perhaps he had miscalculated their rhythms and was in truth looking at a different pair of blind men altogether.

No: next day, the same two passed.

And, next day, the same two.

And just as Bosch was concluding matters could get no worse, one of those dropped off the canvas as well.

Then there was a single blind man groping his way along the lane, palming house fronts, stumbling, unsettled.

And, a fortnight later, he vanished as well.

The young boy felt dreadful, guilty, ashamed. Had he somehow injured them by doing no more than speculating about their existence? Had the very act of studying them somehow changed them irrevocably and for the darker, made them less than they were?

For the following week Bosch slept a sleep thin as moth wings, rising each morning, gobbling his food, hastening to stand watch, only to learn repeatedly that the three were never coming back. After much hand wringing, he finally collected his courage, rolled over in bed one night, and asked Goosen, already aslosh in sleep, what he imagined could have happened to them. Suspicion of a joke being played on him tinting his tone, his big brother told Bosch, pokerfaced, that he had never seen such a group of men. He had no idea what Bosch was talking about.

Unnerved, Bosch approached his father in his studio the next morning. His father's face bobbed out from behind his easel, demanded the boy quit making up tall tales, and bobbed back out of sight.

The boy found his mother cooking in the smoky kitchen. He

asked her the same question. Smiling down on him, wooden spoon in one hand, she mussed his hair and said:

What thoughts you have, sweetheart. What thoughts.

But mommy, Bosch did not say, standing there, looking up at her snaggling teeth, helpless, but—

But—

But there is a devil sunk to its waist in the hole in my floor. My legs have disappeared up to the knees, up to the thighs. A chubby toad with a man's hairy arms is squatting on my belly, grinning, smoking a cheroot, while a pair of meter-tall mice are hunching on the chairs Groot and I occupied only minutes ago, cleaning their snouts with their hoofy paws, while a swarm of cat-sized mosquitoes is burring around a lamp, each sporting the face of a grim elderly priest carrying on a busy liturgy, and mommy, mommy, what do I do now?

Bosch finds the pandemonium noteworthy. All this hubbub, all this mayhem, and yet somewhere nearby Aleyt reads on in perfect peace. What a startling place to be: *here*. Here rather than, say, there, rather than, say, anywhere else.

With his next breath, the painter's energy suddenly becomes an old man pushing a wheelbarrow piled with stones up a hill. It will not be long now, he has time to reflect before his body bucks, his eyeballs pulse, his facial architecture assumes an unusual construction.

And, with that, Bosch becomes a stranger to himself.

The final beast of which he catches a glimpse boasts the head of a rabbit atop the unclothed torso of a young woman with girlishly pert breasts. She is wearing a nun's headdress. That one. Her brown eyes glisten with compassion. Chalky white fluid dribbles from her nipples. She collects it on her long first fingernail and licks it off, pink nose twitching. Bosch conjectures: an itch, season for fleas.

He balances on the very brink of the black absence.

The devil braces, sucks in a lungful of strength.
Gives one last great heave.
And Bosch tips over.
And yet, he thinks, beginning his plummet—
And yet—

And yet, despite all the waiting, the apprehension, in the end the end happens much more rapidly than he ever could have anticipated it might: his stomach lunges, weightless, and then he is freefalling through boundless night—unless, it shimmers through his mind, he is not plummeting, but rather hovering in nothingness, turning head over heels like a slowly revolving fetus. How, after all, could one tell the difference?

More perplexing still, a frantic din has broken out around him. Honks, tweedles, squeals, brays, barks, clacks, rattles, roars, hisses, hoots, yackers, yammers, yawps, bleats, grunts, chirrs, gobbles, coos.

Death, Hieronymus Bosch thinks to himself, is a very crowded affair.

Needless to say, of course, another option is that he has already reached bottom, softer than a bed of breath, is safe, sound, surrounded by God's minions, yet does not know it. Today is nothing if not one for shockers. The painter decides to test his hypothesis by peeping open his right eye, having a peek around, and several tiny luminous white Arabian horses gallop past chased by a large snail with bat wings. Bosch squeezes shut his eye again, settles on the encouraging datum that his throat seems to have quit bothering him—unless, needless to say, this indicates he is already dead, a bodiless spirit with no need for swallowing.

There are so many universes in the universe. It would not be an overstatement to suggest Bosch expected white tranquility, a spotless sense of wellbeing, but surely not this: tumult and bewilderment and an agitated gut. Surely the angels would never make such a racket—and, well, if these are not the noises of seraphs and cherubs clamoring around him, if he is not in heaven, but the other place, would he not feel rather warmer than this? Here the air is frosty and moist as if he were suspended topsy-turvy in some sort of gigantic cavern.

Wherever he happens to be, Bosch cannot shake the corroding awareness of how little difference his passing will make to so many. He calculates the number of people who will not miss him, and the sum is astronomical. Shaken, he begins again, this time trying to calculate the number of people who *will* miss him, and derives such a low sum he is forced to re-reckon to assure himself he has not made an error. Aleyt, undoubtedly. Yes. Absolutely. And beyond her? Beyond her, the children he did not have. His missing children's missing grandchildren. His parents, were they alive. His wife's, the same. His brother, had his brother treated Bosch as something other than an expendable social obligation to be met once or twice a year. Four or five uncles, five or six members of The Brotherhood, six or seven Cathars, each of whom, upon hearing report of his demise, will pause in some lane to remove his hat, lower and glumly shake his head, less out of any sense of real sadness than because removing one's hat and lowering and glumly shaking one's head is what one does upon learning of someone else's crossing the bar in public, regardless of one's own genuine viewpoint on the subject, then reseat said hat and push on into his errands without even the sip from another thought about the deceased except, feasibly, for some minor concern over who the painter's replacement might be on this committee or that, how the listener will phrase his note of condolence to the painter's wife.

Then, swiftly as it thronged Bosch, the uproar dissipates, shoots past, rises away at terrific speed, because—

Because—

Because Bosch has no idea why. He realizes unenthusiastically he is still on the descent, has been for quite a while now, if his sense of time is faring any better than his sense of space, a notion open

to some speculation. He could not say with any conviction, naturally, but he has the general impression his drop has encompassed
minutes, not seconds. Two? Ten? He would not want to hazard a
guess. For all he knows, he may have been at it for weeks already.

Little by little, thinking these thoughts, he becomes sentient of
another body falling alongside him. He can sense the heft of its
company, hear the airstream of its presence. Curious, he opens his
right eye for a second peep and has, he discovers, crossed into an
extensive realm of grayness. Blackness has given up to grainy opal
light as far as he can see.

Opposite him hurtles down the naked burned girl he spotted
from his attic window all those decades ago during the great fire.
He is confident he could reach out and touch her, if only he possessed the strength to raise an arm. Her blond hair flutters in a
large shredded and singed teardrop above her head. One side of
her body is skinless. Wisps of smoke flicker off her blackened flesh,
evaporate quick as a cough in the wind. Her hands cup her privates,
making her appear modest as Eve after the bite. Her eyes, which
are taking in her traveling companion with interest, are precisely
the wisterial of his wife's.

Do you by any chance fancy ginger snaps? she asks.

What's happening to us? Bosch shouts back against the bluster.

Because I simply can't get enough of them. They're my weakness.
I can't help myself. Don't you love how special they make your
tongue feel?

What's happening to us? Bosch repeats at the top of his lungs.

Oh, right. Sorry. I'm dead. You're dying. Not to worry. It
shouldn't be long.

This is what it feels like?

Forever. Yes. Odd, isn't it. Not how they described things in the
least. Then again, they wouldn't have had the faintest, would they?
The stories people tell. I'm happy to say the worst is behind you.
More or less.

The worst?

The shock. The jolt that startles and scares.

I was imagining the most horrible things. Lying on the floor. Swallowing my tongue.

You had. Have. You'll get used to it. Everyone does. But what do you *think*?

About death?

Ginger snaps. The honey. The cinnamon. The ground white pepper. Isn't it extraordinary? Like a street fair below your eyes.

I haven't given it much thought.

Goosen has. I could eat them all day. Gave it quite a bit, in actual fact. Of thought, that is. It has two tastes, doesn't it. The sharp surprise, and then the—the what?—the flood of prospects.

Ginger snaps?

Death. A shame, really. He never was very keen on your paintings. But you already knew that. Always considered them rather . . . *indecent*, I suppose, is the word.

He went behind my back?

No, no. Didn't have it in him. He merely made certain of his sentiments . . . *available*. What I think I fancy most is the texture. Don't you? Crackly and chewy and melty all at once. You were more interested in doing your own work. No fault in that. What sort of artist would you be if you hadn't been?

He called me a heretic.

Everyone does. Did. Because . . . because you *were*, weren't you? Only snag was you believed you were good at keeping secrets. Still, then again, who doesn't?

You're saying our falling won't end?

There are various theories on the matter. Some maintain it's a logical impossibility to keep going and going until the end of time. Others aren't quite so sure. Personally, I've been at it now for—what year is this?

Fifteen sixteen.

More than half a century. Isn't that curious? You meet the most fascinating people. I once fell for rather a long way with an explorer from the future. Blond fellow with a sprained wrist. Trekked though the Far East. What stories *he* had— Oh, dear!

Bosch notices the girl has picked up momentum, is beginning to pull away from him. Her head is level with Bosch's belly, with his knees, with his ankles. Hope contracting, he peers down at the top of her smoking plume of hair.

Can't you stay a bit longer?

Oh, I *do* wish I could! she shouts up at him, exasperated. But I don't believe it's in the cards. Perhaps we'll see each other again sometime.

She adds something else Bosch cannot hear.

What? he calls after her. *What was that?*

Arabella! she shouts, face shrinking. *My name! It's Ar-a-bel-la!*

Goodbye, Ar-a-bel-la! he calls out after her.

She lifts a tiny white hand from her sheltered pudendum to wave discreetly, but does not answer, or, if she does, Bosch can no longer detect what it is she is saying.

Arabella becomes a lost clog drifting down far below him. A marble. A pinprick.

And then Arabella becomes nothing at all.

And then—

And then—

And then, plunging, the painter does no more than tilt back his head and squinch shut his eyes in preparation for his inevitable trip through eternity.

When he opens them again some time later, what he sees startles him: the daedal ceiling of his studio.

The veiny wood.

The non-eye of non-God not peering down.

Stunned, Bosch discovers himself on the floor beside his easel, gazing up, mouth dry as pumice powder. Perspiration saturates his shirt, squiggles down his temples. The notion comes to him that he stinks of oniony sludge and bitter pissoirs. He is lying in a swampy puddle of himself, his heart beating so hard he can see the pulses in his eyeballs.

A grown man, a not wholly undistinguished painter, a detester of the flesh and all earth's excesses . . . and *this*. Satan has one pure pleasure: waiting until you have forgotten him, moved on with your life, feeling, if not a certain variety of cheerfulness, precisely, then at least the deficiency of immediate despair, and stepping up beside you on the street, nestling up behind you in your bed, to remind you in his hissy whisper of just who and what you are not.

Nonetheless, if the truth be known, Bosch would much rather hear that hiss than its opposite, than silence, for its sound suggests by its very presence that Hieronymus is not quite done yet. The painter certainly does not *feel* quite done yet. To the contrary. Lying there, he senses life beginning to trickle back into him.

And so he settles, watching the vision of the market square that has started coalescing above him atom by atom. The spot is packed with people, merry shouts, carnival commotion. Bosch watches Bosch gather into being on a wooden platform in the middle of it all. He is clothed in his finest attire. Across from him stands Goosen flanked by two somber cloudbearded men dressed in the black robes of distinguished scholars. The crowd is chanting. At first Bosch cannot decipher what it is they are going on about. Then his brother steps forward, and the sound resolves into intelligibility.

They are, if Bosch is not wholly mistaken, cheering his name.

Not his brother's. Not his father's. *His*.

What an astonishing fact: Hieronymus Bosch is being honored. He is quite sure of it. Goosen reaches out, and in his slender hand appears an offering: a lambskin scroll—a prize, a decoration, Bosch is uncertain which—and the artist's lungs go light with love.

These people have come to see him. That's what they have done. They have come to pay tribute. All these years. A lifetime of not being seen. And here Bosch is, arriving into visibility.

Placing one palm on chest, raising the other in a sign of mock modesty, Bosch basks in the waves of admiration.

No, no, his gesture says, *I could not possibly,* but, of course, he can. He will. Goosen presses the gift upon him. Bosch accepts it. The multitudes erupt into jubilant roar.

Hieronymus! Hieronymus! Hieronymus!

Hieronymus! Hieronymus! Hieronymus!

Hieronymus! Hieronymus! Hieronymus!

The scholars nod in solemn unity. Bosch undoes the black ribbon binding the parchment, works the scroll open, bashfully turns it out for the throng to savor.

The problem, the painter suddenly suspects, is that something is not quite right. Something is not quite right at all. Rather than meeting the howls of approval he expects, Bosch meets only chirped laughter. He raises his chin slightly, checking. An outbreak here, there, as the few barely literate townspeople up front squint to figure their way through the stubborn alphabet, then pass along the news to their neighbors.

Before Bosch knows what is what, a wall of hilarity surges back and forth before him. His appreciative beam thaws, melts away, and, in its place, a hot confusion overflows him.

Panicky, he looks to his brother for reassurance. Goosen lends Bosch a gummy smile that says *Don't worry—I'll protect you,* then bursts out laughing himself. Head thrown back, stained teeth sharp and unruly, the yokel reminds Bosch of nothing so much as the maw of a predatory fish bearing down on him.

His big brother holds up the unrolled scroll for Bosch to read.

Time hangs.

Time hangs.

Bosch cannot initially pull the nouns, verbs, and prepositions into meaning. Then the appalling information reaches him: he is reading a list, not of his accomplishments, but of his foibles. Bosch is taking stock of the once secret catalogue of his shortcomings. There are, he is somewhat startled to see, remarkably many of them.

And now they are public knowledge.

And now the public is adoring each and every one.

With that, the scholars turn their backs to him, bend at the waist, hoist up their robes, and present their sagging hairy asses for his benediction. Farts tuba out. The crowd's laughter intensifies. Bosch's chest staggers, his face goes on fire, and—

And—

And the vision dissolves in a wintry rush. Bosch is once again back on the floor of his studio, sweating, reeking, waiting for the next humiliation to come calling. Somewhere, he senses his right hand waking up. He watches sidelong as it rises and commences a tottering search over the contours of his body, checking for proof that Bosch is still Bosch.

The painter inhales and exhales, collecting himself by degrees. He slowly lifts himself onto one tender elbow, onto the other. Braces. Waits for Lucifer to take note of him and swoop down. Waits a little longer. Decides, gradually, that he is in the clear, at least for the nonce.

In measured stages, he eases himself into a sitting position.

Lets his head steady.

The entire world remains his body.

And then, cautiously, he commences rubbing his limbs, hoping the heat will restore his identity. Beyond the noise called Hieronymus, he hears Aleyt moving from sitting room to hallway to kitchen, preparing to prepare the midday meal. He envisions the mug of amber ale and bowl of hare stew afloat with leeks, chopped garlic, bay leaves, and sage bits that will be waiting for him on the table. All he has to do, he knows that he knows, is reach it and his life will pick up where it left off. Give him a moment. He will, with effort, rise. He will, with effort, hobble down the hallway, strip, wash himself at the cut-down barrel with the dipper and mutton-fat soap out back. He will change into fresh clothes, make a stab at poise, make a stab at lunch, then take his daily stroll across the market square with his wife. That is what he will do.

Walking beside her, he will carefully explain to Aleyt what

he has accomplished this morning, where he has been and with whom. The ginger snaps. The seizure. The visions. He will assure her he is perfectly fine, then beg her never to mention this incident to another living soul, including Bosch himself, because he intends to engage in an act of extended amnesia at the earliest possible opportunity. This is why God created a charity named Forgetting.

Walking beside her, he will love his wife more stubbornly than he has loved her in decades, and, afterward, will return to his studio for another afternoon's work, because that is how he has been sewn together.

And then?

And then, tomorrow, he will do it all over again.

Someday, he knows, he will bump into hideous Groot on the street, or at a service, or at the fair. They will, by force of circumstances, exchange pleasantries as if nothing occurred between them because, in the only sense that matters, nothing did.

And so, with a grunt, the painter lifts himself tentatively to his feet. His head swoops and whirls. He wobbles, shuffles a step forward.

Staring down at a single point on the floorboards to fix himself to this dreadful planet, he regains his footing, becomes aware of his own lukewarm filth sliding down his legs, the shit he has birthed.

The stench is crushing.

Bosch stands in it bowel bruised, belly sore, knee achy, tongue swelled, thought smeary, life worn. His knuckles throb for no reason that he can say, his right elbow where it must have banged as he went down, the back of his skull.

This is bad, he determines, and yet, given a little time, a little rest and recuperation, it will get much worse. Of that much Bosch is confident. Each hour will always bob up as a sour pill one must swallow until the bottle is empty and lying on its side, at which moment things will turn truly nasty because—

Because—

Because each morning, as you rise from your bed, the belief hums through your head that you are going to die, going to die, going to die, yes, surely, no doubt about it, but not today—an observation that will remain correct every morning of your life, except one, because—

Because—

Because, Bosch sees, this is as good as it gets. Because this is what sorrow feels like. Because for now sorrow is the best Bosch can crib in his hands.

Bosch is, that is to say, not all right, yet he could be much less all right than he is at present.

He is not really alive, yet he could be much deader.

And so—

And so—

And so he pushes off, dragging his feet toward the heavy oak door.

Reaches out for the latch. Lifts. Opens.

Appraises.

Shambles through.

Into the shocking afternoon.

Into the radiant daylight.

His next breath.